HOUSE OF BLUE SKIES PUBLISHING

PRESENTS

NOIR ON EIGHTH

An original, epic, mystery novel in the
grand tradition of a "Penny Dreadful"
by thirteen brilliant Calgary writers,
featuring some of the city's quirkiest
characters and historical events.

A collaborative historical novel by:
Kris Demeanor
Dymphny Dronyk
Cheryl Foggo
Aritha van Herk
Jani Krulc
Dale Lee Kwong
Clem Martini
Natalie Meisner
Lisa Murphy-Lamb
Telmo dos Santos
Ian Williams
Deborah Willis

with a fascinating epilogue by historian
Harry Sanders

Our Dastardly Plan

Noir on Eighth was originally published monthly, at "Long Lunch, Quick Reads 2015" – 10 delicious literary luncheons at Loft 112 in East Village!

And what a fabulous time we had!

Each chapter of *Noir on Eighth* was launched live and in person at Loft 112 over the course of ten Fridays in 2015 – (and the occasional Thursday, when a holiday long weekend got in the way of our Dastardly Plan) May 8, May 22, June 11, July 3, July 24, August 14, September 3, September 25, October 16, November 6.

On each new lunch date, during the hours of 11 a.m. to 2:30 p.m., the latest chapter, printed as a handbound chapbook, and complete with historical photos, was available for those looking to escape the madding world to the comfort of a chair, in a quiet, light-filled space.

The chapters were also available on-line within a week of each lunch date. You can visit the original online version, with photos here:

https://yycpennydreadful.wordpress.com/start-from-the-beginning/

East Village's Loft 112 is located at:
#112, 535 8 Ave SE,
Calgary AB T2G 5S9

Acknowledgements

WITH GRATITUDE TO OUR intrepid authors: Kris Demeanor, Dymphny Dronyk, Cheryl Foggo, Aritha van Herk, Jani Krulc, Dale Lee Kwong, Clem Martini, Natalie Meisner, Lisa Murphy-Lamb, Telmo dos Santos, Ian Williams, and Deborah Willis.

Each writer contributed the wealth of their imagination, enormous amounts of time – for free, and their astonishing integrity to the project. As you read you will notice that each of them also championed certain social issues dear to them. This story is about so much more than just singing the lost history of one of Calgary's oldest neighbourhoods.

Special thanks to our historian – Harry Sanders. Harry's exuberance and generosity, and boundless patience with our questions about the truths behind our fiction, helped the writers bring depth and authenticity to their chapters.

Dale Lee Kwong also earns extra recognition for the enthusiasm and unflagging determination she has for sharing the history of Chinatown. She continues to lead Jane's Walks and walking tours of her beloved community.

Thanks also to Lisa Murphy-Lamb who created space for this ambitious, eclectic project, and who continues to bring the arts to our city, through her work at Loft 112.

Gratitude to Nancy Jo Cullen, whose marvellous book, *Pearl*, was one of the sparks that created this project, and also serves as the namesake for the artist residency at Loft 112.

Thanks to Shelley Youngblut and her fearless, creative team who created a fabulous event for us during Wordfest 2015.

Deepest thanks to Bridget Honch whose excellent technical skills and good humour were the driving force behind layout and printing each month.

We are grateful to all of our readers, at the lunches, online, and now that we finally have a big, fat, paperback.

"Books are the way that the dead communicate with us."

Neil Gaiman

Foreword

THE ORIGINAL CONCEPT FOR creating a "noir" novel, highlighting the lost history of Calgary's East Village in a playful, penny dreadful style was conjured by Kris Demeanor and Dymphny Dronyk late one night while they were cleaning up after an event at Loft 112, an innovative and inclusive art space in East Village, and chatting with its Director, Lisa Murphy-Lamb. There may have been some wine involved.

Lisa mentioned that she'd love to find a way to attract more readers to the Loft, and they realized that for many busy people, committing to reading a whole novel for a monthly book club was too much. They also mused about what East Village must have been like before the skyscrapers, and wondered what ghosts and stories lurked along the streets and alleys. Once upon a time it was the heart of the city, a place of refuge for the marginalized, a place where people of colour could find a place to live. And long before settlement and colonialization, this delta nestled in the convergence of the Bow and Elbow rivers, was home to the First Nations peoples who came to harvest the rivers.

That night, the dreamers at Loft 112 came up with a plan to recruit a few Calgary writers, have them explore the history of East Village, and each write a short story, one per month; a vivid story that illustrated some ghosts, some key elements of a world that had in recent years been bulldozed and paved over.

As is often the case when artists put their heads together, the concept became more ambitious as they dreamed. The next step was when Kris, Dymphny and Deborah Willis met for a very long and fascinating lunch with historian Harry Sanders who filled them with so many East Village anecdotes and characters that they realized they had enough material for a novel.

The core team explored the concept of creating a serial novel, which dates back to the days of Charles Dickens, wherein a new chapter is produced on a weekly or monthly basis. In fact, the history of the "penny dreadful" is a great example of historic serial novels: cheap to buy in weekly instalments, often about sensational crimes and characters, with just enough intrigue to keep the reader turning pages and wanting more.

They researched modern serial novels and found that the concept was making a comeback in places such as New York City. Of course, it is hard to research what goes on behind successful branding on social media, where positives are bragged about, and challenges are more likely to remain hidden. The team did not know, for example, that many of these famous modern projects were not written in real time. While they may publish a chapter or story per week, or month, the entire novel is written and edited and finished long before the first chapter is ever launched to the public. Typically, these projects are written by only one writer.

That was the first mistake, of many other glorious, naïve mistakes. Another challenge is that when you have twelve powerful writers, from twelve very different worldviews and writing styles collaborating on a creative project, plot lines may become divergent, characters and their voices may abruptly change, and priorities shift.

(Also, what IS in the damn package that causes so much tension and violence throughout *Noir on Eighth*?)

But as Neil Gaiman writes in his inspiring essay, *Make Good Art*, "If you don't know it's impossible, it's easier to do.". The mistakes and learning curves do not matter as much as the joy and energy of believing in the magic of creating.

The team plunged in with great intentions and a ton of energy. Kris and Deborah worked together on the introduction and chapter one, partly because they had spent the most time with Harry, taking notes on the many historical facts and anecdotes that he shared in the first planning meeting. Dymphny became the editor/project manager and chapbook creator. Together they fleshed out a rough idea of what the story could become, and the key historical aspects they felt should be included. (The murder! The bones! The recurring impact of floods!)

Calgary's devastating "100-year flood" in 2013, which had had personal impact on each of the writers in one way or another, became a major influence on the story.

As the project developed, each subsequent writer was given the previous chapter, in rough draft format, as soon as it was sent to the editor, along with a "cheat sheet" that explained plot points and rationale, character studies, and any other helpful information – a literary baton passing, if you will. The new writer then had three weeks to write their chapter, plus their cheat sheet ... and so on.

Three weeks might sound like plenty of time. It is not. Especially not when the writers all had "real" jobs too! Especially not when the writers wanted to research and incorporate their own angles on a storyline that became evermore tangled and compelling, and occasionally even confusing. (Those red herrings!)

The editor then had from Monday, (and sometimes "Monday" was a nebulous concept, with drafts arriving closer to dawn on Tuesday, if writers had found the Muse particularly hard to wrestle) to Friday morning to edit, format the layout, fact check, research and procure appropriate photos, print, assemble, and hand bind each chapbook. By Friday lunchtime, the chapbooks were delivered to Loft 112, to be enjoyed by the readers who had arrived for a catered lunch.

Impossible, and yet ... they did it, with enormous talent, integrity, and a collaborative will that may never be replicated.

This first paperback edition is *Noir on Eighth* in its original ragged glory. Handbound chapbooks are much harder for libraries and archives to store, and collectively it was felt that the massive amount of work (a year of time and creativity and commitment by thirteen brilliant, dedicated Calgary writers) was too important to lose to indifference, the way some of the East Village's buildings and voices have also been lost.

The team of writers that conjured Noir on Eighth hopes that this volume will bring the reader lasting joy, and that the ghosts of Calgary's historic East Village will continue to whisper to all those introduced to them.

Archives and Images

ALTHOUGH THE ORIGINAL VERSION of the Noir on Eighth chapbooks included many historic photos sourced from the spectacular Glenbow Archives, as well as original photos we felt added to the allure of the monthly chapbooks, this paperback version of our project does not include any photos.

You can visit the Glenbow Archives here:

https://www.glenbow.org/collections/archives/

You can visit the original online version of *Noir on Eighth*, with photos here:

https://yycpennydreadful.wordpress.com/start-from-the-beginning/

The Calgary Heritage Initiative also has a fascinating website full of the history of the city's streets and architecture:

http://calgaryheritage.org/wp/

Prologue

by Deborah Willis and Kris Demeanor

I⊤ WAS WARM ENOUGH in March that Aaron had ridden his bike to work, and on the way home, he'd almost crashed into the Simmons Mattress Factory. He'd been distracted by the river: the water was high and there were slabs of ice the size of merry-go-rounds. It had been unseasonably warm the past week and he'd heard from his neighbour, Valeria, that there was a big melt coming down from the mountains. How did Valeria know this? She seemed to just hang out on the stoop of her apartment building all day, but also knew everything about the city, about the weather, about their neighbours, even about the developer who wanted to tear down her building and Aaron's house to put up condos. "He's not as rich as he seems," she had said once, narrowing her eyes and scratching her eyebrow with a yellowing fingernail.

He hadn't even brought the bike inside yet when he heard a boom that sounded like the downstroke of a digger slamming concrete. He was used to construction noise, but this was different—so loud it made him jump and trip over the bike, chain grease smearing down his jeans. Then he heard people yelling, and another sound that seemed to come from the river. A low roar.

He dropped the bike in his yard, then jogged down 6th Street and along 5th Avenue. The rumbling seemed to come from under his feet. He passed torn up asphalt and a construction crane, the background of his life for the past three years. A scattering of people stood by the Langevin Bridge—or what had been Langevin Bridge. You couldn't see the bridge now because a huge wedge of ice had slammed up against it. More chunks of ice crashed into that slab, then muscled over top of one another—he could hear the grinding of one frozen beast against another. The ice blocked the river's flow, causing the water to rise like it was held by a dam.

"That's right! I'm at the Langevin Bridge!" Someone—a man in a Gortex jacket—yelled into his cell phone. "There's a blockage here. The ice is sort of piling up."

No one in the crowd got too close to the heaving water, but they were unable to look away from it. The river's cold water was nearly bursting its bank.

"Look at that." Valeria was next to Aaron—had she been there the whole time? "It'll flood."

Valeria was somewhere between 30 and 50, and possibly a working girl. She tended to wear jogging suits that were too small and showed a band of skin along her wide middle. But she had the bossy, comforting demeanour of a mother, and he was glad she was next to him right now because his brain was going blank.

"It's an ice jam." Valeria seemed as cool as ever. Smoke from her cigarette curled up through her bangs.

"A what?"

"An ice jam," she said again, unimpressed, exhaling.

Everyone stood around, fascinated. Valeria finished her cigarette, dropped it, and crushed it under the toe of her sparkly
plastic shoe. There was nothing to do, nothing that could be
done, but leaving didn't seem like an option either. Should
Aaron just go home? Have dinner? Wait for the cold water to
reach his house? He wanted reassurance. He wanted someone
in a uniform to appear and to say, *Nothing to worry about
here, folks.*

"Put that in your album!" Valeria yelled at a young couple
who were taking photos of the rising water on their phone.
That was Valeria's specialty—yelling at people, in a good-na-
tured way that made them uncomfortable. "Taking pictures
of the big disaster," she said. "I get it."

"It's not a big disaster," said Aaron. But as if to prove Valeria
right, the Gortex man—who had called the police and the city
and the fire department—yelled, "Evacuation notice!" Then
he walked through the crowd, telling people that he'd been
talking to city officials, that he'd heard they would evacuate
the neighbourhood. "We have half an hour. If you have any
valuables at home, deal with those now. Does everyone have
a place to go?"

"Is it mandatory?" someone called out.

"Do they mean all of us?" someone else asked. "Or just
the places close to the water?"

"What bullshit," said Valeria. "Right in time for the weekend."

"You have plans?"

"Not really. But this is bullshit."

Aaron had known Valeria since the day he'd moved in to
the house he'd inherited from his grandfather. Aaron was the
only one in the family who wanted to deal with—let alone live
in—the hundred-year-old bungalow in what was considered

3

the wrong side of the tracks. But when Aaron wasn't at his day-job—writing technical documents for a bank—he was an amateur historian, one of the star members of the Historical Society of Alberta. He knew that the East Village had once been a bustling town unto itself, a place of importance in the prairies. He imagined that every Saturday when he strolled to Gruman's for breakfast, he was walking alongside the ghosts of former bakers, shoe-shiners, even Premiers of the province. Each spring he researched one of Calgary's heritage neighbourhoods—Bridgeland, Bowness, and Mount Royal—and led a History Walk through the streets, talking about the most salacious details he managed to dig up. The man who shot his business partner for bedding his wife. The female detective murdered by a jealous real estate developer. The Lieutenant Governor caught with his pants down at an infamous local brothel.

This year, he was working on a walk through the East Village. He would show off the buildings that were still standing: the Cecil, the mattress factory, the King Eddie, the St Louis, and his own house—built in 1914, by his grandfather, who had been a tanner. And he would have to hope people could imagine the rest: the liquor stores, blacksmith shops, the vaudeville theatre, the billiards halls, the laundries and garages. All of that had been razed to the ground. His bungalow was the only original house left standing. He'd refused to sell to the developer; the *Sun* had even interviewed him about it, and then twisted his words so that he came off as a crusading, nostalgic nut. But wanting to keep his house wasn't nostalgia—he just liked where he lived. And yes, maybe there was some hubris: he wanted his little yellow bungalow to stand for the entire East Village, to act as its memory. He also happened to dislike the developer who had tried to buy him out, a guy named Rodney who actually smoked a cigar on Aaron's porch while talking to him about *green space*. If it hadn't been for that cigar, Aaron might have agreed to sell.

A fire truck arrived—how would they help?—then an Enmax van.

"C'mon," said Valeria, turning, and he followed her back up 6th.

"This won't be the first flood around here," said Aaron.

"Duh," said Valeria.

"1897. 1915. The dam almost broke in 1932—"

"You better deal with your books," said Valeria. "Those'll be done for."

She was right—he had to move his books up onto higher shelves. Or bring them with him. Bring them where? Maybe he could call his cousin, Dara. They lived in Tuscany, so they'd be safe. But would she mind if he brought Tommy Douglas? His nephews loved the cat but Dara would worry that he'd scratch her furniture or spray on her carpets.

"What about you?" Aaron turned to Valeria. "Where will you go?"

"I'm not going anywhere. I'm on the fourth floor, honey. The water won't get that high."

"But the power will be cut off. The heat. You'll freeze."

Valeria patted her belly. "That's where this blubber comes in handy."

"You'll be ok?" He realized she probably didn't have anywhere to go. Should he ask her to come with him? But he couldn't ask Dara to lend one of her guest rooms to Valeria—not with young kids running around, and all the expensive electronics in the house. Valeria was his neighbour, but not his responsibility. Right? He didn't even know her last name. "I guess maybe you could come with me," he said. "I might go to my cousin's. I don't know if she'll have room."

"I'll be fine."

5

"Really?"

"Oh sure. I've lived through worse."

When he got home, Tommy Douglas was already wailing at him—stalking through the house, emitting agonized, throaty *mews*. The cat seemed to have a sixth sense, a way of smelling changes in the atmosphere, shifts in the mood. Aaron sometimes worried that Tommy suffered from anxiety. Then worried that he, Aaron, suffered from anxiety due to his anxious cat.

"I'm not going to leave you behind," said Aaron. "Okay? I promise. Just give me a minute to sort this out."

He called Dara's phone, then remembered that she never answered it, so sent her a text instead.

> Hey D, there's crazy flooding in my neigh-
> bourhood. Evacuation notice. Can I stay for
> the night? I'll have to bring Tommy along
> (??!). But I'll babysit the boys for you, if you
> and Sol want to go out for the evening.

Her reply arrived within seconds:

> Oh no flooding! Of course you can stay with
> us!! Esp cause you just said the magic word:
> babysit!

Someone knocked on his door then, a young woman in an orange reflective jumpsuit. "Hey, I'm just here to let you know that there's a mandatory evacuation notice in effect."

"You think it will be bad?"

"We're working on it as best we can. Mount Pleasant and

Capitol Hill community centres will take people in, if you don't have anywhere else."

Tommy walked up to the doorway and yelled at her, a growly, pissed-off meow. He got offended when strangers stood on the porch.

"Sorry," said Aaron. "My cat's distressed."

"We're all distressed, sir." The girl was clearly not a cat person—she stared at Tommy Douglas and backed down the porch steps. "You have twenty minutes."

Aaron grabbed a change of clothes, his toothbrush and razor, and Tommy's food and litter box. What he owned of the family photos, and his grandfather's ledgers. Then he moved his books into the loft space, a low-ceilinged attic that was only accessible by a rickety wooden ladder. He liked to joke that the ladder was 'vintage'—he was pretty sure his grandfather had built it by hand—but the creaky, splintery rungs didn't seem so charming today. He saved his local history books first, the glossy ones with reproductions of old photos. Then the boxes of material he'd printed or copied from the archives: maps of Calgary from the 1870s to the 1920s, newspaper articles, photos of the first Stampede. Then he carried up his paperbacks—Atwood and Ken Follett and Hilary Mantel and Stephen King, a disparate collection that he'd snagged when walking past Little Free Libraries or during Saturday afternoons browsing in Fair's Fair.

What else? He moved his files and some of his clothes up to the loft. Then made sure any perishable food was out of the fridge—he'd bring it to Dara's and improvise a dinner for them. He'd bring his laptop too, the old clunker, but he didn't have much else to carry with him. Would looters come? They'd find a bunch of old postcards and scratchy sweaters and past tax returns. There were so many benefits, he found, to not owning much.

7

Tommy Douglas howled with such annoyance and passion that it could not be ignored. Twenty minutes was probably up.

"Ready to go?" Aaron scooped up the cat, settled him over his shoulder, regretted not putting Tommy on a stricter diet, then walked out to the car. There were cars packed with suitcases and pillows driving down the street, and he could hear, distantly, the sound of a child crying. He waved to his across-the-street neighbours, a young couple who were renting one of the recently built condos and who'd had a baby a few months before. They were just now trying to fit all of the baby's blankets and diapers and jars of food into the trunk of their car.

"Pretty crazy, isn't it?" said the young man. And that's when Aaron took a breath, paused, and noticed that water had already soaked his shoes.

He and Tommy Douglas woke early, Aaron mistaking the stomping, giggling, whispering of his nephews for the usual construction sounds—engines, back-up beeps, hammering, pile drivers. He'd slept badly even though the futon was comfortable, and the guest room was dark. He put on his clothes and walked down the sweeping staircase. The house had four bedrooms and three bathrooms, and he sometimes got lost—ending up in the "games room" when he meant to be in the "study." But he could always find his way to the kitchen.

This was where the muffled noise came from. His nephews—Daniel and David, eight and nine years old—were standing at the stove, watching a pan that smoked over one of the ceramic burners.

"What are you boys doing?"

"We're making breakfast," whispered Daniel. "It was supposed to be a surprise."

The pan had what looked like blueberry pancakes in it, fried crispy.

"Are you allowed to use the stove? Are your parents still asleep?"

The boys giggled, leaning into each other. "Yes," said Daniel. Then he scooped out one of the pancakes, put it on a plate, and poured Aunt Jemima's over it. "For you." He did a little bow.

"Why, thank you," Aaron bowed back. He stood beside them at the stove to supervise, then took a bite. It wasn't blueberries; it was chocolate chips. And caramel chips. The thing was so sweet that it made his teeth hurt.

"You like?" asked David, who then did a spin in his stocking feet on the linoleum.

"Oh sure, I like." Aaron handed the plate to him. "But you have some too. I'm not much of a breakfast man."

"Then why don't you sleep 'til lunch?"

"Good question. Listen, boys, when do your parents normally wake up?"

Daniel shrugged. David said, "Dunno," in a sing-song voice.

"I'm going to drive down to my place, see if I can take a look at the damage, okay? When they get up, tell them I'll be back soon."

"I heard your house got *swallowed*," said David, and Daniel smacked his arm. "What? That's what I heard."

"I hope not," said Aaron. "I certainly hope it hasn't been *swallowed*."

The house hadn't been swallowed, but the street was a swamp of mud. He drove slowly down a road that had once seemed so solid, so permanent, now covered in silt from the river. And his house. He strained to see it as he approached, then looked away. The home his grandfather had built. There was a muddy line about four feet up the siding, where the water had reached. And the porch must have washed away—it was simply gone. Even Tommy Douglas, who was normally so chatty, kept quiet in Aaron's lap as they witnessed the destruction.

Aaron parked, got out of the car, put Tommy on the passenger seat— "You stay here, buddy"—then felt his shoes sink into the mush at his feet. His steps squelched as he walked over what had once been grass and the garden beds he'd been looking forward to planting.

He walked up to the front door. With no porch, the door seemed to float in the middle of the house. He reached up, unlocked it, stepped inside. The hardwood, which was original, had warped and buckled from the water. The line of dirt showed on the inside as well, staining the pale yellow walls. The drywall was sopping, falling in wet clumps, and the place smelled both like a freshly turned garden and like a sewer. Aaron turned, walked back to the car—careful not to slip—and picked up a frantic Tommy Douglas. He needed something to hold onto.

They went back to the house; Aaron took a big breath before entering, then walked straight to the basement stairs. The basement had a hard-packed mud floor and walls to begin with, and now it just looked like a swamp. Two feet of dirty water had settled there. He waded through, gripping Tommy tight. He opened the dryer door and a rush of water spilled out.

He'd stood his ground, kept his house, and now the house would rot out from underneath him. *Bullshit*, he thought. Valeria was right. This was bullshit.

And Valeria? How was she holding up? He went up the basement stairs, outside, then over to Valeria's apartment building. He buzzed her place, number 401. No answer, so he buzzed again. Then the apartment door burst open and a guy in a denim jacket pushed past him.

"Hey," said Aaron. "You see Valeria around?"

The guy looked him straight in the face, then turned and kept walking. Aaron buzzed her again. She was probably out. Probably at the Central library or somewhere else where there was heat. And what should he do? He'd heard on CBC during his drive over that the evacuation notice had been lifted, but what did that mean? What should he do next? Call his insurance company—he couldn't even remember if he had flood coverage. Start moving his things out? Call the city? What he felt like doing was curling up and going to sleep.

He walked over to his own yard but couldn't bring himself to go back inside. The cat seemed to protest too, squirming and screaming on his shoulder. He'd been stupid to bring Tommy Douglas—there was probably dangerous sewage seepage everywhere along the street.

He sat on one of the wooden stumps that had once supported his porch, and cradled Tommy Douglas in arms like a baby. He rocked Tommy back and forth and this seemed to soothe them both.

"What now, TD?" said Aaron, but the cat squirmed and pushed his way out of Aaron's arms and trotted through the yard, paws covered in mud. "Hey, come on, buddy," Aaron called after him, but didn't have the energy for a chase. He stayed on the stump, staring at the ground.

That's when he saw something white poking out of the earth, between the house foundation and where his porch had been. Part of a pipe or a wire? He bent for a closer look. Just a rock. He kicked it, venting his anger on the wet earth. More grey-white showed through. He kicked and kicked, until it became clear that these weren't rocks. This was bone. Broken shards of bone.

This area hadn't been a First Nations burial site, he knew that from his research, so these must be animal remains—a coyote or a deer. He kept digging with the toe of his shoe. What came up, what he eventually uncovered, what he picked up and wiped off on his shirt, was the bottom half of a human jaw.

Chapter One

by Deborah Willis and Kris Demeanor

THE RIVER WAS LOW, to the point where one is reminded that water hitting rock at a lazy pace actually does 'babble'. Mid-morning sun reflected on the tips of the waves like gold coins. Hanging willow branches kissed the surface, cottonwood fluff rode the current. Birdsong saturated the bluffs.

Beatrice quickened her pace. They were drunk. At first, they whistled, then asked her what her name was, then when she kept ignoring them they called her some names of their own. *Boys,* she thought. It was nothing she hadn't heard before. Or done. The men ran on the spot and shouted "Hiya!", like they were spurring on a horse. Bea's throat seized up and she took a few running steps in surprise and fear. The men laughed. The same game repeated. She undid two middle buttons of her coat, her slender hand grabbing the bone handle of a four-inch blade she kept in a sheath. *Try something, pigs.* In her mind she slit all three of their throats and watched them writhe, wide-eyed, full of panic on the dusty riverside path.

Bea regretted hustling down 1st street past the public market in her rush to find serenity by the Bow. Besides the fact these bastards had stolen the promise of a quiet river amble, she most probably could have found the mixture at one of the Chinese shops, and definitely a pastry at one of the bakery stalls. She was famished. Nearing the Cecil Hotel she noticed a small crowd hovering on the street out front, and, with the added company, was emboldened to spin around, plant her feet and scream foul language at her pursuers—but the drunks had stumbled back to the riverbank. She looked to see if the men on the stoop of the Cecil had seen the action—or lack thereof—but they didn't acknowledge her.

She approached the doors of the Cecil Café, right next to the hotel, passing the men who now were now paying her full attention, silently scanning her from bottom to top. It wasn't lascivious; in fact, the men appeared embarrassed and shy, like schoolboys. A couple even wet their fingers and ran them past the hair on their temples in a hapless attempt to look more presentable.

These were the men who had found a home at the Cecil, guys who worked half days or not at all, men whose wives had already fled. Men who were not even in contention for love. The more desperate of them wore brown overcoats that, in the heat, gave them the appearance of glistening, dirty walruses, keeping with them the warmth they would need lest the coat be stolen while the beers and whiskeys stacked up. The most capable of the Cecil barflies were talkers, jokers, the ones who still had enough prospects that watching the sun cross the sky while the glow of liquor washed over them, the city's bustle churning all around, made them feel like they were in on a beautiful secret no one else knew.

Beatrice scanned this menagerie of strange humanity on her way into the café—there was a young man with a patch over one eye. On the patch he had sketched an abnormally large eye in black ink. Another man had only one leg and leaned against the brick wall, rubbing the stump while the wooden prosthetic lay on the pavement. He grinned at Beatrice in a self-mocking, helpless way she found endearing. *My God. Pirates.* Beatrice thought. *Prairie pirates.* Fair enough, they were all looking for a map that would lead to easy treasure. Not looking, perhaps, but waiting.

Beatrice took a seat in the café, on an uneven wooden chair next to an uneven wooden table. On one wall was a deer head with a bowler hat on it, colourful streamers hanging from its antlers, vestiges of a rowdy party. On another wall a large painting of a shirtless Blackfoot brave on horseback in full flight, taking aim at the straggler in a running herd of buffalo. There was no one else in the cafe. A small man with a bulbous, purplish nose approached wearing a blood-stained apron.

'Not quite lunch time yet, miss. The wife is at the market as we speak. But I can try to oblige if you need a snack.'

She ordered a cheese sandwich and a pot of tea. Two minutes later a sandwich with unevenly cut bread and a slice of cheddar came out. She lifted the top piece of bread. There was no butter, nothing.

'Sandwiches ain't our specialty, miss—if you want a nice pan-fried ribeye, let me know. You'll be set 'til tomorrow afternoon.'

On a nearby table was an abandoned newspaper. Beatrice did a cursory look around even though the place was empty, and picked it up, The Calgary Daily Herald. Despite her sandwich's disappointing appearance, it was satisfying. She had let the tea steep until it was strong and black, and while she tipped in the cream she scanned the pages:

Socialist Organizer Speaks - the Socialist party of
Calgary held a meeting of last evening at the Princess

Theatre when an address was delivered by William
Gribble the Dominion Socialist organizer on 'Trusts'.
There was a very large audience who listened atten-
tively to the bitter arraignment of the lecturer who
referred particularly to beef, oil, coal, steel and other
combinations of organized capitalists.

Complainers, she thought. If she knew one thing in her
27 years it was that you have to stick with the fastest in the
herd if you want protection, not the sick and slow.

Walk-Over Shoes – "Seeing is Believing" If you
want to see the fruit of 36 years of shoemaking experience ... trimmer ... longer wearing – Do You Want
to Know?

One of Beatrice's soles was peeling away. It would have
been an easy fix, but she had money now and the The Vici
Kid Blucher Boot Bridge Model looked elegant, sturdy, good
for walking. However, she imagined the next few weeks, there
would be a lot of walking.

A Serious Accident – John Ricks Has Throat Cut
in Horrible Manner – Subject to Epileptic Fits and Fell
Through a Window Suffering a Gash from Ear to Ear-
A distressing accident which very nearly proved fatal
occurred this morning at 618 4th Street East. The house
is occupied by two negroes and a white man. He was
lighting a fire ... situated close to the front window
... taken with a fit ... pitched headlong through the
window ... his throat was cut on the jagged edge ...
gash went to the root of the tongue ... bled profusely
... expected to recover ...

Ear to ear? Accident? Sounds like someone didn't finish a job.

Electric Theatre – Cor. 8th Ave and 2nd Street East
– continuous vaudeville – The Sherrahs: Buck and
Wing Dancing – Ali Zada: The Oriental Necroman-
cer – The Merritt Sisters: Contortionists – Illustrated
Songs – The Dramagraph

It sounded like a class reunion. Beatrice had done buck and wing dancing back home. She was good. And one summer she had a lover who was a contortionist. Nobody knew that, of course. No one would ever know that. Except the contortionist.

She jotted down the address of the theatre, and of Glass Bros Co., 120 8th Ave West, for the Walk-Over Shoes.

The short man emerged from the kitchen through swinging doors and looked around at the empty cafe, then at Beatrice. There was twice as much blood on his apron, and he carried on a napkin what looked like a Danish.

"You must have been hungry," he said, looking at the empty plate. "It was a lousy sandwich. Have this." He had made an effort to at least wash his hands of blood, she noticed, and the offering made Beatrice smile.

"You're kind, sir."

"Ethel makes them. I just have to be swift enough to take them out before they burn, which isn't every time." He winked and offered his hand. "Frankie."

"Bea-etty. Betty." To cover the awkward slide into her introduction, Bea followed up fast "Frankie, may I ask where the nearest hardware store is? I have a fussy sink ..."

"There's one on the Costello Block, just up a few blocks, but I suggest you take a fellow there with you."

"Why is that?"

"You're not from here?"

17

"Across town. On a bit of an adventure. So…the Costello Block?"

"Sort of place that attracts …" He laughed. "I know, I know, who am I to talk?" tilting his head toward the exit and the invisible undesirables on the other side.

"Just make sure you set your dial to 'No thanks'. You get offered a lot of stuff on the Costello Block and none of it's good. Get your washer or your plug or what have you and move on."

"Thanks Frankie".

If only he knew.

On the street, Beatrice adjusted her hat to shade her face and as protection from the sinister wind that was kicking up, sending dust and bits of straw into an annoying swirl. She retracted her parasol and let it dangle as she walked, touching the ground lightly as she stepped, like a walking stick. She wore a long, pleated skirt past her ankles with cambric drawers underneath, lace chemise, white undershirt and the twenty buttons of her jacket done up to her chin, a belt tightly reining in her waist. She hated her body being in a prison. It was absurd. She wanted to be naked as the Polynesian island girls she'd seen in the National Geographic. It wasn't only the women. She looked at the men too in their woollen slacks, starched collars and coats, and wondered what they had all done to deserve this punishment.

Women here, she mused, were not full of options. You're a wife, a country or a city wife—she couldn't imagine what would be worse; a servant or nanny, a shop worker, a waitress, or a whore. If you're young enough, a kept mistress perhaps, and if you're lucky, one with an allowance. Sure, some women were writers, artists. But how many Lucy goddamn

Montgomerys could there be? The only other option was to join the rodeo circuit as a trick rider or the carnival as a clairvoyant or acrobat. But for most women, those weren't options. Those vocations were more like callings, and you had to be willing to be called a lot of other things along the way. No power. No vote. Beatrice had planned, schemed and sweet talked her way this far, and as she ran her thumb through the block of five-dollar bills in her billfold, she felt consolation. She unbuttoned the top two buttons of her jacket, mopped her face, brow and neck with a handkerchief embroidered with the initials GW.

There were two middle-aged opium dreamers lounging on a boardwalk, and a working girl having her morning coffee at midday, but nothing seemed threatening about the Costello Block. A grocery, liquor store, a couple of guest houses, and the hardware store Frankie had told her about.

Bea walked confidently into the liquor store, her boots on the wooden floor inspiring three men who were in lively conversation to stop, go silent, and disperse back to their respective positions, behind the till and arranging stock.

"Help you, ma'am?"

"Yes, a half quart of whiskey, please."

The two stockers looked at the manager and he smiled.

"Husband finishin' off a cigar?"

"Pardon me?"

"Husband. Expectin' him any minute?"

"I'm sorry. I don't … I'm not … I'm here alone."

"From Montreal, huh? Europe?"

"No."

"Ma'am. Can't sell whiskey to a woman unless she got a man with her. The law."

"It's not for me."

"Not how it works. Can't sell spirits to ladies. Lose my license."

Beatrice turned to exit when a fury rose in her belly. She snuffed it and approached the counter calmly.

"Sir, I would not want to jeopardize the integrity of this business. But let me implore you. My father is ill. I have come from out of province to care for him. Besides constant dyspepsia and an evil rash, a toothache won't let him rest. A man will see to the rotten tooth but not until morning. Only whiskey will soothe him—he has an aversion to powdered medications. Please, as the only customer on this quiet day, may I discreetly purchase a flask, immediately conceal it, and take it straight home to my suffering father?"

One of the stockers. "Percy ..."

"Shut up, Cal! It's my neck!"

"I understand." Bea dropped her gaze, made herself appear small. "Sorry to trouble—"

"Hang on, miss. A minute."

Percy washed an empty flask, poured a half quart of whiskey from a tapped barrel tipped over into deep grooves on a wooden bar.

Cal slid the flask across the smooth wood grain.

"I ain't selling this to you."

"Excuse me?"

"I am offering this, so your father has medication while he waits for treatment. Ain't selling' it. Got it?"

"Yes, I do, sir. Thank you. My father thanks you."

The wind had calmed, the day engulfed in thick heat that made all metal and wood too hot to touch. Beatrice stood on the street facing the hardware store, her jacket half open, trying to loosen the billfold, which was stuck next to the flask, when, without sound, a foreign hand plunged with brute force into the cavity, grabbed her wrist, pinned it painfully against her breast. A second hand, with Dickensian speed and adeptness, seized both the flask and billfold from the pocket, leaving Beatrice too stunned to scream. There was a smell of spit and sweat left on her by the man, more likely a boy. The implications of the theft pierced her, and she clocked a thin figure sprinting down a perpendicular street. Beatrice pursued, her hat flying to the dusty ground, leaden skirt lifted high, chest heaving, on the crest of panic—she would be finished without money. Bea screamed, not *Help!* or *Thief!*, but a desperate howl of futility as the boy fled fast. She tripped, striking the ground, clothing and face kicking up a fine brown dust. Looking up hopeless she saw the crook running full tilt back towards her. A second man was chasing the thief to the crime scene. The scoundrel was tripped by the vigilante, launched into midair, horizontal, toward a watering station, his head making full-force contact with a hitching post. His body crumpled to the ground, defeated, still.

Charlie Tucker helped Beatrice up, took out his handkerchief and wiped clean the whiskey bottle, which was still intact, and the billfold, which had its full stack of bills inside, thank the Lord. Glancing at the well-endowed wallet, Charlie raised an eyebrow and grinned, nodded at the whiskey. "You could probably use some of that."

"I think you killed him."

Blood was seeping from the left ear of the unconscious felon. Charlie gave him a kick, splashed water from the trough on his ear which caused him to stir and groan. "Not yet."

Charlie Tucker was a blacksmith, had heard Beatrice's wail and introduced himself to the commotion. He jogged back to the main road, retrieved her hat, and invited her to his shop to wash herself in the sink. He was the first black man she had seen in Calgary. She was struck by how britches and suspenders, which could look comical and incomplete on most men, highlighted Charlie's stature, explained the demands of a job forging hot metal. She came out of the bathroom, her jacket off, blouse still dirty, neck and face clean, revealing freed skin framed by a mane of black hair encircling her breasts. Charlie turned away, feeling like he was in church being lectured on sin.

"Do you make locks?" she asked.

"'Scuse me, miss?"

"Strong locks for… locks that can't be smashed or picked without trouble."

"I do big locks for rail cars, miss, but I don't see you needing that, unless … you … got a train."

They faced each other, glanced at the ground, laughed quietly. Beatrice re-buttoned her jacket, captivated by the sheen on Charlie's shoulders and arms, the moving sinew announcing power as he nervously tossed a dirty rag back and forth.

"What you usin' it for, if you don't mind me asking?"

"Treasure chest," she said, spinning a length of hair around two of her fingers.

"Uh huh … well, look, you show me how thick the shackle needs to be, and I'll have a custom lock for you in two days that even dynamite can't scare."

"Thank you, Mr. Tucker. What's that?"

"That? It's a salting cannon. You put some rocks and just a little bit of silver in the core, then blast it against a rock face out in the woods so it looks like the shiny stuff comes from that very rock face. Then you get a dumb prospector from Toronto to spend way too much money on a claim with a guarantee the silver from the cannon's the only silver he's ever gonna find."

"Naughty."

Prairie pirate. Beatrice would be back in two days.

Corner of 9th Avenue and 3rd Street. *Exactly on the corner? Where the hell is it?* A laundry but no medicine store. The paper had the names of three plants, roots, herbs, something. Had to be at least a grocery … and a name written, perhaps a name, one she couldn't read, or couldn't understand. Two private residences flanked the laundry. Those were the three corner houses. Bea strode impatiently to the middle house, entered to the sound of a bell rigged above the door, approached a middle-aged Chinese woman bundling socks. She spoke clearly and slowly, trying not to condescend.

"Hello. Do you know of a Chinese medicine shop? Here? In the area?"

The woman said nothing, turned gracefully through a swath of red hanging linen into another room. Uncomfortably long minutes passed, when a young man of about 20 came out, baggy silken pants gathered at the waist with a sash, white collar-less shirt unbuttoned to reveal his neck and part of his chest. He had been roused from a nap.

"Yes? Drop off?"

"No, I have a question. I was given this address, on the corner, it says. Is there something else on this corner?" She passed him the note.

The young man looked at the note carefully, turned a dispassionate gaze to Beatrice. His expression was assured, serene, but not serious. He nodded, tapped his knuckles twice on the counter and left, back through the hanging red linen. The older woman backed up past him, carrying two cups of steaming liquid. She nodded at Beatrice and extended one of the cups to her. Beatrice stood anxiously, sipping the hot tea with floating black leaves in it, while the mother returned to her sorting.

The package was square, tied around both sides with twine, a bow at the centre. On the same slip of paper, the young man had written the number 4.

"Four dollars?" Beatrice said astonished, instinctively haggling. The son answered with no response whatsoever, and it frightened her. The mother looked at Bea with urgent compassion.

Bea withdrew a five-dollar bill without removing the billfold. She was conscious of how crisp it was, crumpled it slightly in her palm on the way to the outstretched hand of the son. Unnecessarily. He snatched it from her, had a single dollar coin ready in exchange, yawned, and went back behind the red linen to continue his nap.

I think he knows.

She could admit it. The day was getting the best of her. The river, the pickpocket, the confusion at the laundry, she was thinking of nothing else but the tedious ritual of unlacing her boots, heating water on the stovetop, and soaking her feet. Her next fantasy involved a pillow. Soon …

The St. Louis Hotel had none of the quiet, unorganized charm of the Cecil cafe, but it looked a lot more fun. Striped overhangs shaded the balconies of rooms on the second and third floors. All four chairs in the adjacent barber shop were filled, two other clean-cut men outside looking for trims. A cigar stand out front advertised Tom Moore cigars – "Ask for Tom Moore when you have a dime and Little Tom when you don't have the time," coaxed the sandwich board image of a man in top hat and waistcoat with tight trousers, a bend in one knee. Inside the tavern, heavy drinkers were setting the volume high, billiard breaks like thunder cracks erupted every few minutes from a side room. There were two tables of men immersed in cards, sober frowns on their play faces. The piano was silent, a man sitting on the bench facing away from the keys, beer in hand, on a break. There was a spirit of familiarity—even a table of black men were drinking, laughing.

Bea couldn't ask the bartender where Pearl Miller's place was. She couldn't ask any man. Shielded by her hat, she took out her billfold and from tight between two new five-dollar bills, withdrew a photograph. The woman was young, in a dress made for dancing. The posture was formal, but one could tell she was trying to jump out of her skin. *She could be here.* Bea scanned the room carefully while returning the photograph to the billfold, set her eyes on a woman who was hiking up her skirt to clean a spot on her hosiery with a napkin she had just spit on. Only some women were free enough to do that in a tavern. Bea took her root beer, squeezed between tables, mostly ignored, and made her way toward the woman, who was sitting on a chair, chest opened, arms up on the chair back, smoking a Little Tom. Bea had planned not to make a big deal of it and shoot straight. She knelt to be closer to the woman's ear.

"Can you point me to Pearl Miller's?"

The woman pursed her lips and took a long drag of a Little Tom. She exhaled, grinned and looked toward the bar.

"Maggie! Maggie! Hey Maggie! Lady here is looking for Pearl's! Could you point her there? Pearl's! Lady needs to see Pearl, so it seems!"

The cacophony of the regulars continued, but most around the bar and a dozen more turned and put all scrutiny on Bea. Whispering and laughter. Men uninterested before, leered. Bea froze and ground her teeth.

"Cow."

"Take it easy. Nothin' dishonourable about it."

"I'm not—"

"Fine, sweetie. Neither am I. I know. Look, it's on 9th and

5th. 526, I think. Just a regular house but you can see the shadow of a couple nice looking hats in the window on the other side of the curtains. Nice curtains."

Two men had approached, drunk businessmen, collars unbuttoned, red-faced, cocksure.

Bea ignored them, focused on the woman who had brought on all the attention. She should have been livid, humiliated, but the woman smiled like a sad goddess, and Bea extended her hand.

"May I try your cigar?"

The woman held it out to Bea like a flower. Bea mimicked the woman's smoking mouth, touched the wet tip of the cigar to her lips. She inhaled once, too quickly. When the burn hit her lungs, she stifled a cough, held her breath, opened her mouth and let the smoke creep out.

"Thanks"

She turned to leave the tavern. The woman called after her.

"I only advertised it because I hoped you'd lead all the snakes out of this place like St. Patrick! You'll be fine, sweetie!"

The row of houses along 9th Avenue, bare plots browned in the sun, the quiet expanse south before the rail tracks, the comically blue sky—all conspired to make the city look like a museum diorama of a town. Turning west to see the sandstone bullies of downtown, the faint outline of rocky mountain, settlement pushing the grassy earth out like bacterial culture moving through bread, the city looked so … intent.

Pearl wasn't the image from bawdy books Bea snuck peaks at when she used to visit her auntie's place. Madam. She should be older, bigger—she looked like a school teacher in a school play, on that uneasy high wire between youth and middle age, still playing the game but a little crankier.

"Turn around, honey."

Bea, compelled by Pearl's voice, did so almost unknowingly.

"Are you clean?"

"Oh, no, no ... I ..."

"Want a job."

"No, I'm here about something else."

She plucked the photo from her pocket.

"This girl. My sister."

Pearl didn't take the photo.

"Hold on."

She went to the sitting room and took a pair of bifocals from a card table and put them on. Now she looked like Bea's auntie. Even with the glasses, she leaned in close.

"Alice."

"Yes!"

"Who was Annie-Lou two months ago, Dorothy when I first saw her a year ago, when she wasn't dancing as Carmen the Harem Girl."

"Yes."

"Hmm. Yes what? Which one are you looking for?"

"She was always doing things like that, always pretending this and that. You recognized her. I knew it must be her."

Pearl studied the photo again. She squinted at Bea, who had composed herself.

"We have different fathers but grew up together on the farm. She was my other half. Our mother died, she went to live with her father and his wife. We wrote, then we stopped. It's been three years. I heard she ran off. I heard she was ..." Bea's eyes welled up. She rooted around in her pockets. Pearl waved her into the sitting room.

"Look, honey. Alice is not doing great. I haven't seen her for a couple of weeks, and when I did, she was so out of her mind she could hardly—some clients are supposed to be protecting her but looks like she's just another prop at the party."

"Protecting her?"

"Things got complicated for Alice. She's a popular girl. There was man with a lot going on, a reputation and some big money to protect, who she got in too deep with. He's worried about himself. The girls and I are worried for her. I can tell her you came by and where you're staying—"

"No, please. I'm afraid she'd be too ashamed to see me. If you don't mind, I'd like to come here in a week or so and see if she's found her way back."

"Don't expect anything in particular from this part of town, miss. You kick over enough rocks, eventually you wake up a scorpion or two."

"I just want to bring her home."

Pearl took one more look at the photo. "Sweet girl."

Bea faced the street, saw a man half a block away waiting in the box seat of a carriage, leaning against the rail, waiting for her to leave. She walked down 4th Street then turned west down 8th Avenue towards downtown. The Hudson's Bay Company had fur stoles, she had seen, and it was on the way to her hotel.

It could have been harder. Much worse. She held the package from the Chinese laundry under her arm, took the whiskey from her inside pocket, uncorked it, and in mid-stride, in the middle of the street, put the throat of the flask to her mouth and poured back half its contents. She stopped, closed her eyes to the sun, and felt the generous heat of the alcohol travel from her tongue down to her belly, and spread throughout her body. She returned the bottle to her pocket, next to the billfold with $300 in it and the photograph of the sweet girl Bea had never met.

Chapter Two

by Natalie Meisner

WITHOUT HER MIND'S CONSENT, her feet had taken her to the river. Beatrice felt the last inch of earth under her feet. She watched the textures and eddies of the impossible chalk blue rush past beneath her. The color was preternatural. She understood why some people attributed an animus to the river itself. This colour existed almost nowhere else in nature.

How high had the river been this year, she wondered. How solid was that handful of earth directly beneath her and would the fingers of the clutching roots that snaked through the clay soil of the bank keep their grasp on the fistful of clay under her weight?

She felt all of her body weight taut and poised. The whiskey sang its peculiar soothing song through her body in the pathways of her blood. She was tired. Bone tired, blood tired. It seemed quite reasonable to let go. Lie down; just release the load of secrets, of obligations she carried. She had, after all, not knuckled under. No, she had made it this far and no one controlled her … and, yet did they? No, tired didn't quite cover it. Not by half.

Who would blame me if I were just to let go right now? Who would know or care?

She felt her lips move as if they belonged to another. This visceral movement recalled her to the present moment, and she wondered if she were, now, being observed. There was no one in evidence and yet each rustling bush on a clump of rhododendron along the river, each tinder snap of a twig on a forest floor … Ask not for whom the twig snaps, Bea.

It snaps for thee.

There is was again. A new habit; a disturbing one that seemed to increase with each passing hour in the city. No one had heard her, but then why speak aloud? To whom was she directing her urgent requests for permission to rest? To the chalk blue implacable surface of the river itself?

Perhaps. This was enough. She thought she could extricate herself from what she had seen. Burned the name, the shamed name out of her birth certificate and with Doe became free. But it wasn't like that. She wasn't to be left alone. Each day, hour, minute of living on this planet cost something. Just her being alive cost someone somewhere something.

To whom was she speaking and how shocked was she when a voice rose from the depths?

Kindly step back. The voice commanded. *I cannot hold you, not your body, not your bones. I have too many already. I am thick with bones of the unnamed. And besides. To fall would be stupid, laughable. Please step back.*

It was a liquid voice. Or was it? It emanated from somewhere at the cross section of her jawbone and left ear and yet it also vibrated in the rocks and rustled out from the circular silver dollars of the birch leaves. That sound like laughter when they flip over and rustle together. When the birch leaves flip over ... what was it she remembered? A nursery tale about how when the birch leaves flipped over to silver it forecast a great storm:

Lorsque le bouleau laisse bascule en dollars d'argent d'une tempête de siècle viendra. The voice. Was it her mother's? Half remembered, now obscured this many years she could not be sure that she hadn't blended it with her own. And yet it also hinted at the liquid wave forms of the river.

She wavered over the surface of the mighty Bow. She felt the rising wind catch the edge of her skirts. And this did the trick. She did not want to slip. To slip and drown would be stupid, would be laughable. The river was right This was an indulgence she could scarce afford.

Stick with the fastest in the herd if you want protection, pas les malades et les lentes.

She stepped back and strode purposefully in the direction of her hotel. Away from the greenery and currents of the river now she stuck her nose in the air to breathe in the peculiar scent of the city. Creosote, money and the sizzling fat from a hunk of flesh on the sear.

If a person could only bottle this smell it would be ... vastly unpopular. She thought to herself. And yet it wasn't necessarily malodorous. Bea lengthened her strides and enjoyed the feeling of her legs striking the earth as she surveyed this booming young city. As she let her eyes caress the painted storefronts and promising alleyways of a city still not as old as she was, she found herself indulging in a luxury that she seldom gave in to. She imagined herself a home. She tallied how much it would cost her per week for a permanent room in McGonagall's rooming house. Subtracted what old lady McGonagall might pay her for scrubbing the steps and entrance, for making up the rooms of boarders who'd shifted. It was reputed to be a safe spot for a woman of independent means to lay her head at night. Yes, she could almost feel that this new city—as green as the ill-gotten cash that fattened the wallet that chaffed her—she could almost feel the newly minted city stretching arms out to hold her. She could feel her mind begin to ink in the corners of the blueprint of the future she might have. If only if she were able to get past this one distasteful task.

Worse than distasteful, what she had promised to do was loathsome to her. No one was saying that she, Beatrice de Seychelle was perfect but this ... to sell your own sex down the river in this way ... to these sinister men with their threats, their blood money and stubborn refusal to take no for an answer. What were they going to do with Alice once they located her? Better yet, what did they want with her in the first place? These were questions that she could not delve deeply into without a wholesale excoriation of her choices, life and character ... none of which she had time for at the moment.

It was then that she felt the hairs stiffen on the back of her neck. She knew with the instinct of prey among predators, of one who has spent her adult life in ill-considered situations, hiding and ducking for cover ... that someone was following her.

She quickened her pace and then slackened it, experimenting and the footsteps—they were heavy—did the same. She knew with the vital life lust of the hunted that she could not look back. No, you can never look back, as the past can cut you. She had learned that. For the second time today, she reached under her coat and readied the smooth bone handle of her knife. Her thumb poised just so under the handle to maximize the torque of the blade. Now the gooseflesh was raised along both arms. The footsteps drew closer and while it might be unwise to confront her pursuer in the open street, Bea knew that to lead him back to her hotel would be sheer folly.

She made as if to turn down an alleyway, and then quickly feinted to the left, melting into the alcove of the sandstone façade of the marble company. At precisely that moment, she caught the first bit of luck, the first bright penny from heaven that had rained down on her for many a year.

A black and blue bank of cloud was steamrolling in off the open prairie as it was wont to do this time of year. It was not the kind to glide overhead and pass you by: No, it was the thick wet fist of wind that smacked you around, really had its way with you. The kind that felt personal when it smacked you around or brought down your barn in the night. And what was more:

Hail. Summer Hail. *Oh, let it come down*. Breathed Bea. *Oh yes*.

The street that had hummed along efficiently, with pedestrians on the quick walk each with his or her own particular errant now erupted with umbrellas, people running and dashing for cover, copies of the Calgary Daily Herald tented over the heads of the underprepared.

Beatrice seized her moment and ducked under the ramparts of The Flesher Marble & Tile Company. Be one with the sandstone, she thought as she felt its smoothness along her back. The biggest mistake of prey is the mad dash. That is what the predator wants. She forced her breath to slow. She angled her eyes and her head down to the ground and feigned interest in a pamphlet that become plastered to the earth. *Bow City: The Town With a Future,* block letters exclaimed. The Collieries was selling off lots on the south bank of the river she read as she shifted the paper with her toe.

She willed her breathing to steady and felt time slow down as the hail passed over toward the mountains in the west. She listened through the din, separating each strand of noise and thrusting it aside as she had taught herself to do, stripping the noise polluted din of the street into layers, sifting through the clatter of the streetcar, the hum of voices. She would hole up here for a while and with patience outfox her pursuer. If there is one thing she had learned these past seven years on the road, it was how to be alone. She gathered her coat around her and let her eyes go to half-mast …

Her father's factory hadn't failed all at once and neither had her mother's mind. No, it had been a slow dissolution like a cheese overblown with mould and crumbling.

He had whipped the woman. One of the labourers he and M. Cecile trucked in from Beatrice didn't know where. He had accused her of shirking on the day when it finally became apparent that no one in the new world was now, or would ever be interested in his runny, inferior Gruyere. The woman had stood her ground. She'd grabbed the lash and pulled. Sent the Viscount in his fine brocade trousers head-long into the muck. When he struggled up to muffled, behind the hand laughter of the assembled groups of workers, each huddled with those whose tongue they spoke, it was in an apoplectic fit. Bulging eyes and veins standing out he had his two workmen hold her while he gathered the lash from the ground. He had then exerted himself as perhaps no one in his family these last five hundred years had occasion to. He had whipped the woman until neither of them could stand. All assembled stood frozen in shock. As if they had become a relief tapestry tableau rather than a lot of humans.

This was not the promise of the new world, a voice seemed to say. It was a watery voice, an angry and vibrating one … but it was miles and miles away. As too were the Northwest Mounted Police, who, heaven knows, would only stir them-selves if property were involved.

The whipping continued until it became clear to Bea that what her father was whipping was the clanking and poorly designed machinery of his cheese factory. It was his folly for placing the remnants of a proud family fortune on this fool's endeavour. It was the herd of dead sheep on his back acre that he tore with his lash. At the end anyone but him could see that it was only his own fear, ignorance and impotence that he sought to whip to death. But that would never die. The wind had come up—the fist of cloud on the horizon ... walnut sized hail was coming to beat down what was left of their haphazard vegetable garden. Let it come down, she had thought. It would break up this awful scene. This inhuman curse that replicated itself in old words and new. Had he made Bea strike a blow? Had he shaped her child's fingers around the handle of the whip? Had she struck, or had everyone scattered in advance of the hail? She always saw an aura... a twinkling above the left eye when weather came ... and the French words came along with that.

The past made her head hurt. The temptation to sooth it with a second salvo of Pendleton's Whiskey was fierce. But she was walking the razor's edge now. She could not afford it.

No, in this scant bitter morning light there wasn't much she could afford.

The voices were back, and she knew, without question she had to cut them loose. These vestiges of her mother tongue. *Vous ... amour*, syllables like a slow pouring of cream but stranger and stranger to her with disuse. They were cut off at the throat now and kept only for herself as if it were a language between mother and infant. She had not uttered French aloud since had she left with nothing but the gold jewelry that was her birthright and a wheel of the inferior product in her pack.

In her mind she could still hear the clanking of the badly formed machinery … just as she could hear the failing machinery of her father's thoughts. Noblesse Oblige counted for precious little against sweat and a strong back in this land of meat and wheat.

Now the hiss of the hail was fading. Bea was sure she had evaded her pursuer… if in fact there had been one at all. Had she imagined the footfall behind her? Or had the portent of the storm set the tinder to her imagination?

She crawled out of her hiding place and decided not to return to her hotel, to be on the safe side. The scant belongings she had left there were hardly worth an encounter with Mr. Heavyfoot. And so, what now?

She spun suddenly on her heel. How much longer would her stash hold out while she sat waiting for this Alice to surface? What could Heavyfoot and his henchmen possibly want from her that could be so valuable? Perhaps Pearl had been covering for her and the woman was upstairs the whole time.

Well, she had not run away on her own at sixteen, the only sane survivor from the collapse of an Aristocratic cheese farm, for nothing. It was said of bluebloods in the new world, that nearly all of them to a man found themselves unable to cope with the hand hardening labour that came with all their raw promised acres and they either became despots or ate their young. Her father had (nearly) done both. And further than this she could not afford to ponder.

Her feet had surely and stealthily guided her back to Pearl's. Through the turmoil of the pedestrians ducking for cover; through the mess that the hail had made of the street. And now here she was at the door. Her hand grasped the large iron handle cast in the shape of a ram's horn. As she moved to throw the door open, she had an uncanny feeling, a déjà vu. As if she had been there a hundred times. Or as if she had daubed on the thick turquoise paint herself in a dream ... she yanked the heavy door and stepped inside. Several heads angled themselves her way and she could instantly feel the all-seeing eyes of Pearl upon her.

Under the glow of the freshly lit lamps, Bea could see the business side of the establishment more clearly than she had earlier. A long gleaming wooden table along one wall did service as a bar with stools lined up along it. Women of various ages wearing clothing just a bit more colorful than you would in the street leaned on the arms of men from various walks of life in a conspiring manner. They were all telling jokes or stories, it seemed. The atmosphere was ... could she say jovial ... no, that wasn't it. Congenial? Certainly lively. Certainly civil. She looked again at the row of seated men. They all seemed to tell fascinating anecdotes or raucous stories. The women found each of them hilarious or astounding ... unless, that is, you closely examined their eyes, which in their depths were a million miles away. Where? No one knew. Bea had been blessed or cursed with the ability to feel what other's feel. This was not witchery or ESP as that rip-off artist down the block called it. It was just an overly sensitive nature. It had been what nearly tore her apart as the factory crumbled and her family with it.

It made her senses zing with information. She felt an undercurrent of desperation, need, fear even. At first sniff it seemed to come from the women ... but no, no, she let her eyes pass over several of the men. It was there with them as well. The cast of their shoulders in some cases. The cant of their chins. An unease stalked them that they sought to shuck off for a time, but it dogged them still. All bravado or mindless fun aside, there were men here who fairly leeched sadness into the floorboards. Could the women feel this? Were they too alone in their own personal version of the summer fair corn maze to even observe it? Were they already dreaming of the moment they could relax the calcified smile that was now rigouring their cheeks and embrace the smooth surface of their pillows? Who could know for sure? Under all of it was the inexorable hum of currency. The clink and the rustle. The stirring in the pockets and the dance of want, need, and desire. The pinch where they met: this is what made it all possible.

High above, at the top of the staircase seated at her roll top desk, inking the books industriously was Pearl Miller. She licked the pen nub, finished her last neat figure and snapped the roll top closed. Without seeming to break stride for the stairs, Pearl was at her elbow.

"Ah, you've returned. You've reconsidered my offer. This is most wise of you and I thought you would. You didn't have the air of a stupid girl. And there isn't a better place for a smart one in this town.

"This business with Alice... I can see you are willful person... but I advise you to give it up. You might well be in over your head."

The woman again reminded her of nothing so much as somebody's spinster aunt, yet she had the face and inquisitive air of a bird on the hop.

Beatrice felt her voice catch in her throat as she tried to speak. It had been days since she'd spoken more than a few words to another human being. Now the disuse caused her speech to come out staccato, busted. She sounded like a farm hand.

"A job, yes, I need, but."

Here the woman cocked her head to one side.

"I can't," said Bea. "That is to say I'm not. "

Pearl nodded reassuringly and put a finger to her lips.

"Ah, dear girl. You needn't worry."

"Need I not?"

"Not in the slightest. I see exactly your concern. Sit down. Let me get you a cup of tea while I put your mind at ease." Here a sharp crack of one knuckle sent an urchin running for a tea tray.

"You don't look well, my dear. Now just get comfortable and let us get acquainted."

"I'm fine. I'm really fine. I've eaten. "

"There's more to life than that, my girl. When is the last time someone asked you how you were? When is the last time someone has combed out that wild tangle of hair."

"It is clean. What are you inferring?"

"I don't question you, my dear. But combing it out will really make it shine. It seems to me you have been a long time without tender loving kindness."

"Ah. Tender loving kindness. That's what you dispense here, I am to believe?"

Here Pearl blew air through her lips and peered over the top of her bifocals with amusement.

"For the most part, yes. Ask any one of the motherless girls here if I shirk their wellbeing. I beg of you, do."

Here there was a steeliness to her that lent her words credibility and Bea didn't doubt that she meant what she said. The gentile atmosphere afoot this evening, surely was not the only mood of the place. When the waves of travellers and those just passing through came through; hopped up on bug juice … people who were passing through did not care what they left behind, Bea knew from experience.

"But you're concerned about this" Pearl cocked one pinkie finger adorned with a cygnet ring toward Bea's chest. "Not much there to work with, to be sure."

And then she had given Bea's breast an appraising dispassionate squeeze. Much as if it were a market fruit she contemplated buying.

"Not to worry. In fact, I have a bodice right over here that will reshape you like a mandolin."

"Oh no" Beatrice held up her hand in protest. Pearl had gotten her entirely wrong. "I was thinking I could serve the drinks, maybe sell cigars …"

Pearl threw back her head and laughed and then tilted her head to one side. Her eyes glittered brightly, intelligently like robin hopping across damp earth while listening for the vibration of an insect to snatch up.

"Sounds like an easy way to starve, my girl. But I can see that you aren't quite suited for the feathers and jewels. That's alright. That's perfectly alright. Better yet we can make your boyish form a charm."

Boyish? Thought Bea to herself. She had never quite gone that far, in her own mind … and yet she had never quite felt herself a woman either. In her secret heart of hearts, she considered herself a creature. Yes, something better left to its own devices in a thicket … but here she was, and Pearl was at full bore.

"We are usually better persuaded by reasons we uncork ourselves than by those poured forth by others." Pearl said as she took off Bea's jacket and hung it on a chair. Bea had no strength to counter the compact woman whose certainty was a force unto itself.

"Humanity could be freed from all evil if we just possessed the ability to sit quietly in a room, alone." Now Pearl was winding a length of cloth around her so that even her modest breasts were invisible. Over that she threw a hound's tooth coat from a nearby gentleman.

"Need this for a moment, Ned." She shouted affably into the din of the parlour.

"Take what you need, Pearl." The man sang out. "You always do. Just try to leave me something for breakfast in the morning." He winked and turned back to an amber haired beauty who—true to form—leaned into his story and found it scintillating. A tray of drinks had arrived at her elbow. Pearl placed a shot in her hand and tipped her chin, motioning for Bea to drink. She did and felt her head swim pleasantly. Someone turned on a phonograph in the corner and a lively vaudeville tune enlivened the room.

Beatrice felt loose and heavy as she surveyed this surprising woman who spoke in nuggets of wisdom. She sounded more like one of the philosophers that her tutor tortured her with, than the madam of a bawdy house. Bea felt herself relax her guard slightly for the first time in months.

"Now just look, you'll barely recognize yourself." Pearl held up a pair of breeches in front of Bea as she swung her by the shoulders to look at her own reflection in the polished tin behind the bar and Bea was shocked to realize that in fact, she did recognize herself. Perhaps more than ever before. She averted her eyes from her own reflection as Pearl held forth and grabbed another shot from the tray for fortification.

"Handsome, are you not? Not a man ... not a woman. Man's Desire is limitless, my dear. This, what you feel as a lack, can be turned to a bounty. They have a desire for everything under the great, hot sun. If you learn this, learn how to bend it to your ends, you can be exceedingly wealthy."

When Bea woke up, the most embarrassingly beautiful woman she had ever seen was applying curling tongs with an antler handle to her honey colored curls. The smell of slightly cooked hair mixed with a light perfume and the smell of the woman herself on the bed clothes. She now picked up a tube gleaming gold and dangerous as a bullet. But it was too large for a bullet. It had red stripes on both ends and text in elaborate font: Flavoured with Mary Garden Perfume by Rigaud, Paris. Colour: *Cerise Daylight.*

Bea tracked the path of the woman's layered clothing back to the bed she rested in. She reached under the pile of blankets to discover that she too was as naked as she had first come into the world. Through the haze of the second half of the bottle that she never should have consumed she fought to piece together the events of the previous evening.

"Good morning, Love." The woman turned the full bore of her gaze upon Bea who suddenly felt doubly naked.

"Were you? That is to say, did we?" Only broken phrases seem to sputter from her lips and tumble to the floor.

The woman laughed lazily, through one hairpin held between her lips.

"But of course! Don't be ashamed. Are you one of those from the Church? If so let me personally assure you that this is all sanctified and pure."

"Pure?"

"Yes, you see I am certainly in love with you already."

"Love, how can you speak of such a thing here?"

"My, we are one to split hairs, aren't we?" The woman stepped in long strides toward Bea, her honey coloured curls and generous curves mesmerized Bea in motion, as they now were. There was something familiar about the woman who leaned over and planted a firm kiss on her lips.

When she came up for air, she also grabbed Bea's billfold and spilled out the contents.

"Oh, my, did I pay you, I— "

"Not at all. Last night was my treat. But I would like one thing in return."

Beatrice felt her face turn scarlet. She was out of her

depth and she knew it to the tips of her toes. She could not answer.

"I would like to know how you came by this." And she held up the photo uncurled, unadorned, but now the resemblance was clear.

"I guess it is a bit late for formal introductions, but I'm Alice. Or Annie-Lou or Dorothy depending on who is asking. And who is asking, if you don't mind me asking?"

The Voice of the River:

Glassy, unblinking. I am looking up through the depth. The blocks of stone, the tower of babel you thrust toward the sky. Your scaffoldings erected and tumbling down again year by year.

Down here am I, immaculate cold, violated and enraged. What you deliver unto me. The unholy things that you deliver unto my arms to bear away.

And I throb. I throb now for your blood. All you who walk with blades at your boot. All you who trade in the misery of others. With my teeth of ice, I will tear.

I want to feel you enter me now. Enter me now with less violence than you have in times past. You must supplicate. You must fall on one knee ...

For I can see now, I can see back through these filmy scales of time. When you raised yourself on hind legs for the first time. You picked up your first stone. Your first flint. How long before you used it upon one another. I can see now, and I can see future. What you will cast forth, what you will pour into me until my blue filmy surface runs black with old bad blood?

Yes, I can see black blood that flows up when you puncture ... the black and brown, the yellow blood, and finally even blue. Now you have given me a taste and I thirst for the rust of the spikes of the tracks cutting north. Slicing north. You do not want to follow my lines; you make your own. You score them against me.

I will rise up. You will see. For now, I am quiet. I accept your unsanctified offerings. Your cast-off things, your soiled boots, your excrement, your filth.

But now. Now. What you have given me to take away.

What you lay down upon my breast and expect me to transport .... I will not. A girl. A woman. Another and another. Who you used as a receptacle until she was broken. You lay here and expect that I will take her away. I will hold her.

I will not lay her down on the bottom to settle on the hard stones. I will not spirit her body away down river to the secret silent forest of the Canadian Shield. No. She, her. All of them. All the tender shades of skin of their bodies.

The deeper shades marking further outrages.
Brown, black, blue. This is the palate of their
lives. This is what lies under your liquor breath,
your parties, your good time gals. At the end you
throw them into me. Until my waters run red
then black with blood, and I will not transport
them.

No. I will hold them here suspended in the cur-
rent. All of them. A forest of bones, thick with
outrage. A forest of skeletal fists raised, here just
under the surface of the water. If you care to look.

Along my bottom I am covered with perfectly
suspended women's skeletons—their fists raised.
A forest thick with bones. When the time is right,
I shall heave them up and they will walk again.
You will feel their bony wrists at your throats as
you sleep.

I. Will. Be. Back.

Chapter Three

by Ian Williams

A: Aaron

THEY WERE ALLOWED TO, but not advised to, occupy their houses again. So said 660 News.

"All clear," Aaron announced to his cousin.

"You got through?"

"No," he said. He was also on hold with the insurance company. They were playing 90-second loops of Kenny-G-sounding contemporary jazz. "The City says we can go back."

"CBC said that last time and the house was uninhabitable." Dara was loading the dishwasher before heading to work.

"They just said the power's back. And the heat," he said.

"But there might be mould." She closed the dishwasher door and began to mother him. "I'd wait a little bit more. You just don't know what you're going to find. I mean, if you had nowhere else to go, then yeah, fine, whatever. But if I were you I'd give it a few more—"

The jazz stopped.

"Hello?" Aaron said.

❖

Aaron had flood insurance—everyone in the area was required to have it—but the service representative notified him that his policy did not include coverage for personal articles.

"I don't own articles," he said. He was fifteen minutes into a circular conversation. "I own stuff."

"I'm sorry, sir. Your stuff is not covered."

"Don't call my stuff *stuff*," he said. "It had value."

"Your property, sir, was not insured under your current policy. If you like, I can upgrade your policy to protect you in the event of future—"

"Do you cover jawbones?"

"Excuse me?"

"Jawbones." Aaron stretched out the word. "Do you insure jawbones?"

"I'm sorry," she said. "I don't understand. I understand this must be a very difficult time for you. We're processing a number of claims from East Village."

Aaron recalled the damage to his yellow bungalow. His porch had collapsed. Two feet of water in the basement. Everything he had stored down there would be lost. The washer and dryer would have to be replaced. The earth was belching up skeletons and now this lady from insurance—what was her name? She had given it at the beginning—was telling him that his coverage did not in fact cover anything important.

His bungalow was the last hold-out on a street sold out to condo developers. All his neighbours had taken the bait. The City had rezoned the area for mixed-use residential and commercial. He had no mortgage but his property taxes had increased to force him out, he believed.

"But no, no, we don't cover body parts," she said. That's what she said. Then the service representative pattered on some more. "Is there anything else I could help you with today?"

"No." Defeated.

"Thank you for calling Assurance Insurance. We appreciate your business and look forward to serv—"

Aaron hung up.

His cousin had already left for work by the time he got off the phone.

"I mean, if you had nowhere else to go," she had said.

Aaron thought of Valeria, the (former?) prostitute who lived next door. She had nowhere else to go, yet when he checked on her yesterday, she was elsewhere.

All right, Aaron would collect Tommy Douglas and be on his way. What else would he need? He opened his sister's linen closet. It was a cornucopia of bodily delights. He figured he might as well take some soap and, why not, some toilet paper and toothpaste and body lotion and, sure, a few lightbulbs and some post-its and Saniwipes and, oh look, her husband used that expensive shaving cream for sensitive skin. *Don't mind if I do.*

One last thing. He went up to the guest room where he spent the last two nights and retrieved the jawbone from between the mattress and box spring. He held it to his nose, then a few inches from his face like a book.

It was as close to a woman as he had been in weeks. Not true. There was his sister and Valeria and women at work. Correction, then: it was the closest he felt to a woman in weeks.

It was going to be a long drive all the way from Tuscany at the height of rush hour.

He loved Tommy D, make no mistake, but it would be nice to have a human in the passenger seat, preferably one that did not need a carrier.

The last woman Aaron dated was Whatshername. He found her on Tinder. Her profile photo was blurry and dated. She had attempted to crop a man from her side, but his arm was still around her.

Clearly, she was a woman who had things to hide.

When they met, he wished he could swipe left over her in-focus, up-to-date face.

And before Whatshername, there was another Whatshername. Began with B. Beatrice? Or maybe P. Patrice? Katrina? There was a train emerging from the fireplace of her name. She was against paying a little bit more in taxes to fund Calgary transit. She said she always voted Wild Rose.

Swipe left.

He had found her on Tinder too.

And before that Whatshername, there was, you know, Whatshername. With the muddy roots.

She was a French teacher who said she couldn't shake the feeling that everything in the world had a gender.

"Cats?" Aaron asked.

"Yes, cats too," she said.

"You mean like male and female cats," he clarified.

"No, like the entire species of cat. Cats are female animals, although *on dit* un *chat*." Whatshername twirled her fork through her endive salad. "Gender has nothing to do with

50

actual gender."

She may have thought she was being quirky, being memorable, but Aaron could see an ax falling on her neck, on the future.

"Tommy Douglas," Aaron said, pointing his fork, "is male."

"Still, as a cat, he's a female."

"You just said *he's* a female."

"It's just in my head, Aaron."

But, no, he saw Whatshername's gender reassignment of Tommy Douglas as total disrespect for reality. And for his cat. *You gon' take that,* Tommy Douglas said in his deep cat voice.

Swipe left.

http://www.whatistinder.com:

> Tinder is the hottest new social app for online dating and hookups.
>
> The Tinder interface is very simple. Swipe right if you like the profile you are viewing, swipe left if you don't. If you and another user both swipe right it creates a match and you can begin chatting with the user immediately.

But why did Aaron see it as some kind of insult to be called a woman?

That wasn't the problem. It was that she was telling him that Tommy Douglas, his own cat, was something he—"He's an *it*, technically speaking," Whatshername said later that evening and he nearly lost it—was not. That was the point.

"It's like if I called you a man, you'd be offended" Aaron explained to his cousin. He was sitting in traffic still. He could tell she was trying to get him off the phone so she could go back to making money.

"Not really," Dara said.

"If I told you you looked like a man, you wouldn't get pissed?"

"That's different," she said.

He didn't forget the women, Aaron told himself. He just forgot their names. A rose by any other name.

He was not a misogynist for forgetting their names, Aaron told himself. He was just bad with names. Relax.

Felicity Sargent, **"Are Tinder-Style Mobile Apps Left-Swiping Away Our Humanity?"** *Vogue*:

> And that's why I'm deeply disturbed by Tinder's
> establishment of the left swipe as the definitive gesture
> of permanent rejection in the digital age.

He had taken one of the Whatshernames to the James Joyce joint downtown. Had an Irish bloke for a waiter and Aaron thought to himself that he'd (Aaron would) be sexier if he had an Irish accent.

Whatshername asked the waiter, "What's good?"

She didn't ask him (Aaron) that and from that point in the evening he knew he would swipe left over their future. She had valued the waiter's opinion more than his (Aaron's).

His cousin, Dara, still trying to get off the phone, accused him of having a self-sabotaging inferiority complex masked as perfectionism but really just a Bohemian, wannabe-hipster romanticism of and nostalgia for and perpetuation of his own suffering. And Aaron replied, "Well, you're a, well, you live in, you're a Stepford wife hick," by way of a comeback. She had really hurt his feelings with that *hipster* bit.

And now the James Joyce Pub was probably being pumped dry by a giant vacuum.

The Ting Tings, "That's Not My Name," a song on Aaron's workout playlist:

> *They call me hell.*
> *They call me Stacey.*
> *They call me her.*
> *They call me Jane.*
> *That's not my name.*
> *That's not my name.*
> *That's not my name.*
> *That's not my name.*
>
> *They call me quiet.*
> *But I'm a riot.*
> *Mary-Jo-Lisa.*
> *Always the same.*
> *That's not my name.*
> *That's not my name.*
> *That's not my name.*
> *That's not my name.*

Left, left. Right.

And now he was driving up to his grandfather's, his mother's, his yellow bungalow.

Aaron's grandfather loved his whiskey and his women and some of his children more than others. He had willed the yellow bungalow to his third daughter, Aaron's mother, without explanation or apology.

Aaron parked in front of Valeria's building and decided to check on her before re-possessing his house. He took Tommy Douglas in his carrier to the entrance of the building.

He buzzed for Valeria downstairs. No answer.

He called her cell. No answer.

Luckily, someone was entering the building and he snuck in behind her. He walked up to Valeria's unit on the fourth floor (the elevators were down).

He knocked. No answer.

"Valeria," he called.

He turned away and began walking to the stairwell when something told him to try the doorknob. Who does that? he said to the something. *Try the doorknob*, something said again.

He did. Lo. The door was unlocked.

Great, he said to something. He pushed the door open an inch. The scene all had the feeling of a horror movie, the spoof of a horror movie. The door even squeaked. Aaron tried to summon real emotion but could only summon spoof feelings, as if his fear were wrapped in a Ziploc freezer bag.

"Valeria," he called again.

No answer.

Keep going, something said. It sounded like the river, if the river had a voice.

Her floor was untouched by the flood. Her power had been restored 1:54 ago, according to the blinking clock on the microwave.

Aaron turned toward the bedroom. He pushed the door open with his toe, expecting to find Valeria overdosed on a combination of prescription pills and whiskey.

Don't be stupid, the river voice in his head said.

There was indeed a bottle of alcohol on the carpet next to Valeria's bed. Who you calling *stupid*? He smelled the bottle and winced when the stench hit him in the eyes. Whiskey.

Valeria's imprint was on one side of the bed, and on the other an open album. It seemed so quaint to have an album in this age. He turned his head. The album was open to a page of black and white photos. All of women.

Most of the women were a little jowly. Square faced, frumpy bangs. That was the style then, Aaron supposed. Their expression had the timeless mixture of confidence, forthrightness, and boredom that beautiful women wore.

In one of the photos, a woman with tightly curled hair was standing in front of his grandfather's, his mother's, his his bungalow.

So Valeria wasn't in her apartment.

Tommy Douglas's carrier was getting heavy. The cat needed a diet. Aaron switched hands and began the walk to his little yellow bungalow, sandwiched between apartment buildings.

That morning, his cousin had said: "I mean, if you had nowhere else to go, then yeah, fine, whatever."

Where could Valeria be?

Where do you go when you have nowhere to go?

55

Where do we go? Where do we go now? sang Guns and Roses in his head.

Go home, the-something-he-was-calling-river-voice said.

❖

Aaron let Tommy Douglas out of the carrier once he got home.

As he did last time, Aaron went straight to the basement stairs to assess the damage. A box must have burst because he saw papers and photographs bobbing on the surface of the water.

At the bottom of the stairs he turned around to examine the rest of the basement.

He found Valeria among the photographs.

She was floating face-down in two feet of muddy water.

❖

B: Beatrice

THERE WAS A TIME to drink milk and a time to drink whiskey.

There was a time to keep a knife in your garter and a time to plunge it into a neck.

There was a time to lie and a time to lie down, Beatrice was learning.

A time to be a woman and a time to be a man and a time to be neither.

The woman next to her, did she, did she say she was Alice?

"Or Annie-Lou or Dorothy," the woman repeated. "Who you want me to be, sugar?"

❖

Alice. Beatrice was searching for Alice.

This honey-haired, perfumed woman couldn't be who she was searching for. The Alice Beatrice had in mind did not smell like Paris or hold hairpins between her lips or have lips, for that matter. She was not inch after inch of softness.

Hung-over, unsure of the past night, Beatrice asked something ridiculous: "Is that your body?"

"What do you mean?" Alice looked down at her breasts.

"Is that your body over there with you?"

"I sure hope it is," Alice said. She was still holding the photograph. "Is it yours?"

Beatrice sat up. Her head. A bowl of hornets.

"Why you carrying around a photo of me in your billfold?" Alice asked.

"I was looking for you," Beatrice said.

"This is from before I was here." Alice examined the photograph then turned back to the mirror and tightened her curls with the curling tongs as if fortifying herself against slipping back into the plain girl in the photograph.

"I like your hair curly like that," Beatrice said.

"What's your name?"

There was a time to lie and a time to— "Beatrice."

Alice approached the bed. She smiled and started plucking the hornets out of Beatrice's head. "Tell me, sugar. What does a girl like you want with a girl like me?"

Beatrice lowered her head, but Alice tilted her chin upward.

Alice asked, "What does a girl like me need to know about a girl like you?"

There was a time to be mysterious and a time to— Beatrice was tired of being mysterious. Of wearing her hair over one eye.

Here's what Beatrice knew.

1. She was in Calgary. 2. Calgary was cold. 3. Men looked her up and down the same way everywhere. 4. There was a package sitting in her hotel room, near the Hudson's Bay. The package would remain unopened until the right time.

5. Her father could die. Of natural or unnatural causes. As could she.

6. Her father was a half-French, half-Bavarian viscount who never spoke German, so completely had he renounced his German side and its generations of land for Beatrice's mother (dead) and her land. Not *renounced*. *Liquidated*. (Drowned, her mother.) He was not a fool. There'd be trouble in Europe soon enough.

"He likes cheese," Beatrice said to Alice.

"What decent man don't?" Alice said.

"Gruyere," Beatrice said. "It's not exactly like the gruyere you eat here."

"No?"

"Yours is more muscular," she said. "Ours is lighter. Cloudier."

7. Her father was not very good at cheese. He blamed the cows. Their milk was "like drinking a drunk rat's piss" is a rough translation from the French. Beatrice knew the farm failed because her father would not take basic advice from farmers in their town on the border of Alberta and Saskatchewan, farmers who'd been making cheese—"if that's cheese then I'd sooner eat a brick"—for generations. 8. Her father was not very good at taking advice in general.

Which leads to 9. Clouds don't make good cheese.

"But eventually," Beatrice said to Alice, "my father paid some Canadians. They were from elsewhere."

"Was this before or after your farm failed?"

"Before. A last-ditch attempt to save it."

"Since there's been farms, there've always been people trying to save 'em."

"He really couldn't afford to pay them well," Beatrice said. "Well, or at all, eventually."

10. The quarters for the farm workers burned down last year. Two years ago? The workers were supposed to live with the cows for part of the winter. It was April and surely it would be spring soon enough.

11. It was winter all year, in some form or another.

Beatrice had intended to tell Alice only up to the part about cheese. The conversation would be cheese-centered, but here she was going on about herself.

"I asked," Alice said. "Don't go faulting yourself for talking."

"It might be the whiskey still," Beatrice said. "Loosened my tongue."

"I could get you some more," Alice said.

Beatrice shook her head. Alice went out the door calling after the other girls and Pearl to get some coffee brewing. "The good stuff."

Beatrice had been running, drifting, escaping, searching, starving, pursuing, avoiding, lying for months. In the stretch between Saskatchewan and Alberta, she felt like she had travelled to Europe and back. She had slept indoors and out. She had become adept at squatting out of eyeshot to relieve herself.

She had met all sorts of eyes—inquisitive, suspicious, sympathetic, beagle—and said nothing, yet here she was spitting out her soul to Alice or, what did she say, Annie-Lou or Dorothy.

Beatrice reckoned that she talked so much about the farm now because she missed it. No, that couldn't be true. She talked so much because in Pearl's house she was among women who wouldn't harm her.

But if she was divulging all of these details about her life now, what had she told Alice the night before when she was drunk and safe and excited and dressed up in someone else's clothes?

Alice set a tray of coffee, bread, a tiny jar of jam, and a hunk of cheese before Beatrice.

"It ain't gruyere," Alice said.

"You eat well here," Beatrice said.

"We manage."

12. A 16-year old, one of the youngest workers on the farm—

Alice stopped Beatrice. She held a finger to her lips and tiptoed to the door. She opened it quickly and looked outside. No one.

"Sometimes the girls like to listen if they suspect rumour's flying. Go on. Go on." Alice waved Beatrice's story onward.

—died among the cows. 13 (this one was not, in fact, a fact, but more of a hunch). He had a thing for Beatrice and when he lay there during the interminable winter and she begged her father to let him stay in the house, she felt like he was a wounded soldier she would tend, would open her vein and pour her blood into, but no, her father said, he would not have peasant manimals in his house (hard to get the viscount out of the viscount), he was running a farm, not a brothel.

Alice sputtered on her coffee.

"I didn't mean—"

"No, it was *manimals*. You mind if I use that?" Alice dabbed at the spilled coffee. "It's actually quite comfortable here at

Pearl's, whatever you want to call it. There aren't too many places even in these big cities—I mean, we're not in London or Paris, wouldn't you love to" and Alice lost the rest of the sentence to daydream.

14. Beatrice had been to London and Paris yet found herself unwilling to trade this moment in this bed with this woman in the East Village for either.

"All I'm saying," Alice said, "is a brothel is one of the safest places for an independent woman."

"Do you consider yourself independent?"

"I do," Alice said. "Don't you?"

"I do," Beatrice began, "feel safe here."

"No one harassing you."

"True."

"No one telling you to fetch this or fetch that or do this or do that or don't sit like that or don't laugh so loud or eat your elbows." Alice nibbled at Beatrice's elbow.

"True."

"No one trying to marry you."

"True," Beatrice said. "There's that."

Beatrice was so open, she realized, because there were few women she could talk to. Even among women, there were particular women who listened as effortlessly as breathing. Each breath was a gust of empathy.

You tell: I listen :: You breathe out : I breathe in.

15. So she left the farm, but not because she loved a 16-year old boy.

There were things that Beatrice knew but could not tell Alice.

"You ever kill anyone?" Alice asked Beatrice. Direct like that.

What was the truth in that case? This was before the days when people said things like, *Define kill.*

"I saw your knife."

16. A knife was an incredibly useful thing to keep, especially on one's thigh.

"I've thought about it," Alice went on. "Someday it might be nice to feel what the tip of a knife feels like going into someone's skin. I picture it like diving into a lake." Then as suddenly, Alice changed the subject, "You been out to Lake Louise yet?"

But the subject came back as they were feeding each other slices of cheese. (Acceptable, the cheese.)

"How many bodies you think are in the Bow right now?"

"Swimming?"

"No, dead." And Alice's eyes took on that faraway look it had when she had said *London* and *Paris*. "I bet the Bow wasn't named the bow for nothing."

"You know, there are a bunch of people like us here in East Village."

Beatrice knew exactly what Alice meant by *like us*.

The hornets flared up. Beatrice was tired of mystery.

17. She said, "I was supposed to kill you, Alice."

Alice said, "I know."

Then Alice reclined on her side of the bed and licked the corners of her mouth.

"Well, what are you waiting for, sugar?" Alice asked then laughed obscenely. "Gimme a little death."

Beatrice said, "I'm not fooling. They want you dead."

"They who?"

Beatrice restrained herself. They'd want her dead too if she divulged that.

Alice said, "There are lots of men who want me, dear, but none of them want me dead. I reckon I'm a whole lot more useful 'live than dead."

Beatrice took one last gulp of her coffee.

"And you?" Alice asked. "How'd you prefer me?"

> *They call me farm girl.*
> *They call me whore.*
> *They call me daughter.*
> *They call me shame.*
> *That's not my name.*
> *That's not my name.*
> *That's not my name.*
> *That's not my name.*

Beatrice knew that it was all right to name dairy cattle but not beef cattle. She had drunk too much, gotten too close to this Alice, and now to kill her would be impossible. She'd hear Alice's voice, that laugh in her head, forever. If only Alice had remained abstract.

63

The plan was to lure Alice to the river and make it seem like she (Alice) lost her footing and drowned in pounds of petticoats, but only after she (Beatrice) had secured the deed for her (Alice's) land her father owned, that she (Alice, oh that name) owned. Beatrice still had trouble thinking that a woman could own so much land.

Yet rich as Alice was—she didn't know about the oil, did she—here was Alice working in a brothel. Something didn't make sense. It was time for Alice to start talking.

Alice asked again, "You'd prefer me 'live or dead, Miss Beatrice?"

"Alive," the hornets said.

"Then alive I shall stay."

"But you don't understand," Beatrice said. "If it's not you then it's gon' be me. My father's in a lot of trouble."

"He made his bed, why you goin' go lie in it?"

"You know what it's like on the border."

"I don't," Alice said. "Never lived on that farm. Never even seen it."

"These men, they want what's theirs—"

"It's not theirs. It's my father's. It's mine."

Beatrice was becoming exasperated with Alice's logic.

"Look—" Alice began.

"No, you look. I know my father's a terrible mule and that he done angered or swindled half the province. But where I come from my father's problem can become mine right quick" —Beatrice snapped— "whether he is walking on the earth or swimming under it. And I come here with the intentions of making things right for my family."

"By killing me?"

"I admit, it's not ideal. And so, I confess the truth to you—"

"I think you had too much whiskey."

"I confess the truth to you with the hopes there might be 'nother way. They don't want you dead, Miss Alice. They just want your land."

"There's no way."

"And you just said you never seen it. You never stepped foot on that property. I meanwhile lived my whole life making gruyere, making cheese, you hear me, me and my father and some migrants. They already have most of our land."

"I need to know who these people are you talking 'bout."

"I laid my situation as bare as I can for you, Alice. If you just give me the deed to the land, I'll tell 'em I robbed you but you put up a mighty fight and got 'way or I can tell 'em I killed you and flushed you in the Bow like I was planning but I need to get that deed from you else they gon' devour me. They already—I can't tell you what they already done me."

Alice didn't respond for a long time. They had finished eating. The dishes and cups sat empty and imploring.

"It's not my land they want," Alice finally said. "It's what's under it."

"You just speculating."

"I know oil and I know oil people. And you might be one of them, I suspect." Alice took the tray and went to the kitchen.

When Alice returned from the kitchen, Beatrice was dressed in her original clothes. The change must have piqued pity in Alice.

Alice said, "You do have an option. You can stay here at Pearl's."

"They'll find me," Beatrice said. "Just like I found you."

"That's exactly what we want," Alice said. "You gon' kill somebody before the season's through."

19. The men pinned Beatrice's hands behind her back and pulled up her skirts. Beatrice drank whiskey whenever she came to this point in the memory. This was before she started wearing a knife around her thigh. The whole time, she looked into the eyes of a cow. She tried to count its eyelashes but ended up counting thrusts instead. She got as far as 19.

They told her, "Give that message to Alice."

A: Aaron Again

AARON WAS ON THE phone with the police.

That he didn't remember the women he dated didn't mean he killed them. He never killed a woman his whole life. Honest. He wasn't a pig farmer.

As if in refutation, Tommy Douglas entered through the front door with the upper part of a femur in his mouth. He dropped it near his travel carrier and ran outside again.

"Sir, are you still there?" the dispatcher asked.

"Yeah, no, yeah."

Tommy Douglas came back with a smaller bone, part of a humerus.

"Sir?"

"No, it's my cat."

"Please keep it away from the body. The police are on their way."

Was it too late to hang up without being suspicious?

Was it too late to remember all these women he forgot? To shovel the snow off their names?

Tommy Douglas returned with an intact radius and fractured ulna and spat them out near his carrier.

"Was there any trauma to the body?"

Aaron heard sirens, very faintly, in the distance.

"Sir," the dispatcher said.

"My cat," Aaron said.

"Was there trauma?"

"I don't know. I didn't look. I didn't do anything. I—"

Tommy Douglas came back with a mouthful of small bones, like finger bones.

"Sir? Stay on the line with me."

There was a hashtag for all of the Missing and Murdered Indigenous Women: #MMIW.

1200 MMIWs.

"Sir? Can you hear me?"

"I'm here," Aaron said. He hadn't heard the question.

"Do you know the victim?"

His old high school didn't even have 1200 kids.

"Yes," Aaron said. "She lived next door."

"Do you know her name?"

"Yes." Aaron lost his voice for a moment.

"Sir? Do you know her name?"

"Her name was Valeria."

Tommy Douglas returned with a thin, flat bone. A pelvis?

"My cat keeps bringing in stuff," Aaron said to the dispatcher.

"What kind of stuff?"

"Like articles," Aaron said. "Articles of people."

Tommy Douglas came back with his final gift: part of a ribcage.

This cage, meant to protect the breath and the heart, in the end protected only itself.

TD sat down and licked himself.

And just like that, Aaron's cat had managed to produce most of a female skeleton in the hallway as the police entered.

Chapter Four

by Jani Krulc

Aaron

"So, this Valerie, she was what, your girlfriend?" Police Officer Stansky looked like every jock Aaron had spent his high school career avoiding: chiseled jaw, spiky brush cut, bulging biceps. Stansky was also developing the suggestion of a beer gut, and his hair was much thinner than it would have been when he was, say, star of the football team. He leaned forward across the scratched-up metal table.

"You were, what, girlfriend and boyfriend?" Stansky repeated.

"No," Aaron said, frowning. He folded his hands together, placed them on the table. The steel was cold and he almost flinched. "Absolutely not."

"So, what, you knew this Valerie chick through business? You were associates?"

"No," Aaron's voice snapped, and he clenched his hands together, the knuckles whitening. "We were friends." The skin on his throat started to get hot and, as it always did when he became upset, blotchy.

"And her name was Valeria."

Officer Radar had been standing behind Aaron, so still and silent he'd forgotten about her.

She had come up to him at the house, said they should talk, clear up a few things.

"What about my cat?" he'd asked. Radar assured him another officer would take care of his pet.

He knew it was a mistake to go with them as soon as he got into the police car. He craned his neck, could make out a stocky officer trying to scoop up Tommy Douglas, who was trying to get back to his skeleton. Completely wrong approach. TD hissed and swiped, and judging from the officer's audible yelp, TD's aim was as good as ever. The cop car peeled off before Aaron could reconsider.

Now Officer Radar slid out from the corner of the room and leaned on the table until her ice blue eyes were level with his.

"You were friends," she said. Stansky smirked, his lips pulling apart to reveal stained teeth. Aaron bet he chewed. Maybe he would get antsy for nicotine and end this farce. Aaron had been waiting in this bare room surrounded by windows he couldn't see through for hours. He was being cooperative. He was the one who had called the police in the first place!

"You were friends?" Officer Radar wasn't challenging him. She wanted to know more.

"We were neighbours. She kind of looked out for me."

"You're saying that a broad like Valerie there, she took care of a guy like you?" Stansky walked around the room with his hands on his hips.

"Looked out, I said."

"What were you doing that she needed to look out for you?"

"I wasn't doing anything. But it's not the best of neighbourhoods. It helps to be neighbourly."

"What were you doing in a place like that, anyway? That

land's valuable. You could be living in a brand-new house out in Walden with a two-car garage. Instead, you're still living in that slum."

A knock at the door, to which Officer Radar responded. Muffled voices, the exchange of some papers. She walked back to the table.

"I like the history. It's my grandfather's house." Aaron's voice was becoming hoarse. His t-shirt and shorts provided little warmth in this barren space. "It's gentrifying."

"Witnesses put you in her apartment," Stansky said.

"I couldn't find her yesterday."

"You were in your house yesterday?" Officer Radar spoke evenly.

Shit. Should he have said that?

"Yeah, I went back to see what it looked like. If there was damage."

"You thought there wouldn't be damage?" Officer Radar clicked her fingernails against the table.

"I wanted to see the extent of the damage."

"And that's when you saw Valerie in your place."

"Her name was Valeria. And I didn't."

"Maybe she was stealing some things. A thief. Maybe you didn't like that."

"No, no, no. I did not see her." He pushed his fingers through his hair. His scalp felt prickly. Why had she been in his house? Was she trying to find him?

"I want to know where my cat is. Has someone found Tommy Douglas?"

"The cause of death has come back," Officer Radar held up the file.

Sudden collapse, he hoped. Painless aneurism. No, screw that. Mistaken identity.

This is not happening.

71

"Blunt force trauma to the head."

They were studying him now. Officer Radar placed a photograph on the table.

"Oh, god." A deep gash in the back of a skull. Was it hers? Of course it was.

Earlier in the day, when the police showed up – because he had called them! – Aaron crouched over the pile of bones in his front hallway. Like an idiot, or maybe a sociopath, he had been carrying the jawbone with him, all over downtown and north Calgary. He hadn't imagined he'd spend the rest of the day here.

"You'd better get comfortable, Mr. Cohen. We haven't even gotten around to the business of that little crypt in your front hall."

Beatrice

RED BROCADE CURTAINS BLOCKED sunlight, moonlight, muffled sound. Weeping candles flicked shadows up the crimson walls.

By the second day, it was clear that no one ran a tab at Pearl's. But Beatrice felt flush and parted with bills: for meals of cheese and bread and fried meat, for the room, for Alice, for time.

How long, how long could she stretch this out? She found a whole world in the fine white hair that coated the fronts of Alice's thighs (not the backs, which she confirmed over and over again).

"You're so soft," Beatrice repeated. No callused heels or torn up fingers to catch threads or skin.

It seemed easy to become soft. Bea's belly full, head heavy with sleep; was this what it felt to be rested?

On the third day, Alice brought coffee with whisky, and news.
"Gladys at the bar says your room's gonna be vacated."

Bea sat up in the bed, pulling the sheets to her neck, and slurped. The liquid struck her hard, her stomach burning.

"What room? Who's Gladys? What bar? Come back to bed."

"Your room at the hotel. No bother, if you got nothing in there." Alice faced her vanity, dipped her finger in a little pot.

What room? The coffee or the whisky started to burn away the fog: indeed, a room a few blocks away. Not the room that's important, but what's in it.

Bea dropped the sheets, hoisted herself out of the bed. She started rifling through a pile on the floor: dress (Alice's? her own?) wool coat, hat, trousers. The cloth smelled stale. In fact, the whole room carried the odour of sweat permeated by grease from the unwashed plates piling on Alice's vanity. Bea needed air.

She dressed. The wool itched; the pants pinched her. She tied the strip of cloth around her chest as tight as she could, until any suggestion of female curves vanished. She slid the knife into her boot; not very useful to strap a weapon to your thigh if you're wearing pants. Into her jacket pocket, she pushed the diminishing roll of fives. Knotting her hair into a bun on the top of her head, blind because Alice was using the mirror, she slid pointed pins to secure her locks, then slipped the cap over top.

Alice approached her; arms open like she wanted to embrace. She had made up her face: black kohl around her eyes, rouge on lips and cheeks. She'd smoothed flower scented oil over her mop of curls and contained them with a ribbon.

"Pretty lady," Beatrice said.

"If you're gonna go out there, at least do it right." Alice flicked the brim of Bea's cap, then knocked it off. Bea's hair cascaded down her back.

"Wait here," Alice said.

Beatrice perched on the side of the bed, ready to spring, tongue scratchy. She chewed the inside of her cheek.

The door swung open and she started. Alice chuckled.

"Easy there," she gestured to the vanity and Beatrice obeyed.

"Take off your jacket." Bea hesitated. "Don't want to make you itchy."

The straight razor flashed silver in Alice's hand.

"You planning to shave me?"

"One gust of wind and you're a goner."

Beas's hair reached the small of her back. Had she ever cut it? Not in years. Not exactly top of her mind.

"Give it here," Bea said. Alice pressed the razor flat in Bea's palm. Bea pulled a fistful of hair straight, sliced a clean foot off. The remaining hair sprung up to her chin, weightless.

"Finish it," Bea said. Alice nodded.

"I used to cut my pa's hair."

When she was done, Alice placed the razor on the vanity and unbuttoned Bea's collar, blew to lift the short hairs off Bea's neck.

"Perfect," Alice said. Bea's cheeks hollowed without the weight of the hair; her forehead widened.

"Just don't claim to be older than 19. You can't grow a whisker worth a damn."

Aaron

"I'M SORRY, DO YOU not watch cop shows?"

Dara was spreading soft butter onto slices of bread. She was working from home because of the flood and she'd had to cut short her day of conference calls to pick up Aaron from the police station in the far northeast quadrant of the city. She'd brought the boys with her because the school had closed, and no one had eaten lunch.

"You don't volunteer to talk to the cops! Everyone knows that."

In fact, Aaron spent most of his free time on his historical research. He didn't own a TV.

"I'm not a criminal, so it didn't occur to me," Aaron pressed his fingers deep into his temples. "I wanted to clear some things up. Christ, I had questions for them!"

"Words!" The boys were lurking outside the kitchen, waiting for their grilled cheese. They tittered in unison, hiding smiles behind cupped hands.

"What? Jesus." The boys gasped and ran from the doorway.

"You're something else, you know that? I'm really looking forward to everything just getting back to normal," Dara pressed the bread into the pan. The butter sizzled.

"The point is they couldn't hold me. They didn't arrest me. That Stansky officer looked like he could just cry when they had to let me go." Aaron was rubbing his hands together.

"You okay there?" Dara was staring at him, and the boys, who had returned to their post at the door, were staring, too.

"I'm fine. Well, I'm probably traumatized, but I'll be out of your hair very soon, as soon as possible." But was that true? Even if his house didn't have a cracked foundation or permanent mould spores in the walls, he couldn't live in that place again. Where would he go?

"How did you know that woman anyway?" Dara was teasing the bread with a spatula, trying to see if she could flip the sandwich. Impatient, Aaron thought. Dara looked paler than normal, as though the march to the office from the LRT was the only sun she got during the day. In fact, it probably was.

"I gotta go."

"You don't want one?"

"I'm not hungry." In fact, he was starving.

"You're not returning to the house, are you?"

Aaron was almost out the door.

"I need to rescue Tommy Douglas," he said.

"Don't you know anything? You never return to the scene of the crime!"

Alice

ALICE HAD ARRANGED THE hair into a bundle and secured it with a piece of twine.

"Gladys, some whiskey." She set the hair on the bar. It was mid-morning and the room was unusually empty.

"What in heaven's name? Did you skin a critter?" Gladys pushed a tumbler towards Alice and poked the bundle with her finger. "That's not some black magic nonsense you're doing?"

"Magic's not required." She took a gulp of the brown liquid and relished the burn. "Gladys, do you believe in luck?"

"I believe certain folks got more of it than others." Gladys wiped the bar, which was already clean. "Sometimes that's just called smarts, though. Hey, that friend of yours asked me about a room in a hotel somewhere. What was he on about?"

"Three days of lovemaking causes some men to go a little funny in the head." Alice tipped the last of the drink into her mouth, set the glass down with a flourish, and grabbed the hair.

"What you plannin' to do with that pelt?"

Alice grinned.

"Consider it my good luck charm."

Aaron

HIS HOUSE, SODDEN AND sallow, looked like it was sinking into the mud. Bright yellow police tape highlighted its anemic pallor.

"Tommy Douglas!" Aaron skirted around the tape, obeying the perimeter.

"TD!" He pulled out a packet of Fur Friends Cat Treats in Sardine, TD's favourite, and shook it. If all else failed, Aaron also had a can of low sodium tuna and a can opener in the car.

"Looking for someone?"

"Gah!" Aaron dropped the bag of treats in a puddle, which the radio had told him was festering with e. coli.

"Damnit." He picked the bag up by its corner and continued to shake it, splattering mud onto his legs.

"I already talked to the police," he called over his shoulder.

"I'm not the police," the voice, a woman's, said.

"Then get off my property." He shook the bag with more energy.

"I'm on the sidewalk."

Aaron clenched his teeth, "Would everyone just leave me the hell alone?" and wheeled around.

"My name is Chester. Phoebe Chester. But everyone just calls me Chester." She stuck out her hand.

Chester's bobbed hair fell over on eye in a dark lazy wave. She wore a gigantic brown leather messenger bag across her body, dwarfing her small frame.

"Chester?" Aaron blinked. He'd never seen such a deep green eye before. "I'm Aaron." He extended the hand holding bag of cat treats. "Oh, sorry. Don't touch that."

"I'm with the Herald."

"Oh," he said, and turned away. "No reporters."

"I'm not, I'm just researching. The murder."

"I gathered that," he said. "Tommy Douglas!"

"Researching, that's it. I don't have a story."

"Well, I'm not giving you one."

"I want to do a profile on Valeria. Make her more than a dead body in a basement. Make people care."

"The last time someone I didn't know said they wanted to talk to me about Valeria, I ended up spending six hours in an interrogation room."

"Oh, I didn't know they arrested anyone."

"Um, they didn't."

"You know, you don't have to talk to the police if they don't arrest you?"

"It was a misunderstanding." Aaron cleared his throat. "TOMMY DOUGLAS!"

Aaron began stomping to the back of the house, mud making his boots heavier with each step.

"Why did her photo album have pictures of your house in it?"

He paused.

"Who told you that?"

"Why was she looking at them right before she died?

Aaron sighed.

"I don't know." His resolve was failing.

He sighed.

"What do you want from me?"

"Who is this in the photograph?"

Chester held a police photograph of Valeria's bedspread.

"How did you get this?"

Chester stared at him.

"I don't know," he answered, honestly. "And I have no idea why she was looking at this."

"You were her friend. Did she have many friends?"

"She knew everybody. Everybody loved her."

"Not everybody, apparently."

A crash sounded from inside the house.

"What the?" Chester started.

"Tommy Douglas!" He strained to hear the inevitable meows that would follow such a commotion.

"Come on!"

"What?"

"It's my cat, come on!" he started to run, then stopped and grabbed her hand.

"Come on!"

"There's police tape!"

"I can get in through the side door. Come on!"

"It's illegal!"

"Hey, you want a story or not?"

Beatrice

At FIRST, SHE AVERTED her eyes when men passed her on the street. But soon Beatrice realized they just wanted to share a nod or size her up. Better to look forward, untuck her chin, and amble on.

It was a short two block walk back to the St. Louis, but Beatrice wanted to stretch her legs. She felt a pleasure in taking long strides unencumbered by the choke of a corset or the weight of petticoats. True, the wool jacket itched her neck, but she could slip a finger under the collar and scratch without arousing suspicion about her character. The package could wait.

Outside, earth crunching under her still unmended boots, she was able to think. She had two choices: stay or go. If she stayed, she couldn't exactly keep a residence at Pearl's, not without paying a fortune or working herself. Either option was too risky. So, she'd go, west over the mountains, maybe all the way clear to the ocean. And Alice?

Beatrice couldn't begin a long journey on an empty stomach. It was already late afternoon. She strode to the Cecil, pushing her chest forward, her shoulders down. Was that the key to this? Just make yourself look as big as possible?

They were serving steak; it was late enough. She would not have to make do with another hastily sliced cheese sandwich.

"Whiskey," she said when the waiter came. "And one of those rib eyes."

"You from around here?" It was the same man from days earlier, his apron dirtier. "You look familiar."

"Just arrived. Lookin' for work."

The man squinted at her, tilted his head.

"There's work, even for someone your size."

She kept the hat on, didn't think manners mattered that much in this place. A couple men sat at the counter, slumped over their food, elbows up next to their plates.

The steak was bloody when it arrived. Bea mimicked the other men. She fisted the fork and cut a large chunk of the meat, thrust it into her mouth and chewed with vigour. Even when she was on the road, rationing food and starved, she ate like a lady: small mouthfuls, setting her fork down between paltry bites, patting her mouth clean with a soiled handkerchief before sipping water out of a canteen. Not for the sake of appearances; she thought eating slowly would make her feel fuller.

She paid, checked her pocket. Outside, a large cloud threatened rain and obscured the sun.

The river was starting to rise, spring runoff from the mountains. She walked down the bank to the edge, knelt and picked up a flat rock and pitched it across the water. It skimmed the surface and skipped, three times, and then sunk. Plunk.

And Alice?

Alice would be fine. She knew how to take care of herself. And anyway, first they'd have to find her. She was probably packing up herself.

The sun peeked from behind the cloud, the reflection off the water a dazzling prism. Right in the middle of it, a shadow.

Bea spun on her haunches, ducked a punch that just grazed the side of her cheek. She slid back in the mud as the man, a burly beast wearing black, charged forward. His foot caught a rock and down he went. OOF, he grunted, the reek of his breath spinning her round again. She gained ground, almost up the bank but he seized the edge of her pants. Flayed a tree branch of its leaves as she tumbled down, landed on her back. He straddled her, holding her arms in one paw as he reached back for her foot and pulled off her boot. The knife went with it. Grinning, he flipped her jacket open. "You's a wee strange thing," he wheezed. "Now where's the gold?" He plundered her pocket, tucking money into the back of his pants.

"You's better be a quiet one," he leaned his weight forward to undo his buckle. Bea turned her head away from his stink, took a deep breath.

"Pig," she hissed, then lunged. Her teeth cleaved soft flesh, ripped the tip off his earlobe. He leapt back, hands cupping ear, wailing. Torso free, she rocked forward, clenched her fist, and slashed.

Beatrice rolled the cretin off her. Blood pooled in the divot their bodies had made. She snatched her money back and shoved it in her pants, found her boot and slipped it on, tucked the knife back in. The straight razor she cleaned on a rose bush, clicked it closed and slid it back up the sleeve of her shirt. Stripped off the ruined jacket and started to heave the body into the river.

"Who's the pirate now," she whispered.

Valeria

"REGGIE, GET YOUR ASS on that bus."

They were clearing out the village, packing up all the Drop-In residents and sending them to the Northeast. But Reggie, good old Reggie, didn't want to go.

"How about you, V? You're not going."

"I'm staying here to make sure them zoo animals don't get out," Valeria guffawed and lit a cigarette, Du Maurier, King Size.

"I can't go, V. I gotta stay here, gotta take care of my stuff."

"Reggie, we both know that everything you own is in that there Spiderman backpack you're wearing." Indeed, the bag was stuffed full of festering clothes and a week's worth of Sun newspapers.

"Oh, you're right, V. You got it," he said, then leaned in and whispered loudly, "I'm talking about the treasure!"

"Reggie, Reggie," she leaned in, too, and whispered back. "That's what I meant when I said I was taking care of the zoo animals. I'm staying here to make sure everything is on the up and up."

Reggie grinned, stood taller by an inch.

"Oh, good. Okay. Okay," he turned his attention to the bus. "Wait for me! I'm getting on! I'm getting on the bus!" He left Valeria to her cigarette, ploughed into the last couple of tired men waiting to get shipped out.

"There's room for you, too, Valeria. An extra bed." Pete, a social worker at the DI, offered. He was a smoker, too, and they'd chat occasionally when she had time to kill and was just hanging around.

"I'm good Pete, thanks. Just keeping an eye out."

"Stay dry," he said, and waved. The bus drove off.

I'm the only person on the planet, she thought. Or, the only person in the East Village.

The sirens had stopped and the river, still swollen and angry, wasn't rising. She paused at the Langevin bridge. Dirty water sucked a tree trunk downstream. It got stuck right underneath the bridge and wouldn't budge.

"Mother Nature's pissed," she said, to nobody, tapped out her cigarette and threw it in a garbage can on her way back to her apartment. Her grandmother had always said only idiots would build a city in the middle of a river, and Valeria was inclined to agree. Although no one was asking her opinion.

The four story hike up to her floor didn't faze her; the elevator hardly ever worked anyway.

Inside, she poured herself a drink and lit another cigarette.

The power wasn't on yet and looking out her window at a dead downtown got old really fast. She took out her memory book (as her grandmother used to call such things) from the top shelf in her closet and started flipping through the pages.

She was the only one left. One cousin in Whitehorse, last she knew. But she was the only one in the city. When she came to the photo of the house, she paused.

That Aaron was a good kid. Maybe a little naïve, but a good kid, nonetheless. Although, considering how much he liked his history, maybe a little dumb, too.

Nostalgia gripped her, carried her out the door and down the steps to the little yellow house.

The muck stuck to her shoes. It wasn't mud, or sewage. It was the innards of the river, come spewing forth every few generations.

She tried the door handle, and, to her surprise, it opened. Aaron must have forgotten to lock it. "Dumb," she muttered, but smiled.

Fresh muck had been tracked through the entrance. She followed the fading foot steps to the basement entrance. Something behind the door was sloshing around. The door opened.

"You," she said. "It's you."

Chapter Five

by Aritha van Herk

SHE HAD TO GET away, as far away from the river and the spinning hump of his black shape as possible. Had anyone seen him following her? Was he being followed? It felt like the whole town was watching, sizing her up, measuring her vulnerabilities. Before, she had been a passing stranger, now she was a killer and a victim, both. Pitiless, Calgary was pitiless.

She tried to recover her breath, think of what to do next, even while she stumbled, ran, stopped and looked back over her shoulder. The river moved as the river moved, carrying its depths and secrets, dead branches and discarded whispers. She wanted to vanish, but then thought she should try to make sure that she was seen so that if his corpse snagged on a branch and bumped into the bank she was far away, far away and with no connection to him, to whatever curious person would find him and develop suspicions.

She had zigzagged away from the river and now found herself in front of a solid building, brick, with a long veranda that looked hospitable for a factory. Alaska Western Bedding

Co. Limited. The entrance stairs at the side looked like they led to refuge. What had Frankie said? Lots of work, even for someone her size. How did she look to them? Young, too weak to haul and carry. She could try here; stuffing mattresses couldn't be too difficult. But jacketless, she felt naked, stood out. She needed a jacket, a coat to hide behind. Without the jacket, her shirt was too obvious, and she looked like a young woman in trousers; it was the jacket that gave her male stature. And boots, the loose sole was starting to flap even more.

She dodged away from the river; cap pulled low. The houses to the west huddled blank and meager, and she strode quickly, whistling as if she were an errand boy, eyes alert for a clothesline. Nothing, she could see no potential camouflage at all.

She moved south and east then, passing empty lots and small bitter-faced houses, almost despairing but calculating, watching, and at last met luck, for there, behind Mrs. McGonagall's rooming house with its capacious veranda and side-leaning porch, was a clothesline, flapping the arms and legs of men's pants and shirts—clearly the landlady did her lodgers' laundry for a fee, and Bea yearned to strip down, and into clean clothes—and yes, a coat that looked like a grown schoolboy's, a possible fit. Bea checked the house with a surreptitious eye, walked past, slid down the back lane, and saw her chance, hopped the picket fence. She smelled the ripe aroma of the outhouse, the lilac bush not enough to camouflage the lye and urine mixture and hovered beside it, considering whether the windows of the house showed movement, and then, like a shadow, crouched behind a flapping sheet, and fumbled with the pins scare-crowing the coat to the line. It was still damp, and smelled of carbolic, but she pulled it on and whisked up the lane as quickly as she dared, hoping to be invisible. She had to resist looking over her shoulder, had to slow her steps so that she seemed purposeful but not in flight.

Now, the decision she had to make. She hot-footed back toward the stores, across Centre street, determined to find Glass Bros. If they had Walk-Over Shoes for ladies, they'd have good hobnailed boots for men.

Leave town or stay? Try to finish her business with Alice or let the whole matter slide, change her name, become Ben instead of Beatrice, head west through the mountains for the coast. She felt light-headed with choice, with the new freedom of walking with an open stride, once you got used to them, pants so much easier to move in. She had enough money for the train fare, could lose herself in Vancouver, find profitable work there, or even take the new railway north to Prince George. She needed to start over, this whole mess unsolvable, and she couldn't see forcing Alice to give up the deed to anything.

When she shoved her memory away, it seemed she could escape the men waiting to get their hands on the deed, but then she remembered again the feel of their threat and the hard hands they had laid on her, and she knew they would never stop looking for her, would never stop until they held the title, the deed and the mineral rights. And then would do away with her.

Logic. Small steps. First the shoes. She needed to be able to run.

"You," said Valeria. "What are you doing here? This isn't your house."

"What are *you* doing here? I could ask you the same question," he snarled, his perpetual snarl, the one that made her shrug and tap out another cigarette in an effort to deflect him from his bitterness. His jacket was dirtier than usual, as if he'd slept in the mud. Mud everywhere, mud coating streets and yards and the sides of houses, cars that had been left stranded with mud as high as their windows.

She stood and looked at him as he emerged from the basement, his jeans wet to his thighs, his face creased with frustration. "Aaron hasn't got anything worth stealing, Chase."

"And how would you know that, you old slag?"

"Don't—" said Valeria sharply, "call me names, first, and second, Aaron doesn't own valuables, just books and stuff. He doesn't even drink much. There's nothing for you here."

"And why are you so determined to protect his stuff? Something you know that you don't want me to know?"

She stared him down. "You're trespassing and I'm not leaving until you get out. He's a friend."

He opened the freezer top of the fridge and twisted the top of a tin of frozen condensed juice, now thawed, which did not open. He tossed it back and shut the door, then came towards her, quick despite his sodden jeans, and grabbed her arm. "And we are too, Valeria. You've even given me a free ride once in a while. And I need to know where he keeps his valuables."

"There are no valuables!"

"Sure. What about in here?" He moved to the smaller room behind the kitchen, one that seemed tacked on to the house.

She followed him. "Chase, he hasn't got a bean. He's a historian, for Christ's sake." She tugged at him, trying to distract him.

He turned and pushed her, and she stumbled against the ladder that was propped in a corner of the alcove. They both looked up. The trap door to the loft stood open.

"Dumb," Valeria said.

"Dumb." Chase grabbed the ladder and pushed it up into the loft opening.

She shoved the ladder away from the access, but he was too strong for her, too determined. "You," she said, pulling at his legs while he wedged his way up the ladder, "you don't care. Someone's sent you to find—"

She grappled with some faint memory of Chase taking a piece of paper from a man with a lethal-smelling cigar, how she'd thought the man wasn't as rich as he pretended to be, his weasel chin, his eyes hidden behind cheap sunglasses.

"Shut up," Chase snarled. "Shut up, shut up." Standing on the second rung from the top of the ladder, he pulled a box from the loft space, and it flew open, papers cascading around him to the floor, newspaper articles, photographs, copies of maps, ragged clippings.

Valeria scrambled to gather them, as if she could erase Chase's tracks. "Just old papers, nothing worth anything. He wouldn't keep money or important stuff here."

Chase pulled another box toward him, and his balance on the ladder swayed.

Valeria bent, scrambling to gather papers, huffing, "There's nothing, there's nothing—"

A fat crate of books, heavier than Chase was prepared for, thudded against his chest, and the rickety ladder seemed to hesitate before slowly pitching back, falling with Chase, in a heavy thump, directly on the back of Valeria's head.

The boots felt marvellous, as if her feet could fly.

The proprietor had looked at her oddly, but focussed on her feet, which she blessed for being broad and sturdy, not feminine and shapely but calloused and road-worthy.

He sold her a pair of thick woollen socks and a pair of brogues that laced up over the ankles, with a tongue so sturdy that she felt it was an ally. She'd fumbled the money out from the inside pocket of the wrinkled and still damp jacket, all the while shielding her face under the cap and hoping that he was more interested in the money than in her.

"And these?" he inquired, nudging at her worn boots.

"Please discard them for me," she said, remembering to lower her voice to a rasp.

Her new boots carried her down the street with a strong whiff of speed, so that she reached the Costello block as if on wings. Back to the hotel now, her feet had given her strength to go to her room and decide how to handle that package, what to do next.

She should have tipped the brim of her cap up and slowed down, because she bumped—smack—into a solid body, and when she tried to dodge around, saying, "Excuse me," he dodged with her and blocked her way.

"I'm sorry, I'm in a hurry."

"You seem to be," said a deep voice. "In too much of a hurry to honour your orders, I guess."

She looked up into the square and honest face of the blacksmith. She had ordered the lock and never returned. How long had she been adrift at Pearl Miller's, how could she have lost days, nights, too much time, her plan, her package, her escape and redemption, all muddled now.

"Charlie Tucker remember?" the man said.

"I'm sorry, I lost track of time."

"Seems you lost yourself too."

Beatrice blushed. "Yes, I — But how did you know me?"

"Takes more than a pair of trousers to fool me. You look different, but you don't *look* different, if you know what I mean."

"I don't know what you mean."

He had a firm grip on her upper arm, in case she decided to run. "Ever notice how if you look at people from the corner of your eye, you can read more about them than if you look head-on?"

"No, I haven't."

"It might be a useful skill to cultivate. You don't do well with the head-on encounter, if my memory serves me right."

Bea felt shame. He had saved her money and whiskey from the pickpocket, let her use his sink to clean up, promised to make the lock to her specifications, and she had not bothered to remember him or to return. Even in a town as raw and rough as Calgary, this was bad manners.

She lifted her eyes to him. "I owe you an apology. I should have returned yesterday."

"I thought you would appear eventually. And there were no reports of lost or missing women circulating. Not that you would be missed, especially now that you are" — he tilted his head— "a young man?"

"I had to disguise myself," she muttered. "And skirts slow even a racehorse down."

"No doubt they do." He seemed to muse, hesitate. "Well, here's my shop. Would you care to appraise the lock I fashioned?"

Inside the big double doors, a horse nickered in a stall, waiting to be shoed. The smell of metal and red-hot coals was so warm, even comforting, that Bea thought she might sink into a corner and cry. She trusted Charlie Tucker. She wanted to trust Charlie Tucker. He seemed the one person who didn't want to deceive her or confuse her or hurt her. But she didn't dare. She felt the edge of her razor up her sleeve and remembered how easily she had swiped it across the throat of the black-coated man, felt his sudden collapse as if it had happened in a dream, a nightmare, another life.

Anyone could be looking for her. With an effort, she squared her shoulders and lifted her chin. "Yes," she said.

"Will it withstand prying or breakage?"

"Oh," he said gently. "It will that. And it might even do for the crate that's waiting for you down at the train station freight office."

A chill raced down her neck. "How—- It wasn't supposed to arrive for a week."

"Well, it's there. And you might need a wagon and horse to fetch it."

"And you? How— How do you know — ?" Beatrice felt the ground tilting.

Charlie shrugged. "I'm the man they call when they want something heavy moved from one spot to another. I've got the workhorse and haul wagon and the space to store loads. They naturally think I'd be the man who knows where Miss Beatrice de Seychelle will want that crate delivered. And although you neglected to tell me your name, I thought you might be the same Miss Beatrice de Seychelle."

Aaron tugged open his side door and called in his most persuasive voice. "Tommy Douglas!"

Chester laughed. "Why don't you just call him Tommy?"

"He won't answer. He only responds to Tommy Douglas, the whole name."

"Seems anti-socialist."

"He just has strong character." The kitchen where he'd stood, talking to the police on the phone, looked the same. They'd obviously taken Valeria's body out the front door, despite the missing porch, hadn't dragged it through here. "TD! TD!"

"But he answers to his initials? Too smart."

"Look," Aaron turned to Chester. "Don't mock my cat. He's the best friend I've got. And he is smarter than most humans. He's the one who found the bones. He knows when things aren't right. He communicates."

He moved through his creaking little ship of a house, noticing that objects were awry. He'd been so upset about Valeria floating in his basement that he hadn't registered, hadn't seen that a little table was overturned, a chair tipped back against the wall. He opened the door to the alcove that gave him access to the loft and stopped dead. The floor was littered with papers, his papers, his maps and books and research flung everywhere, photographs curling and stuck together, his beautiful old history books scattered, spines broken, priceless plates bent. The ladder was splintered on top of the mess.

With a throaty *meouwww*, Tommy Douglas leapt from the open loft space, landing with enough force to make Chester jump and give a repressed scream.

"Tommy Douglas, what are you doing up there?" He picked up the cat and cradled him. Tommy Douglas yowled and complained, lashed his tail and stretched out his claws.

"Scared me half to death," said Chester.

"Tommy Douglas, what happened here? What happened? Did the police do this?" Aaron knelt, still holding the cat, and tried to close a flayed volume of sepia-tinted photographs. "Who did this? Bastards. Not enough that my basement's flooded, but this too, what a mess, my research."

Chester looked from him to the loft access and back. She clutched her messenger bag close to her chest. "Someone was looking for something. It must have been the police."

"But not this way, surely – besides I thought they left with me."

"When they arrested you?"

"They didn't arrest me, just asked me questions."

Thomas Douglas arched his back, clawed at the throw rug and let out another yowl.

"Okay, okay, food." Aaron went back into the kitchen, dug through a drawer for a can opener, took a dish from the shelf and dumped the tuna into the dish. Tommy Douglas switched his tail and ate as if he hadn't been fed for weeks. When he had licked the bowl clean, Tommy Douglas lifted his head and yowled again.

"Right. Don't have any milk, buddy." Aaron opened the fridge and squinted into the dark interior. "Ah, how about some mayonnaise? And water?" He put a dollop of mayo in the dish and Tommy Douglas licked it clean, then still switching his tail, daintily lapped half a bowl of water.

Aaron and Chester watched as if his hunger was a clue, or he was a trick cat video.

"The police?" asked Chester, when Tommy Douglas began to prowl the edges of the kitchen.

"No way," said Aaron. "They seem to think I'm responsible. I have to figure this out myself. Help me collect my books and papers and get out of here. I can't stay. I'll never get Valeria out of my head."

"You found her in the basement. Can I look?"

"Sure," said Aaron. "But there's two feet of water. Be careful." With Chester, he went and stood on the stairs, looking down into the wet ripple and stink of stagnant water. Valeria was gone. The photographs that had been floating around Valeria were gone – just one snagged behind the edge of his washer.

"I'll get it," said Chester, as if reading his mind.

"But I've got the boots on," said Aaron.

"So do I," said Chester. "Boots are the only practical footwear."

Somehow then, they were holding hands as they sloshed into the water, stretched for the curled and water-damaged photograph, climbed the stairs again, and dabbed the blurry image with paper towels on the kitchen table.

"So frustrating," said Chester, holding the blurry photograph toward the window. "What is this? Your house?"

"Half of it seems to have washed away, but that looks like my porch."

"So you keep your photos down there. Not good when it floods."

"But that's not a photograph I remember. I don't have a photograph of my house way back in the thirties."

Chester peered at the photograph again. "Is it the thirties?"

Aaron felt his historian-self launch into explanations that rested on clothes and the style of photo and the pose of the subjects, then stopped.

"I don't have any pictures of my house from that era. Maybe this was somewhere in the basement and the flood dislodged it. I've never searched the house in that much detail."

Chester peered at him. "So, Valeria. How did you know her?"

"She lives in the neighbourhood. We're friends. We see each other on the street, exchange pleasantries. People here look out for one another."

"Friendly enough that she ends up dead in your basement?"

"Maybe she came over to check on my house and fell somehow. I don't know." As if to agree with his frustration, Tommy Douglas yowled.

"How did Valeria get down into your basement?" recited Chester gloomily.

"Stop it," said Aaron. "The police already asked me these questions. I don't have the answers. I didn't kill her."

In the end, after walking miles and miles across the not-flat terrain of the prairie, sleeping in a poplar copse one night, Bea had ridden the train into Calgary. The CPR uncurled smoke west, stopped at every siding and small town, took forever, it felt like. She clutched the photo inside a pocket, tried to forget the weight of the men, the threat that they left her with, while she waited on the wooden platform of a side-station under a relentless sun.

When the train came, she climbed aboard with a mixture of relief and fear. Calgary was only a few hours away but what if the woman in the photo was untraceable, had left already, what if the town, growing every day, was impossible to navigate, filled as it was with workmen, industry, immigrants, travellers, all the people attracted by the magnet of the boom city.

She paid the conductor her fare, all she had, and huddled on the hard, wooden seat, trying not to think, trying to think, imagining her strategy, how she would find the woman in the photograph. She stared and stared at the face, as if to memorize it, as if to communicate with the picture, force it to reveal its trace.

Across the aisle a lanky man in a ten-gallon hat watched the prairie unfolding, bent forward when he saw a pronghorn leap away from the racket of the train. "Beautiful," he muttered, "indescribable. Vanishing."

At that last she looked over at him just as he looked back at her. He gave her a toothy smile and nodded. "Don't mind me," he said. "Can't get this place out of my imagination. It's a beaut." His accent was broad, peppered with enthusiasm.

American, Bea thought. Had to be.

"And you, young lady? On your way to Calgary?"

She shook her head. Couldn't trust him or anyone. "Farther."

"Why? Calgary is the destination. Going to be the destination for thousands. Going to be the site of the greatest outdoor show on earth."

Vaudeville then. He might know how to find this Alice in the photograph.

"I can't stop in Calgary," she said, "but maybe you can tell me if you've seen this woman. She is a showgirl, I think." She extended the photograph across the aisle, and he reached for it, scrutinized the picture thoughtfully.

"I may have seen her once or twice," he said. "But I can't be sure. My Flores is the one with the memory for faces. We can ask her once we get to Calgary."

"But I'm not –"

"Once you smell that Calgary smell, you'll want to stay. It's potent as good whiskey."

"What smell?"

"Creosote and money and horse piss. Wonderful."

"Doesn't sound wonderful."

"Like anything, you need to smell it to understand." He took a flask from his hip. "Want a sip?"

She reached for the flask without a second thought, tipped it up and swallowed hard before handing it back.

"Thought that might put your mind at rest. You seem a bit – desolate."

Careful, she thought to herself. Careful. He's to be trusted no more than any man. Probably less, with that drawl and that handsome face.

"I'm fine," she said, thrusting out her chin. "I am perfectly fine."

"You've been sleeping in your clothes. The sole of your shoe is coming loose. You gave the conductor your last two bits."

She stared at him, tilted her chin up.

"Come on," he chuckled. "I know a woman on the verge of tears. Try this handkerchief." And he passed her a white monogrammed cambric handkerchief, larger than normal, as if it would do for a bandana.

"I don't need it."

"Ah, keep it anyway. It'll bring you luck. By the way, where are you getting off?"

He was insufferable. She fought to keep her voice steady. "I plan to go to the coast."

He laughed, an easy salesman's laugh that she would remember as expansive and confident, filled with anticipation. "You've got to stop in Calgary. Work everywhere. Men looking for company. New houses going up by the minute."

"Do you think I'm a prostitute?"

He seemed surprised, as if her prickliness was unwarranted. "No, you look like a trick rider to me. But everybody looks like a trick rider when Flores isn't with me." He looked out the window, his eyes following a horse and rider far on the horizon. Then he looked back at her and resumed his patter. "And my *"Frontier Days and Cowboy Championship Contest"*. They're clearing the grounds for it right now, getting ready. Going to happen in September. You'll want to be there. A spectacle. Indians, ponies, roping and riding, cowboy art, thousands of people, even royalty are coming."

A trick rider. She'd need a horse, she thought bitterly.

In Calgary, she stayed in her seat, waiting for him to rise. He did, took a battered valise from the ledge above, and hovered beside her. "Well, I'll say goodbye then. Even if you go on now, make sure you come back for September. It's going to be glorious. I've got the backing. From McMullen and Burns and Cross and McLean. And Lane—he's the biggest! It's going to be something."

He bowed then, oddly gracious in his high-heeled boots and the ridiculous hat, and turned away, down the carriage to the door. She saw him pass the window, talking and gesticulating with an even taller man, the two of them deep in conversation.

She waited until she was sure he was gone, gathered herself to stand and disembark before the train continued, and there on the seat beside her, my god, a thick wad of bills, a stack of bills so crisp they felt like soda crackers just out of the package. She tried to call, raise her voice, shout, "Mr? —" but the words died in her throat.

She picked up the money, walked quickly to the rear of the car, and stepped down, onto the splintery wooden platform of Calgary, Alberta. And yes, it smelled of creosote and horse piss and money.

The next morning the river was shrouded in a cowl of mist, damp hanging like a scarf along its edges and banks. Bea could not stop herself from walking along its edge, the rustle and whisper of the water under the coil of fog seeming to speak, to murmur solutions and possibilities. The fog hung thick and spooky, a blanket, a fox stole that rode the river's curves. The sun would burn the mist away in an hour or two, but now, in the rising light, the mix of cold and warm air made a shroud, a mourning coat for all that the river carried.

At the laundry, the same woman seemed to be folding the same socks, quietly and efficiently, behind the worn wooden counter. The clean smell of starch and sunlight hung behind a deeper, earthier smell, like mushrooms or cut hay, like gunpowder or old trunks.

"Hello," said Bea. "Can I speak to your son?"

"Not my son," said the Chinese woman, in perfect English, continuing to fold her socks.

"The young man," said Bea, "who was here a few days ago."

The woman ignored her, eyes on her work, while Bea waited for at least ten minutes.

"Please, can you call him?"

"No," said the woman. "You are trouble."

"Hello," shouted Bea into the back of the shop. "Hello?"

The young man appeared instantly, as if he had been waiting for her shout. "Yes? Drop off?"

"No, I need the same thing you gave me before, when I had a note. I've lost it, I need to replace it."

"No note?"

"No. The package, the note, they were stolen. From my hotel room. I need another the same."

The young man looked her with his dispassionate gaze, as serene and assured as before. He did not tap his knuckles on the counter, did not go through the hanging fabric to the back of the store.

"I'm sorry I was surprised last time. I'll pay double."

His eyes did not leave her face. "No," he said in a flat tone that brooked no disagreement at all. "No. One chance." And he turned, walked back through the curtain.

And when Bea pushed open the door to Pearl's place, it felt different. As if a change had happened, as if a cold wind had blown through some hours before, as if the place were no longer warm and well fed, and safe.

The stools along the wooden table were empty. One girl sat listlessly, alone, staring into a coffee cup. Gladys was not behind the bar. And Pearl was not at her roll top desk at the top of the staircase. The roll top was closed as decisively as the door slammed behind Bea.

"Hello?" said Bea.

The girl at the bar raised a shoulder but did not turn her head.

"Where's everybody?" asked Bea.

"Napping," said the girl.

"Pearl? I need to talk to Pearl."

"Gone to the Market."

"Where's Alice?"

"Alice? No Alice here."

100

"I'll wait," said Bea, and pulled out a stool, settled herself. She wanted a drink. She wanted coffee. No one offered her anything.

She wanted Alice. She waited.

When the door blew open an hour later and Pearl entered, laden with new radishes and a side of bacon, Bea stood so quickly she almost knocked the stool over.

"Pearl?"

Pearl shooed past her. "No room here," she said, as if she'd never laid eyes on Bea before.

"But Pearl – Alice. I need to speak to Alice."

"No Alice here."

"Yes. Alice. Or Annie-Lou or Dorothy or whatever other name she goes under."

"None by that name here," said Pearl steadily.

"The woman I stayed with, the woman I slept with, the woman I paid for!"

"None by that name."

"She's upstairs."

"You can look," said Pearl.

Bea climbed the stairs as angrily as her new boots could take her, threw open the doors to every bedroom, every closet.

Alice was gone.

Chapter Six

by Cheryl Foggo & Clem Martini

Aaron

AARON TESTED THE AIR and frowned. He reflected again that the fragrance of river water could only be considered refreshing so long as it was actually flowing and in a riverbed. Once it was stagnant, scummy and pooled in your basement, the odour took on a special kind of awful.

That's how his entire house smelled now – a rank mixture of wood rot, pond scum and week-old cat poo. He had rented an oil generated pump to propel the viscous liquid from his home; and it was with considerable satisfaction that he observed it gush from the hose into the gutter, and slither in amber rivulets down the street. As his eyes followed the evacuating waters, he listened to his cousin on the phone.

"No," he promised, "I am not disturbing the crime scene by pumping my basement out. I consulted the police and they congratulated me on my initiative. They agreed that the water is noxious. They sloshed about in it and are as happy as I am to see it removed."

"No, I don't feel nervous staying here overnight," he assured her. This was only about three-quarters true. "And

NOIR ON EIGHTH ✦ CHAPTER SIX

yes, I will be careful." He wondered how she had come to equate the East Village with the worst excesses of Hell's Kitchen of the Prohibition Era. Although, to be fair, someone had been murdered in his home. Someone. Valeria, he corrected himself. A week ago, the bungalow his grandfather had built had been the safest place in the world. Now it contained a steaming cesspool where his neighbour had been found floating face down, the bones of some unknown ghost had bubbled up and an intruder had trashed his life's work like it was toilet paper. "I will call if I need help, but honestly, you've done more than enough and I don't want to impose on you anymore."

He heard a door click shut, turned and was surprised to see Chester stepping away from her car. "Life returning to normal?" she called as he bid Dara good-bye.

"Normal," he answered, pocketing his phone, "is relative. Nothing in my life has seemed normal for ... Remind me when it was normal?"

She said something, which was drowned out by the revving of an old truck by a man in a denim jacket who had just exited Valeria's building.

"What?"

"I said where's your political cat?"

"Tommy Douglas has been sequestered. Until I get this place mucked out there's too much that's unhealthy for a curious kitty."

They stood awkwardly looking at one another, then Chester reached into her purse. "I brought this. Thought you might be interested," she said and handed Aaron a newspaper clipping.

"Thanks," he said as he read the short announcement of a funeral service for Valeria. A week from today. He wondered who was planning it. He wasn't aware that her middle name was Delorme. Mind you, he hadn't known her last name either,

104

until the police had told him – Claxton. Seeing it on paper, it was ringing a bell. Why was it ringing a bell?

"You can keep that," she added, "Do you have a moment?"

"Well…"

Chester decided to take that as yes. "I've got a couple of follow up questions."

"Questions," Aaron sighed. "Of course you do."

She seemed to sense his discomfort, perhaps realizing that several days of dislocation and upset had depleted his question-answering tolerance. Still, she plowed ahead quickly. "Any further discoveries about why Valeria was in your house the night she died?"

"No," he replied brusquely, "That's a question only she could answer. And being dead, she's unable. So."

"Or the intruder - do you have an idea what he was doing in your attic?"

"Again, no."

"The photo found in your basement – anything to do with you? I thought there was a bit of a family resemblance."

"No one I'm familiar with."

"Further leads on the bones?"

"No."

"Do you know now if the intruder took anything?"

"No." Aaron blew a lock of hair clear of his forehead. "As you can see, I don't know anything. I'm just cleaning up. I've tried to take inventory, but between the kicking the intruder gave the place, and the wreck left by the flood, there's a pretty godawful mess – files upended, papers soaked, doors wrecked. There was never much to take and no one was ever going to get rich sifting through my old files in the attic. So, who knows what he/she was thinking? *If* he or she was thinking." Aaron felt the frustration of the last few days rising. "Honestly, I appreciate that you brought me the funeral notice, but it's been a long day, following a couple of brutally long days and I'm not sure I'm in the mood…" He hesitated, and another thought seemed to occur to him. "But you know what? Hold on."

Without hanging about for an answer, he turned and dashed into the house. Moments later Aaron returned hauling a large, metal rectangular case. Chester had waited.

"Take a picture of this," he grunted, and dropped the heavy case to the sidewalk.

"Pardon me?"

"I want you to take a picture of me with this," he repeated.

"Um. All right," Chester agreed, withdrawing her camera. "And, why?"

"I kept my most important files and archives and historical photos in this carryall. Who knows what the intruder got or what they were looking for – and I know it must seem petty - but in the end, I'm a bit of a history nerd, and I feel like saying, yes, someone trashed my home, and killed someone, murdered a friend, right in my own home, but at least I saved my best historical material. I kept that safe." The wayward lock slipped over his forehead and he blew it back once more. "Which in retrospect, doesn't seem like very much. I mean, I may not even be able to save the house, as it turns out. Had an inspector come by today, who said she couldn't tell for certain how seriously the foundation has been compromised. I'll find out in a few days."

Chester snapped a couple more quick shots, and was reviewing them when they heard the pump gasp, and the water gushing from the hose slackened to a dribble. Aaron switched the pump and generator off. Silence fell. Aaron considered the daunting task of shoveling up several wheelbarrows of smelly silt and river sludge. He missed Valeria. If she was there she would have lined up a brigade from the neighbourhood to help him by now. Sensing his lack of enthusiasm for the project, Chester took the initiative.

"Look. You must be exhausted. Do you want to go for a drink?" she asked.

Aaron considered the mess downstairs. A drink had never sounded so good. "Sure," he replied heaving the carryall back up. "Why not? You're a journalist, so you can expense this, right?"

"You have a very confused perception of journalism," she answered.

Beatrice

BEATRICE REACHED THE BOTTOM of the staircase without remembering how she got there. The woman at the bar had traded her coffee cup for whiskey and was looking at her funny – as though Beatrice had slid down the banister and she was now waiting to see another trick.

Pearl was watching her too, ash from a cigarette falling on the tablecloth she was ironing.

Keeping her footsteps to a dignified pace, Beatrice crossed the floor without a look at either of them. As she reached for the door handle Pearl said, "I'll be needing those clothes you're wearing."

Beatrice felt the heat rise. Her anger was with Alice. But Alice wasn't here. Pearl was here. She turned to face Pearl and pulled off the crumpled jacket that had never recovered from being worn damp. She hung it on the brass coat hook behind the door frame, then proceeded to strip herself of everything that smelled of Pearl Miller's place, and Alice. The cap, the slightly too-big shirt, button by button, the suspenders, the cloth binding her breasts and finally, after removing the lock and her money, the trousers. Stepping on the pile she could have easily stepped over, she retrieved the jacket from the hook and shrugged into it.

"Tell Alice the razor's in the river," she said.

She slipped through the door into the porch and parted the lace curtains on the window that looked out on 9th. It had begun to rain in the interval since she'd arrived. A downpour of the sort she had not experienced other places she'd lived, not even when she was in London as a 17-year-old, working for Foster and Wilkens. It had rained more often in London, but not as hard. She was glad for the rain in this instance. The street was busy with people riding by; the rich in their warm, dry automobiles, the less rich hunched in their horse-pulled buggies. Delivery boys with goods piled high in baskets, pedals flinging mud from the wheels of their bicycles, honking their horns at mothers trying to gather children under umbrellas on the wooden sidewalk. She hoped no one would have a glance to spare for the pant-less youth she would appear to be in their eyes, as it would be highly inconvenient to be arrested for indecency. *Or murder.*

"Maybe they'll think I lost my trousers in a card game," she muttered to herself, buttoning the jacket from bottom to top. She was sorry now that she had opted not to wear an undergarment that morning, as she hadn't planned on finishing the day without the binding cloth. The cheap wool of the jacket rubbed uncomfortably against her nipples, fuelling her anger – at the god-forsaken town, at Pearl, at Alice, who had messed up her plans. And as soon as the thought came – "Alice, who messed up my plans," her anger shifted to where it belonged. Alice was just looking out for Alice - sticking with the fastest in the herd. Beatrice had spent her first hours in Calgary sharp and focussed. She'd found a hotel, procured the herbs, ordered a lock, tracked her prey to Pearl's. She dredged up another of her mother's platitudes. *Qui n'avance pas, recule.* If you're not going forward, you're going backward. She had blown into town all business, then stood still, treading water in the glorious stream that was Alice. All the trouble that had followed was her own fault. She pulled the photo from the pocket of the jacket. Alice was much younger when it was taken. Less beautiful, less hard. If Beatrice had allowed herself, she might have spent some time wondering what had brought Alice from there to here. But she didn't allow herself. Beautiful, wicked Alice. It was a game of cat and mouse now. "It's her or me."

She peered out the window again. The heavens were still belching dirty water. There was no point, after her grand exit, in lurking there to be found by Pearl or whiskey girl.

She couldn't return pant-less to the new hotel where she'd checked in with her things. Charlie Tucker's shop was close and, if she was careful to slink between houses and down the alley, could be reached in 50 paces without getting her seen.

She tied the GW handkerchief over her head. Through the outer door she slipped, along the side of Pearl's house, across the alley at a dead run, she splashed through the rain to the back door of the blacksmith's.

"Charlie!" she pounded with her fist. "Charlie! It's Beatrice!"

He was probably at the front of the shop, unable to hear over the thunder. She tried the knob, which previous poking around when Charlie wasn't looking had shown her, locked only from the inside. To her surprise it was open.

Charlie was standing near the fireplace, from which blasted the more welcome than ever flames. The horse was gone, but two men were there. One, about Charlie's age, a violin on his lap, was seated on the chair beneath the lantern. The other, younger man stood near the wooden table next to the window. Beatrice recognized him from the Chinese laundry.

She'd caught them in mid-laughter, which died abruptly when they looked up. She could imagine how she looked; her bare knees, still scraped and scabbed from the scramble up the river bank in her attempted escape from Alice's hench-man. The sodden jacket. Her boots caked in mud, the scarf plastered to her face, the smell of wet dog she was giving off instantly amplified by the heat from the brick fireplace.

"It's me," she announced. She was shivering.

"I see that," said Charlie. "Something wrong with the lock?"

"Yes." She clutched at the explanation for her presence. "It's not working. The locking part."

Charlie's eyes were skeptical, but he only said "I'll have a look. This is Spence Lewis." He indicated the man with the violin. He nodded toward the other, younger man. "And Yun Kee."

Yun Kee's hand was resting on a cook pot. Behind him on the wall hung other pots and a heavy frying pan. She could tell from his eyes that he recognized her too. But he said nothing.

"Take them all," Charlie said to Yun Kee. "As many as you need. There'll be a lot of people. Use the barrow."

The man who had been introduced as Spence Lewis set aside his violin and stood to help Yun Kee load pots and the frying pan into Charlie's wheel barrow. He was not as tall as Charlie. Lighter skinned, looser, longer hair, lips shaped like angel wings.

Charlie held up a bow, which Beatrice assumed went with the violin.

"I can fix it easy," he said to Spence Lewis. "I'll bring it tonight."

The two men, neither of whom had spoken a word, moved toward the door with the laden wheelbarrow. Spence Lewis placed his violin in a purple-velvet trimmed case that was resting against an anvil.

"It's raining," Beatrice said.

The moment of silence that followed was filled by the pounding on the roof. They looked at her as water dripped from the jacket onto the planks of the floor, then at each other, then at Charlie - Yun Kee with a raised eyebrow. Spence Lewis picked up the violin case, held the door for Yun Kee and they left.

Charlie laughed. "That'll be one to tell the boys at the bar. 'White girl wearing nothing but her little brother's church coat shows up at Charlie's to tell us it's raining.'"

Beatrice glared at him defiantly.

"I was trying to make conversation."

"And speaking of that, why are you here? There's nothing wrong with the lock."

"No. It's fine."

She hardly knew where to begin.

"I need to borrow some clothes. To get back in my hotel. And I need. Well, you seem to know things. I had some medicine that I bought for my sister and it got stolen. I thought you might know where I can get some more."

"What kind of medicine? Why can't you just go back to the druggist?"

He knows.

"Ya. You're right. I should just do that."

"What happened to your pants?" He looked her over. "And your shirt and everything."

"Lost them in a card game."

"That's a rough crowd you're running with. Send a girl out in the rain with no pants."

Charlie walked to the back of the shop and returned with a towel which he handed to her. "Take that wet jacket off and

111

get yourself warmed up. Put your boots and socks on the fireplace, they'll be dry in no time. Under the bed in back, you remember where the sink is?"

She nodded.

"There's a trunk under the bed where I keep extra clothes for the nights when I stay over here. Nothing'll fit, but you can take what you need and get on your way. I'm not going to help you get your medicine back. I don't do business with liars."

Charlie turned his back to her and went to his work table, where he busied himself over Spence Lewis's bow. She stood for a moment, anger bubbling up again. Screw him.

It was a great relief to remove the jacket and her sopping footwear. She wrapped herself in the towel, knocked a little of the mud from the boots onto the floor. They were probably ruined, and they had cost so much. She loved those boots. She placed them, alongside the socks, the handkerchief and the jacket on the fireplace hearth, close to the fire. Her socks sizzled and stank.

Drawing the drape that separated Charlie's sink and cot from the rest of the shop, Beatrice sat on the bed and dragged out the trunk. The rain seemed to be slowing, content now to drum rhythmically against the grimy window. A few seconds of rummaging revealed a pair of green trousers and a soft undershirt that would do. She sat for a moment before dressing. What would it be like to be a blacksmith? With your own fire and bed and grimy window to prevent eyes from the alley from seeing in. Maybe when all was said and done, when this business was behind her, that's what she would do – get a place near a mining town. Ida could be her assistant and they would have tools and tongs and hammers on the walls and drink coffee and pound things on anvils. Seven years on the road looking for a situation that would work for her and Ida. This seemed like a good one. She pulled on the too big pants first and rolled the cuffs, while rethinking her anger with Charlie. Maybe it was good he knew she was lying. Maybe she could use that. She buttoned the undershirt, tucking it in and gathering the excess material of the pants in her fist. A beat up fedora, dusty from its residence under the bed, she placed on her head.

"Look, I was at Pearl's place." She stepped out from the drape, moving to the fireplace to examine the boots, which were still damp. "She dressed me up in men's clothes for fun and one of her ... Somebody there cut my hair."

"For fun?"

"You wouldn't understand. Anyway, that's how it was. Things went sour and Pearl asked for the clothes. She probably didn't mean right then and there but I was mad, so I took them off. To show her. This jacket I got from somebody else."

"What's in the crate?"

She didn't even think about making use of the lie – that it was full of things from home - that she had prepared back when she'd ordered it.

"Nothing. But you knew that already. Did you pry it open?"

"No. Could tell by the weight."

Charlie appraised her appearance. "You can use this to hold them up."

He snagged a coil of rope and tossed it.

"Thank you."

Beatrice pulled the pants up as high as they would go, tied the rope around her waist and folded the waistband over. Not elegant, but under the jacket it would be good enough to get her back to the hotel and up to her room.

"So, the lock is for the crate that has nothing in it."

"Yes." She pulled on the socks which were dry and soothingly warm.

"And the herbs?"

113

When she didn't answer he went on. "You don't have a sick sister. Are the herbs connected to the lock and the crate?"

He waited again but got nothing from Beatrice.

"I can't help you get them back unless I know what they're for. Kee told me what was in the package he stole back from you. On their own, each of the herbs is medicinal. Combined, they're a little more lethal. Unless you know what you're doing. I've got enough troubles of my own. I don't need to get involved. Neither does Kee. He doesn't need anything that can be traced back to his mother's laundry."

"He took my four dollars."

Charlie shrugged. "That's between you and him."

"You just told me he broke into my room and took the package I'd paid for. That's theft twice over."

"So. What are you going to do, go to the police?" Charlie laughed. He had such a great laugh. Deep and rich and real.

"You would help me if you knew what happened. I know you would."

"Maybe. Tell me."

"Can't." This was the truest thing she had said in days. She could not speak out loud what her father's 'business associates' had done to her. If she did, she would find herself on the riverbank again, wondering if she should throw herself in. That might be all right for her, but then what about Ida?

"I do have a sister. You can believe me or not. Ida. And the herbs are for her. And they aren't. Both. If not for her I wouldn't be here. I would let my father swing in the wind and good riddance."

Charlie had been working on the bow when she came out. He went back to it, made an adjustment, held it to the light and ran it through his fingers.

"There's something you can do for me. Then maybe I could help you."

Beatrice snorted. She was disappointed in him. *C'est toujours la meme histoire:* Same old, same old.

Aaron

ONCE AT TEATRO'S, AARON found himself grateful for the opportunity to quench his immoderate temper with cold drinks. The frustration of the past days had been mounting, but he hadn't been able to discuss matters with his relatives. Dara was naturally high strung and sharing troubles around her would be like throwing gasoline on all the fires of Hell. And though Aaron understood that Chester was pumping him for information, the result was that she just seemed like a really good listener. And, it turned out that since she had cultivated connections at City Hall, she had some sensible, and immediately actionable suggestions about where he could turn for assistance in terms of putting his home in order. One thing followed another and drinks naturally turned to dinner. They migrated to a quieter corner table, ordered the pasta of the day and a bottle of Pinot Grigio, and argued about the police. Aaron expressed the opinion that they were either slow-witted or obdurate and weren't searching for any leads in the murder other than him. Chester maintained that was the impression the police always gave, not the substance. It would be impossible for them to reveal the identities of suspects without threatening the integrity of the entire investigation. Even as they argued, though, Aaron could feel himself unwinding. The food, when it arrived, was piping hot. In the background he heard the brooding opening chords of Nina Simone's "Feeling Good" and as she broke into "*It's a new dawn, it's a new day, it's a new life for me - and I'm feeling good,"* the muscles in his neck relaxed.

As Chester dug into her pasta, she revealed that she had him pegged for a history nerd the moment she toured his house.

"Toured my house," he repeated, "When have you ever toured my house?"

"When you dragged me behind you to find your cat. Which was kind of forward - grabbing my hand - by the way," she said. "Do you do that with every journalist you meet?"

He peered over his plate at her. "Forward?"

"Yes," she answered, twirling the spaghetti around her fork.

"Really?" he asked. "*Forward*? Who says forward? What are you Anne Shirley of Green Gables?"

"It's a perfectly good word with respectable Old English roots, and it describes your presumptuous manner."

"And my guiding you – "

"Guiding me? Now you're the legendary Jerry Potts."

"- to find a cat constitutes crossing some kind of imaginary social barrier?"

"Pretty much," she said, and popped a forkful of pasta in her mouth.

He stood away from the table. "I suppose," he said as he exited for the washroom, "that it's fortunate, then, that I didn't go with my first instinct to grab your ass."

In the washroom, as he cleaned up, he glanced at himself in the mirror, and realized that he had neglected shaving over the past few days. "What a shaggy dog," he observed, rubbing a hand across his cheek. Despite the scruff, he had the feeling Chester found him attractive. Or at least, she might have before he made the joke about her ass. Did she know it was a joke? He became aware of how much he'd had to drink. He'd have to slow down or risk passing out on his plate.

When he returned to the table Chester surprised him by asking if he would be attending the funeral.

"Probably." He didn't care for funerals but thought it would be disrespectful not to attend.

"The paper wants me to cover it. Maybe we could go together?"

So she still liked him, despite the joke. And the scruff.

"Did you know her well?" she asked.

"Well enough," he said, "She was nice. First person I met when I moved in - brought a house-warming gift of bread and bourbon. Some nights she drank a little more than she might, but nobody deserves to die with their head bashed in."

The meal drew to a close. They stood and squeezed between the tables and out onto the street. The restaurant exhaled a puff of steam behind them as the doorway swung open. "I'm going to have cab it, and leave the car to fend for itself till tomorrow morning," Chester confessed, "Share a cab?"

"Sure."

"Do you want to spend the night?"

"Thanks," he said. "Although I've been crashing at my cousin's place, I don't really need shelter anymore."

"I'm not offering shelter," she replied.

He stared at her.

"This is the part in the movie where the journalist makes a pass at her subject," she laughed.

"Oh! In that case." He grinned wide. "Yes."

She kissed him.

Beatrice

SHE WALKED A BLOCK past the turn-off to her hotel, stopping twice on 8th, between 1st and Centre. First to buy a curling tong, perfume, hair ribbon and a brown purse at the General goods, then at White Lunch for a cheese sandwich and a Coca-Cola. She was hungry and ate the sandwich as she doubled back to 1st, turned right toward Atlantic, then headed east for the hotel. Passing the Hub Employment Agency, which she had not noticed before – it was tiny and squeezed between a barber and the Grand Central – she made a mental note to stop in one of these times and enquire about work at the mattress factory. A brief linger outside the livery stable next door to the Alexandra, to smell the horses.

Beatrice moved quickly through the lobby past the leather panelled, fur-trimmed walls, not wanting to talk to anyone or be noticed, and hurried up the staircase to her room on the 4th floor. As concerned as she was that her stash of five dollar bills was looking thinner by the minute, she was glad now that she'd paid extra for the private bath.

The next two hours were spent turning herself back into a woman. A perfumed bath, the application of powder to her face, rouge to her cheeks and lips and a smudge of charcoal around her eyes. The corset pinched, as did the blue satin dress that squeezed her breasts. She had to curl her hair standing up, finding it impossible to breathe seated on the bench in front of the mahogany dressing table. Short though it was, her hair resolved into an acceptable bob. With the addition of the ribbon, she felt she had done all she could to transform herself into "the pretty thing you are" as Charlie had put it. Her boots, though, she would not give up. She collected them from the radiator, raised each foot in turn to the bench, and tied them on.

To her request to have him meet her at the hotel, Charlie had responded that he wouldn't get past the front door.

"Really?" she had said.

"Yes, really."

He seemed to find her naïve, which she did not like.

Aaron

BACK AT HOME THE next day after picking up Tommy Douglas, Aaron opened the paper to the City section. On the third page he found the photograph of him holding the carryall. Beneath the byline Phoebe Cardinal Chester, the caption read: "Owner rescues precious documents from flood and thieves."

Aaron sat on the stairs, placed the paper between his feet on the lower step and brushed the picture flat with the tips of his fingers. He looked at the carryall.

Tommy Douglas meowed and rubbed his head on Aaron's knee.

He obliged with a scratch behind the cat's ears.

"Well, TD," he said. "Who will take the bait?"

Beatrice

THE ADDRESS CHARLIE HAD given was several blocks away, and difficult to find. She walked past the mattress building and the same two tinsmiths three times, before realizing the house was set back a good distance from the street, tucked, *or more like hidden,* behind a green fence that blended into the tall trees surrounding it. She reached over the gate and unhooked the latch. Although it groaned noisily when she pushed through, the young couple kissing on the porch swing jumped when she said hello.

The boy stood. "You got an invitation?" he asked, in an official tone that told Beatrice he was supposed to be keeping a better eye on the gate.

"Charlie," she said.

"Okay, just a minute." He disappeared through the door to the house, through which Beatrice could hear laughter and music as soon as it opened. The girl swung back and forth, looking Beatrice up and down and over.

When he appeared accompanied by the young man, Charlie looked her over too, although with more appreciation than the girl on the swing. "Very nice," he nodded.

The party inside reminded Beatrice of Paris, *la fete apres le parti*, as her best friend in the Foster and Wilkens Ten and Thirty Cent Circus troupe used to call the free-for-all late night soirees they would attend with entertainers of every stripe, following their shows in Montmartre. A jumble of hastily kicked-off shoes, the smells and splutters of cooking, blue haze of tobacco encircling the heads of dancing bodies. Music you could shake to. She stood in the arched doorway next to Charlie and looked around, guessing that this was the common room in what appeared to be a large boarding house. They had entered off a long hallway with several closed doors on either side. The modest furnishings had been pushed against walls, except for a prominently placed food table that seemed not to be getting in the way of the dancers. She recognized a number of people in the room, Kee for one. He was bustling around the table, shifting dishes to make room for others, along with a portly, chocolate-coloured man wearing a bowler hat and a large aproned woman with what looked like a nightcap on her head, who seemed to be bossing the two men. She tried to catch Kee's eye to feel him out, but he wasn't biting. With a little jolt of guilt about the money strapped inside her corset, she spied the man with the ten-gallon hat from the train. Charlie saw her looking at him.

"Guy Weadick," he said above the music. "That's his wife Flores talking to their buddy, Will Pickett. She's a trick rider – saw her drink a cup of coffee standing up backwards on a horse one time. Other cowboy's Tom Three Persons. They're all here trying to stir up interest in some big thing they're doing in the fall."

Beatrice nodded, making a mental note to keep Weadick on the other side of the room at all times if she could. He might have dropped that money on purpose, but then again, he might not have. She wasn't surprised when Charlie pointed out Spence Lewis as part of the music ensemble. Along with him and his violin there was a woman who resembled him across the mouth – same angel wing shaped lips - banging on a piano. Rounding out the trio was a very tall, broad-chested young man of about 18 playing a guitar.

"Spence's sister Jesse and their nephew, Bobby Ware," Charlie told her. He was steering her by the elbow across the room toward a group of people sitting in a small parlour filled with bottles of whiskey, gin and beer. He tossed names her way as they moved through, although none of them meant anything to her. "Mary Darby, that's her husband Herbert at the food table, he's the cook at the Vulcan Hotel, you oughta try his ribs; Charles Daniels, he's the chief inspector at the CPR; oh there's Bertha, she's busy, I'll introduce you later, she runs this place with her old man."

They reached the parlour. Charlie offered her a bottle of beer with a buffalo head on the label from a steel tub packed with ice. She took it, as the occupants of the room stood to greet her. She had the feeling they'd been waiting for her.

"I hope I wasn't late?" she said, looking around at them all.

"No, no," said the man Charlie had first introduced. She thought he'd said William King, but they were closer to the music and it was hard to hear. Robert Clayton, Clinton Ford, she wasn't sure which name went with who. Or who was the president and who was the treasurer. They shouted brief instructions at her, sometimes leaning over to yell directly in her face. Charlie had already told her what they wanted her to do, and they quickly seemed satisfied that she understood. It was a curious way to do business – she supposed they needed to be seen but not heard, to appear as though they were just making small talk at a house party. Kee appeared through a door in the parlour that must have led from the kitchen - he was carrying a plate of dumplings. He nodded at her, and although he wasn't smiling, she thought he looked friendlier than he had in the past.

"Are you a member of the Colored People's Protective Association too?" she shouted.

"They have their own," Charlie offered on Kee's behalf.

"Same fight," Kee said.

The bossy woman's voice carried across the room. "That chicken ain't about to turn itself!"

Kee left them.

"All right, I'll get to work then," Beatrice said to the various board members. "Charlie, care for a dance?"

He nodded. She was pretty sure the song the musicians were half-way through was 'After the Cakewalk' – an old one. She moved into a quieter corner of the party room.

"So that's it?" she asked.

"Yes, I told you. That's all."

"Nobody's expecting me to meet them in a bedroom?"

"Don't meet anyone in a bedroom. Don't go outside or upstairs or downstairs by yourself, especially after the money starts coming. Bertha and Harry try to keep an eye out, but there's no way of knowing everyone who's here. Most times we're all friends, most times nothing happens all right? But you never know. Keep the purse where everyone can see it. If you need to go to the bathroom tell me and I'll stand watch at the door."

"You make it sound dangerous."

Charlie shrugged.

"And I can drink and eat and talk to people."

"The more you look like you're just a guest at the party like everyone else, the better. Don't get drunk."

"What if someone flirts with me?"

Charlie laughed his great laugh as the song ended. "That's between you and them."

She watched him as he made his way across the room to a woman who had waved.

Over the years she had become a good judge of class, and as she began to mingle, she wasn't sure if she'd ever been in a room with a wider representation of all its variants. Black and brown people dominated, some be-suited and bejeweled, others looking down at the heels, mixing with white people she guessed were lawyers or politicians or other kinds of pirates. One or two women she thought she'd glimpsed at Pearl's.

Beatrice wondered what she would do if she saw Alice. She *knew* what she would do if she saw Alice. Pull Charlie to the middle of the room and kiss him, hard and fast and wet, like the kids on the swing outside.

Easiest twenty bucks I've ever made. And Charlie hadn't given any detail, but he had strongly implied that in addition to getting a cut, she would get her herbs. She still had trouble believing all the precautions were necessary. They raised money at these functions through "donations." Only people who donated could get a drink. She had been given very specific instructions about the type of purse to buy. It had to be brown – that's how guests would know she was the donations lady of the day - it had to hang over her shoulder, it had to be big, it had to be open. People would slip money into the purse and give her their order, she would saunter to the parlour and tell whichever of the board members was there that "The man with the red carnation in his lapel would like two whiskeys neat" and the man with the red carnation would get his whiskeys. Her most important job was to make sure it didn't look like the proprietors were selling booze. That was all.

The money raised was used to help members of the community, Charlie had explained. Sometimes with food and lodging, to buy clothes for their babies, sometimes with bail or for a lawyer. Anyone in trouble knew where they could go.

"We can't raise funds openly," he had said in answer to her questions. "You have no idea what it's like here, once you get branded a rabble-rouser."

She didn't understand. But it didn't matter. Charlie was a nice man, but Charlie's problems were Charlie's problems. She was enjoying herself; she'd get enough cash to live on for a few more days, she'd get her herbs, she'd get her business settled and she'd get out.

An hour later Beatrice's purse was bulging. She was in the middle of a conversation with Tom Three Persons about horseshoeing when the room went black. The music stopped abruptly. It was the signal.

There was a soft click and a few lights came back, enough for people to be able to see where they were going. She could hear shouting at the front porch, but remained where she was, as Charlie had asked her to do if this happened. She was just a guest at a party.

124

"They never mess with the white folks," he had said. "They might break a few chairs, haul Bertha and Harry out, maybe get a little rough, but they won't trouble themselves with you. Even if they ask to look in the purse, you've got your story. Just don't do anything that looks suspicious."

Most of the pirates began to melt toward the back of the house, toward the kitchen where she assumed there was another exit. Beatrice had the feeling that, despite what Charlie had said about the police not being after white folks, white folks didn't want to be found here.

"There's a cop out back too," one of them said to the woman who was holding his hand.

"Harold paid him off to disappear for five minutes," someone else whispered. "We can get out that way."

Still she remained where she was, behind the food table.

The shouting got louder. Three uniformed officers burst in, clubs at the ready.

Beatrice's stomach dropped. One of them was the man who had followed her downtown the day of the hailstorm.

She couldn't see Charlie anywhere. She slipped into the parlour unnoticed and through the side door. There was no one in the kitchen.

A door to the back yard stood open, still swinging from its most recent escapee. She tiptoed down a flight of steps to a garden. Beatrice could hear the river and began to run, the brown purse flapping against her hip.

Damn corset.

Chapter Seven

by Lisa Murphy-Lamb

Aaron

Peace Bridge 2013

IT WAS THE PEACE Bridge over the Bow River that held the only beauty on this grey Calgary day for Aaron as he stood, at odds with his thoughts. Earlier, as he walked along the pathway and his mind unfolded over the events of the past few days, he had felt defeated by the sludge in the basement, visions of the past few days and his own indecision.

An old couple passed by as Aaron stared at the basket weave of metal, unable to make the decision to keep walking towards Chester's apartment or return east to his own home and the god-awful mess he shouldn't avoid, but did. He had found himself increasingly despondent with each hour he stood ankle deep in the sludge with a broom and a mop and his thoughts of scattered books and papers.

He should hear today whether the house, his grandfather's house, 100 years old to the month, survived this flood. Even if the foundation had weathered this month's watery intrusion, there would be another and another swamping. Both he and the house knew it. There would be more knocks on the door with cash incentives proffered to demolish the yellow eyesore and make way for —what was it? A coffee shop or a diamond manicure salon or probably a hybrid knowing Calgary's fickle tastes.

Of course, now, he also held the image of Valeria face down in the basement and that skeleton that Tommy D had dragged in piece by piece. It had been, at some point, a body under his front porch and before that, a person. Aaron's considered the weathered couple before him and knew they, like his house, had both suffered and triumphed. History, he was well aware, was full of the dead and their stories. This was the first time the dead had bumped up against his own life, made him a suspect of one murder, his family a suspect, perhaps, of another. It was difficult to remain an objective historian when two bodies had been found below the very place he and his family had lived for a century.

Maybe the skeleton had ridden an earlier flood. That could be true. Who knew how many snagged bodies anchored themselves against the powerful, wild waters of the Bow.

Bones and ghosts. Valeria would definitely come back to haunt. Aaron laughed at this thought. There was no way that Valeria, with her loudness, her plastic shoes, her opinions, her genuine way, had spoken her last word. Aaron looked towards the river's movement, older than the flow of human blood, and felt a tingle at the end of his nose. Really, he was being selfish, and he knew it. His life had been inconvenienced, but Valeria's life was taken. There was no comparison. What other mysteries laid buried within the walls of his grandfather's house?

One puzzle for sure. Among his birth certificate, his passport, his parent's wedding certificate, the paperwork to change his surname back to his mother's maiden name (after his father created a permanent new last name, the artificial progeny of a short lived flirtation with Numerology), Aaron had something of significance in the photographed metal case Chester had published in the newspaper. Carefully preserved in acid-free paper, slipped in a plastic sleeve, an original deed from the early 1900s to some land in the Turner Valley-Longview area, lay safely preserved. Aaron had discovered it under a loose floor board that he kept stubbing his toe on after moving some of his mother's furniture around. Through research and conversation with his mother, the deed didn't appear to belong to his family. The circumstances surrounding how his grandfather came in possession of this deed remained murky and unpleasant. Until Aaron completely understood those circumstances, he had kept the deed a secret, locked up and stored. If legit, that deed was worth millions, if not to him, to someone.

But maybe Aaron was mistaken about the deed being a secret.

Perhaps others knew the deed's whereabouts and that's why he had found the contents of his house spiraled and Valeria dead. Someone was after the deed. He had absolutely nothing else worth stealing in the house. Even his furniture had been handed down from his mother.

At Chester's apartment, the two had sat on her blue velvet couch. Seduced by her vast knowledge of the East Village, drugged by the wine, her beauty and the fact she had invited him back to her apartment, Aaron let his guard down. Then Chester had said something that sobered him up.

"Who is the man with denim jacket who hangs around your place?" She asked this as her foot rubbed Aaron's calf.

Aaron had seen a man in a denim jacket twice. Once, leaving Valeria's apartment and later in Hear's my Soul cafe nursing a beer. Did Chester hang around his place and watch him come and go? If she did, should Aaron be freaked out by it, or turned on? Aaron said he didn't know the answer, only shrugged and said he should go home. The kiss at the back door after he put his shoes on made him forget that she might be a stalker.

In his pocket, a vibration brought him out of his head, back to his place by the bridge. He answered his phone.

"Where are you?" For once, the female voice on the other end was not his cousin Dara's.

"Walking towards your place."

She laughed. "Turn around." I'm standing on your sidewalk. I'd sit on your porch step and wait, but you know ... " More laughter.

"Get a coffee at Hear's My Soul. It's the new coffee shop in the Orange Lofts. I'll be there in fifteen, if I hurry."

"Don't hurry on my account."

"Don't flatter yourself. Nina makes a good cup. I'd sprint for her."

Beatrice

Auto Club, St. Patrick's Island

THE SILENCE OF THE night enveloped her as she walked with a brisk stride beside the shuttered Public Market. The night, beautiful and starlit, kept Beatrice calm as she snaked her way from the raided house with a purse full of money, first down an alley, before taking one street, then another, towards the Auto Club on St. Patrick's Island. Others on the island at this time of night would not pay her any attention. This would allow her to collect herself on the banks of the Bow a moment and listen to the intelligent songs of its current before returning to her room at the Hotel Alexandra.

At the corner of Third Avenue and Third Street she slowed to a stop, glanced over her shoulder, saw no one. With streets as empty as wild prairie, Bea took a moment and breathed in the horseshit-lilac scent of the night. In the distance she heard voices, lifted her head ready to bolt again, but they quieted. She moved north towards the river and ambled quickly across the footbridge to St. Patrick's Island.

"Are you a man or a woman?" A voice called from a bench up the embankment

Beatrice didn't need to see who said it. She knew Alice's voice.

Alice joined her, matched her stride and looked at Bea from every angle, forcing Bea slow her step. "I think I like you better this way."

"It doesn't matter how you like me," Bea said. "I won't dress or undress for you ever again." She took a step around Alice.

Alice grabbed her arm. "What's this?" Her hand slid down the brown strap and rested on the bulge of the purse. "Is this where you've stored the herbal medicine?" She asked, the buildings in the East Village across the river congregating behind her.

Bea's hand rested on that of Alice's, her fingers clenched. Alice drew closer.

"What do you know about my ... about medicine?"

"I know that a little of those herbs at a time are a party. Too much, well, too much is a contract between the devil and his servant." Alice leaned her forehead in to rest on Bea's, her curls tickling Bea's cheek. "It's my birthday, Bea. Let's have a little party. Just you and me."

Alice's breath was heady with liquor. Bea felt Alice's fingers wiggle beneath her hand, hungry to get inside the purse. Bea pulled away, squeezed Alice's hand to a point that she hoped caused pain. Alice arched her back, smiled, narrowed her eyes, just a touch. She knew how to work it. Sweet Alice.

"I don't know what you're talking about. I don't have any medicine, herbal or otherwise."

"Let me see." Alice took her free hand, ran her finger along Bea's jawline. Bea smelled Paris on her fingertips, felt Pearl's sheets with her touch. "As your friend, Bea. I could use a little party. Couldn't you?" She glanced over her shoulder to the Bow, "You must feel the weight of killing a man, letting his body sink to the bottom of that river." Alice smiled. Bea saw her dimples form in the gloaming. "I recommend a party to ease any guilt you might have." She laughed. "Take the night off, Bea. Forget you want me dead for a bit, give your conscience a break."

Bea closed her eyes, swallowed.

"What's that? You didn't get my invitation. Not to worry, I always carry an invite list with me." Doing a pantomime, Alice ran her finger down a large list in the air, stopped, made a checkmark, then continued down the space between Bea's breasts, now a valley where before it had seemed a young boy's chest. "Yes, Bea, you are invited."

"No." Bea stepped back, furious at herself for how quickly her knees buckled at Alice's calculated touches, how tempted she was at giving her mind a break. She knew Alice sensed her weakness.

"An exchange, perhaps?"

Beatrice grasped what Pearl meant when she had told her that Alice spent days messed up. Beatrice could see it now, a desperation she hadn't noticed back at Pearl's place. She could use this desperation to her advantage. She straightened and thought of the deed she knew Alice had, felt the threat of the men rush through her and hoped, only for a snap that this was her out. The quantity of herbs she would offer Alice could be small at first, enough to relax, seduce, talk her into surrendering the deed and then, once the exchange complete, one final, lethal dose.

Alice looked to the leafy slope, lifted her skirt a touch and Beatrice understood the nature of her offer.

"I've just been with this man." Alice leaned in, confided. "A most wonderful lover but despite his fine clothes and family, he's got some dark habits that he shares with me. He also," Alice's voice got low, "won't let anything happen to me, so watch yourself, Beatrice."

Despite her vices, Alice retained the control. "What do you say, Bea?" And with a blink of an eye, Alice uncurled her back, tilted her head just enough, "those herbs—"

Bea heard footsteps. "Police are coming."

Alice's arm fell slack and she released her grip. Bea lifted her skirt and continued along the riverbank a few feet before turning inland into the depths of St. Patrick's Island.

Aaron

Hear's My Soul Café

CHESTER WAITED FOR AARON on the second floor of the café at a table in the corner, her latte nearly finished by the time Aaron arrived. "Cafes are the first sign your neighbourhood is being gentrified," Chester said as way of greeting when Aaron approached the table with his cup of dark roast. "Although, I like the feel of this place. It's messy, full of seniors and graffiti, like it's sticking it's middle finger to the grand plan." Chester pointed to the boot hanging above the entrance. "It's no Starbucks you know?"

"Uh huh," Aaron wasn't sure if the right thing to do was to kiss Chester before sitting, but she didn't lean forward or even towards him, her focus was on the walls of the café. So he sat, no kiss.

"Do I dare ask?" Her head tilted towards his house a few blocks over.

"Tommy Douglas hasn't been granted access yet."

"Status understood." Chester reached for Aaron's arm, gave it an encouraging squeeze. "I've got ninety minutes if you could use some help."

"Coffee first?" He'd take her help, why not? It beat the gloom the stench brought and there was probably only about two hours of work left before TD could return home. Having his fat feline moping around the house would be welcome.

Both put coffee cups to their mouths.

Chester said, "Your friend Valeria, she's lucky."

Aaron looked up from his cup. "You're joking, right?"

"I don't mean she's lucky to be murdered. She's lucky because she has family to keep her name alive and she has an obituary to mark her passing. That's more than most in her line of work have."

Chester nodded, thought he understood. "I suspected what she did for a living, but we never talked about it."

Aaron watched Chester bite the edge of her coffee cup. "We're so quick to treat women like her as whores, like throwaways. Forget them when they die as if they had no worth while they were alive."

"Did you know," Aaron said, "one block over from here, there was a brothel?"

"The infamous Pearl Miller. I do. Now there was a woman who dared use the female body for economic gain outside of marriage. She was some woman, I figure, with a mind for business, who did what she could in both the rich and the lean times."

"And a good business she had. Single men made up this area for decades."

"True. But it's not only single men who pay for sex. One of the wealthier, married Calgarians gave her the money to buy a house and move her brothel to Mount Royal. I wonder if Valeria would have had it easier in a brothel, under Pearl's watch."Aaron looked into Chester's eyes. "You didn't even know Valeria," Aaron said, "I thought this was a story you'd been assigned."

"I didn't have to know Valeria to care about her and about how she died. She's my sister, my neighbour, part of my community. Every last nameless murdered woman out there is. But I'm pleased Valeria has a name that will live on and a family to keep her memory alive. Her whole memory." Chester caught Aaron's eye, looked at him when she spoke. "For the record. I wasn't assigned this story. I demanded it."

Beatrice

Hotel Alexandra

BACK IN THE HOTEL the next day surrounded by the solitude of clean sheets and spotless surfaces only a new hotel could offer, Bea opened the *Calgary Daily Herald* in hopes of finding out what had happened after she tumbled down the garden stairs to escape the raid inside the house. Charlie had told her to return to her hotel room until someone, not him, contacted her for the money. She found the article and read:

Negro Dive Raided
In a raid upon a Negro dive at 611 1st Ave. E. last night the police arrested the homeowners and three

persons present in the house. This morning fines aggre-
gating $220 were collected from those arrested.

For several months the house has been known as
an immoral den, but it was not until yesterday that
the police were able to walk in at the right instant.
Detective Hodgkins accompanied the officers to the
house and as the result of finding numerous empty
beer bottles a charge of selling liquor without a license
was preferred.

The keepers, Harry and Bertha Palmer are known
to the police and this morning pleaded guilty to selling
liquor and to keeping an immoral report. In default
of payment they will spend eight months in jail. The
other three persons arrested were let go as there was
no evidence against them.

The charge of selling liquor against the Palmers
was again remanded.

But how could they prove they were selling? Bea paced the
room. She had the money. She looked towards the night
table to confirm the purse, still full of money, remained. It
was right where she had left it last night. There would have
been no money to be found at the house during the raid.
They had taken precautions. Charlie had laid it all out for
her, everyone had known the plan.

Bea's thoughts turned to Charlie. Charlie! Was he one of
the three arrested? It tortured her to remain inside and wait
but she knew she owed it to Charlie to do so. She owed it to
everyone in the house last night. She had only been a guest.
This was not her cause to get riled up about and head out
to the streets to cause more trouble. Trouble had been her
escort since she had disembarked the train and set foot in
this Cowtown and had smelled the farrago of creosote, money

and horse piss for the first time. Last night, she had simply been hired as the donations lady because she had owed it to Charlie for his kindness. On the road, Beatrice ached for the sort of kindness Charlie offered. She would listen and remain in her room until someone came.

Beatrice sat on the bed, picked up the paper, read the article again but it only served to make her feet want to run. She turned the page and read only a few sentences under the headline **Watkins Blames Wife for Alimony Breech.**

While it made her laugh aloud that Watkins' complaint against his wife was that she intentionally made a racket while washing dishes, Beatrice threw the paper down when Mr. Watkins found this offense worthy of a beating by broom handle. She found herself at the window again under the heavy curtains looking out when there was a knock at the door.

Aaron

Basement of his home

"I HALF WISHED THE decision to knock down my house was out of my control. But this old house is fit to remain a house if I choose to keep living in it. I just got the word." Aaron put the bucket of hot water on the basement floor next to the furnace.

"Tell me what you're thinking."

Aaron looked across the basement at Chester, who true to her word, had come over to help him move the clean-up along. She also, he had discovered, had a way about her that opened him up to talk about himself, about what mattered to him. She was different from Dara who constantly told him what to do and how to think, or the women he'd unsuccessfully

137

dated who challenged him but who seemed uninterested in getting to know him.

"I'll tell my cousin Dara and get an earful. She knows what price I've been offered. With the money I can still live in the East Village, if I want. And I do. It's home here. I could afford something on the tenth floor or higher with new floors, new appliances, many windows.

I'm not Dara, though. Let her live in her fake Italian community with its 2.5 bathroomed houses and manicured yards. She's got kids to think about. This house belongs here more than and frozen yogurt shop or a yoga studio."

Chester handed Aaron the mop. He plunged it into the bucket. "You live in this house for a reason and you've kept it. There must be something about it you love."

Through narrowed eyes, Aaron said. "Tell me you don't already know how I got this house."

Chester laughed. "Call it fact checking then. Let's see if my sources are correct." She pushed the large broom a metre in front of Aaron working to get the remaining sludge down the drain so he could mop up the last of the mess. "Talk and work. I've got to leave soon."

Aaron slopped water across the floor. "My grandfather built this bungalow."

"Name and Year?"

"Chaz Cohen, 1914"

"Correct, go on." Chester kicked at a stubborn lump of mud on the floor, kept sweeping.

"Chaz married a woman named Sally Perelman in 1912. They had two daughters, Ruth and Willa, born in 1915 and 1918, who both grew up in this house. When Chaz was 55 years old he began an affair with a very young woman named Mary Bannister. Mary became pregnant by Chaz and gave birth to Felicity Cohen. That was in 1947." Aaron impressed himself every time he was asked to give names and dates. His mind was made for remembering these kinds of details. Too bad he hadn't figured this out until after he'd finished four years of university. "Chaz cut ties with Mary but not Felicity. The two grew quite close. He willed her this house even though she never lived in it as a child."

"Guilt?"

"Maybe. Felicity married Adam Barsky in 1980 and they had a son."

"You."

"Correct." That marriage didn't last a year and only my dad remarried. I'm an only child. I lived here with my mom until I turned twenty-one. She gave me the house when she moved away to Victoria for some warmer weather. Now I live here with Tommy Douglas who, I think, thanks to your help, can move back in today. How did I do?"

"Spot on."

"Glad to hear it. You're a bit of a historian yourself."

"When the topic interests me." Chester stiffened after corralling the sludge around the slow-moving drain and gathered some of the larger chunks onto a large square of corrugated cardboard. "After you mop, I think this place will hold until the service company gets here. Tomorrow is it?"

"Yes, at ten. I think we've done what we could to stop mould from settling in."

Chester tied off the garbage bag into which she had dumped the last of the sweepings. "Don't sell this place, Aaron."

Aaron pushed the mop into the final corner of the basement chasing the two of them to the bottom stair. "Now you tell me why."

"You know the history of this place. Don't let them bulldoze over this last place of story like they have all the other houses and the bakeries, the fish stores and the Variety Theatre."

139

And the skeletons, Aaron thought. At the top of the stairs, he took the bag from Chester, put it by the bucket and said, "You've got to admit, this house will look pretty shabby among all the gleam and sparkle."

"Sure, a single house that has seen it all over the years and has had its knocks. Not the kind the East Village wants in here. You know it. Your history walks must be difficult to run these days, asking participants to imagine every little detail because nothing is left. Not even plaques to remember what once was here. Let this one house stand as a nod to East Village's storied past."Aaron smirked. Who was this girl? "I complain, but I'm not going anywhere."

"Good to hear." With hands washed, Aaron walked Chester to her car. Once it was unlocked she turned and said, "One more thing. You are going to Valeria's funeral, correct?"

"Yeah. I told you."

"One more question. You two were never intimate?"

"No. Never. You're starting to bug me. Like Dara and the police."

Chester lowered her voice, slid into the car. "I'm not judging. But you never paid—?"

"She was a friendly neighbour, nothing more."

"That is good. Very good." Chester started the car, looked at the clock on the dash. "Shit. I'm late.

Beatrice

Blacksmith Shop

BEATRICE FOUND HERSELF STARING out the window when three loud knocks sounded on her door. She composed herself, took a deep breath, checked her appearance in the mirror before she answered. She did not know who could be on the other side of the door. There had been many people at the party the night before, from the humble to the rich, and all fighting for a cause.

When her hand reached the handle, she also remembered Alice's threat. She supposed it could be another henchman to settle the score or Alice herself come for the herbs she so desperately wanted last night. Or Guy Weadick. Certainly he had noticed her at the party last night. He might have been the one to volunteer to come and get the money this morning. Both sets of money—the Colored People's Protective Association money and his own that surely he knew Beatrice had. Beatrice checked that her knife was secure and ready inside her snug against her calf, inside her boot. She opened the door.

Standing on the other side of the door was a well-dressed woman who Beatrice recognized from the party crowd. The woman made a scene at the door as if the two were good friends. "Oh, it's so good to see you, Beatrice. You are looking wonderful this morning," she said before bustling into the room with skirt swishing. "Close the door," she whispered once inside. "I'm Lily Taylor, school friend of Jesse Ware." she looked around the room. "You doing all right this morning?"

"Yes. I'm fine." Bea said.

"Good. Police raids can be nerve-wracking."

"Don't worry about me," Bea said. "I've seen worse. Would you like a seat?"

"We don't have time. Charlie is expecting us."

"He wasn't arrested then?"

"He was and two others but they're home now. We will need last night's donations to help pay the fines." Lily walked towards the purse. "Do you have another handbag to carry this morning. We don't want anything to connect us to last night's party. Were you seen?"

"I don't think so. I left through the same back door the others left by."

Lily nodded and began to place several of the dollars into her own purse and some down the front of her corset. "In case."

Bea did the same.

Out on the street Lily Taylor hooked her arm in Bea's and the two bent their heads low together as if in conversation. They passed by the stables and Grand Central, the Hub Employment agency and the barber, keeping a steady but casual pace. Charlie was out front of his shop sweeping the entrance when they turned the corner. As soon as he saw the two women, he put his broom down and entered through the door. Beatrice recognized the sheen on his skin as she did the first time she met him. She followed Charlie into his shop, Lily close on her heel.

Charlie looked at Beatrice. "Everything all right?"

"The money is all here and accounted for." Lily answered

"And you?" He directed this question towards Beatrice.

"I'm fine. I left without any trouble." Her thoughts went to Alice in the dark, but she dismissed them. She certainly wasn't going to drag Charlie and Jesse's friend, Lily into this part of her life again, if she could help it. "You were arrested?"

"I was. Released within a few hours. In this town it helps to be an honourable businessman."

Lily began to pile the money on the table by the fire so Beatrice did the same. Charlie counted it, then handed twenty dollars to Beatrice.

Heavy boot steps on the front porch made the three inside Charlie's shop freeze. The door opened "You should lock the door when dealing with that much money," Spencer Lewis said and stepped inside. "Is it ready to go?"

Charlie located brown paper and string, packaged the money and handed it to Spencer.

"Thanks for the repair on the bow," Spencer said. "It was a fine party last night before we were shut down." With Lily on his arm the two left the blacksmith's without much talk.

Beatrice turned to Charlie once the door closed. "My package?"

Charlie walked to the back of the shop and returned with a brown paper package quite similar to what Spencer Lewis only just left with. "I said it before and I'll say it again. It's a rough crowd you run with."

"No, it's not like that," Bea said and thought to her sister Ida and her father. She wanted to convince Charlie she could be trusted, that he should forget about what he had seen so far of her. She looked at the package in his hand. She took it and said nothing more. What could she say? She had been sent to Calgary for a reason. Her mind immediately raced to her sister Ida.

When Charlie handed Beatrice the herbs he promised in exchange for her work at the party, he said, "Something else came for you on this morning's train."

Beatrice cocked her head, tried to think what it might be. "For me?"

"Two men on the west-bound train asking questions about you. They've got two rooms at the St. Louis."

Beatrice sat. It was time to make a decision before decisions were made on her behalf.

Aaron

Golden Age Club

IT HAD BEEN A week since Aaron had needed to put on something nicer than rubber boots and sweat pants, or if he got away with it in March, shorts. Chester texted him after he finished knotting his tie.

Won't risk heels in the grime. Waiting by the car.

He found two socks that matched, did a quick polish of his shoes before locating his house keys on the fridge top. He locked the door behind him ignoring the disgruntled look on Tommy Douglas' face.

The library in the Golden Age Club had seating for about twenty guests and half the chairs were already taken. Sitting, Aaron opened the funeral program he was handed at the entrance of the room. The photo of Valeria on the front was not a recent one, but not really that old. Her hair looked browner than he knew her to have but the smile was the same. Under her name the years (1964-2013). Fifty. She was fifty. He sometimes guessed that was her age, but mostly he thought her younger. Still, fifty was too young.

Valeria Delorme Claxton. Claxton. There was her last name again. He felt Chester's eyes on him, pointed out the name by placing his finger under the type. She nodded.

He said, "My grandmother Mary married a Claxton."

"Any chance it was David Claxton?"

Aaron looked up at Chester.

The service was delivered by an old friend of the family who worked in a community church in the Beltline. He talked of Valeria as a young girl full of promise, one who was hungry for adventure. Aaron looked around the room during the first hymn. He noticed one neighbour but the rest were strangers to him and older, closer in age to Valeria's mother. He wondered if some in attendance were from the surrounding apartments. He heard sometimes people crashed funerals to get out of the apartment for a couple of hours and for free coffee and a date square.

Valeria had never married, had no children. She ran away at sixteen, hitched a ride to Vancouver where she raised homing pigeons. When Patricia, her mother, required a wheelchair, Valeria moved back to Calgary.

Aaron felt a need to stay for a sandwich, not because he was hungry but because he wanted to meet Valeria's mother, let her know that Valeria was an important part of the neighbourhood community and that she was important part of his life—and that he would miss her around his place. He would also offer a hand if she needed one to clean out Valeria's apartment. He felt he owed the family something since it was in his house that Valeria was found dead.

Each with a cup of coffee, Aaron and Chester found a place by a bookshelf to drink. When Patricia Claxton stopped over the plate of sandwiches, Aaron excused himself from Chester, walked over, introduced himself to Valeria's mother. "I'm Aaron Cohen, Valeria's neighbour."

It took a moment for Valeria's mom to look up, for her eyes to find Aaron's. She didn't speak, not at first. When she did, Aaron understood the hesitation. "I hoped you might come. I'm pleased to finally meet you. There is a connection between our family and yours, and the house Valeria died in. Can you stay? Maybe between us, we can discover why she had to die."

Aaron

Blackfoot Truck Stop

SITTING AROUND THE TABLE at the Blackfoot truck stop with coffee poured and patty melts on rye ordered, Aaron began the conversation. "I only just discovered today that Valeria and I shared the same grandmother."

Patricia, a small woman with years of hard living chronicled on her face, smiled. "I hope you don't have to confess anything to your priest." She laughed a low, husky laugh. "You weren't a regular of Valeria's?"

A T-shirt. I should have a T-shirt made that says, *I never slept with Valeria,* Aaron thought. Instead he explained himself once again. "No. Valeria was my friend. A neighbour. We looked out for each other. There was no sex between us."

"You gay or something?" Patricia's friend, a woman caught in the 1980s with feathered hair and a ruffled dress asked, deadpan.

Aaron ignored this comment, pushed the conversation away from sex to the family connection. "On the drive over, I figured out that Valeria was related to me through my grandmother. I am the eventual product of my grandmother and an affair she had with Chaz Cohen who she never married and who didn't raise her. Valeria is the eventual product of my grandmother Mary and David Claxton whom she did marry."

"Yes, both my parents. My mother is your grandmother." Patricia confirmed.

Aaron took a fry from the mound on his plate that had been delivered without him noticing. He washed it down with a long drink of coffee. "Do you know my mother?"

146

"Yes. We were introduced by your grandmother Mary at your grandfather Chaz Cohen's funeral."

Aaron considered this. "Why were you at my grandfather's funeral?"

"My mother dragged me. I was only fourteen at the time, mind you. A hell of an age to discover your own mother had a secret past. Why the hell she decided to confide in me, I don't know. I guess she needed an ally to attend the funeral of a man she had an affair with. So I went. She failed to tell me she also had a child with the old fool. Met her there, your mother. Felicity was a year older than me and we, well, we fell in love with each other. We were sisters. Half. But sisters."

Aaron had to release his grip on the coffee cup. His fingers hurt. Hell, his head hurt. Valeria's mom was his mom's half-sister. He thought back to the familiarity in which Valeria moved through his house from the first night they met. He had questioned a couple of times why, when he moved in, she came over with bread and whiskey. Surely, he had thought after she left, she didn't offer this hospitality to everyone. And yet it never was about sex like people were so quick to assume. Ever. She was only Valeria, bossy, motherly Valeria with a sense of fashion only she could pull off.

"Are you still in touch with my mom?"

"Christmas cards mostly. You know how it goes."

Aaron didn't.

"My father. He got jittery with me keeping in touch with your mom. He wanted to forget, once he found out, about my mother's indiscretion. Oh. If only that was the word he used. He wasn't kind to my mom once he found out about her affair and that she had a daughter out there being raised by her lover's relatives. My father was hard. I left home. Got pregnant. It got difficult to find time to hang out with your mom. She was still in high school, I was raising hell and then a baby."

Aaron slumped in his seat. The smell of the patty melt didn't sit right with him. "This is a lot to take in. You say that you think this connection has to do with Valeria's death?"

"Murder. It sure the hell does."

Chapter Eight

by Dale Lee Kwong

Alice

Alice leaned into the hand mirror and checked her skin for any signs of age or blemish. It was as if her life depended on it, and in many ways, it did. This face had saved her before, but would it get her out of this pickle?

Alice could pass for anything from 16 to 26, depending on the eyes of the beholder. Many were smitten; life at Pearl's was not half bad. Pearl was fiercely protective of her girls, and prominent clients helped give the establishment a legitimacy and respect that even money couldn't buy.

Of course, there were plenty of other things money could buy. Pearl kept her girls in fine clothes, fancy bedding, and delicacies that did not come easy in a prairie town. The whiskey was smooth, and the cheese well aged. There was even a good selection of fruits in the middle of winter. If you looked closely, nearly everything had a silver lining. She put the mirror into the vanity case and pulled out the matching hairbrush to start her daily ritual of 100 brush strokes.

For a pretty penny the girls gave their clients a reprieve from their dreary lives. Each felt he was a king in the arms of his princess. Safe from the cutthroat sink-or-swim business practices of Cowtown, the men shared their deepest personal and professional secrets with their girls. Business deals gone sour, and risky investments that paid big. How to get around the rules and make a financial killing.

What seemed to be idle pillow talk between lovers was rarely wasted on the girls. Some took mental notes that would later be shared with the others. Together they would pool their savings and multiple it tenfold. A few schemes had not paid off, but others had proved lucrative. A lot of the girls would never get out of the life – but dreams and schemes gave them hope.

The brush caught on a small tangle. She frowned, recognized the familiar ache in her body, the way her skin again felt as if a thousand maggots writhed under its surface. She hated it. Hated how badly she loved the opium dreams, how she needed it now. Perhaps her father had been right all along. She was shallow, fickle, and weak. Why had she ever been weak enough to be seduced by pretty clothes, baubles, and opium? It had been delightful at first. An escape. But now it ruined any chance she had for redemption. Now her father was dead, and it was too late to earn his forgiveness. Worse, she had borrowed against the family land she'd only just inherited. Borrowed from the wrong men. If only life's tangles could be smoothed over with steady strokes.

She had promised Tina a piece of the dream. An escape together. And now it was too late for Tina. Too late for the baby. Alice remembered the first time she met Tina.

"Tina Whiskeyjack."

"That's a strange last name for a white girl."

"I ain't white, I'm Plains Cree from Northern Alberta."

"I see. Your Grandpa Jack had a thing for whiskey?"

Faster than a dog on a bone, Tina tripped Alice and pushed

her into a chair. "No. Whiskeyjack like the bird. Got it?"

"Sister, I won't ever forget it." Alice stood up and towering over Tina proclaimed, "From this moment forth, you are 'Tiny Tina' my little chickadee."

The tension broke when Tina chuckled. She knew it is always better to have friends than enemies, especially for an Indian woman. Even an Indian woman with fair skin that helped her pass as white. "You ain't the first to say somethin' like that."

"Clearly it's a sore spot." Alice chose her words carefully, "Okay, Miss Chickadee, let me suggest some better alternatives than saying 'ain't' in conversation. You ain't doing yourself any favours if you speak like a savage."

Thus began a special friendship. Alice helped Tina learn the rules at Pearl's, and Tina kept the best business and investment tips she heard for her trusted protector. For a time, the two thought they might head further west together, but Tina became a favourite of many clients and it was hard to turn away from the steady money.

"Don't get too confident; never forget you're just a rich man's plaything."

"What I never forget is that my people had their land stolen by the white man. All I need is a few good years, and I'll have enough to buy back some land that belonged to my people to begin with."

It wasn't a new rant; Alice had heard Tina rail before. "I gotta keep to my plan. Gotta save enough for some seeds, a few laying chickens, a dairy cow and some cattle. I gotta get back to the land."

That plan started with Chaz Cohen. A mostly generous man with good intentions, Mr. Cohen had given this very brush set to Tina. Yes, he had good taste. Yes, he knew what he wanted. He loved having an Indian lady with exotic looks, but he didn't like having to share her. Tina's popularity prevented him from buying her way out of Pearl's, but he managed to move her into a room of her own at a Chinese rooming house.

It seemed like things were falling into place. Then Tina got ill. She couldn't keep any food down but for the rice gruel that Chaz brought her from Yun Kee. As she gained strength her head cleared, and she realized she was with child. Perhaps from Chaz, perhaps from another client. Either way, the child would be a half-breed. That much she knew for sure. If they were lucky the child would be fair like herself, but it could also be dark-skinned like her sister's children.

Chaz wanted to do right by Tina, but it was impossible to extricate himself from his marriage to the daughter of a prominent lawyer. The scandal would be in the Calgary Daily Herald for months. The news would travel throughout the province.

Then Chaz asked Tina to hold his stakes in a strange Chinese gambling game. He believed her to be his lucky charm. She believed him to be her ticket out of town. The promissory note hastily scribbled in the heat of the game, was to give the holder the deed to the land in Turner Valley. No questions asked. The catch was that the note was torn in two, as was the promissory note for land in Chinatown. It was to be a gentlemen's bet.

The promissory note for the Chinatown deed was the stake put up by longtime Chinese businessman, Hop Wo. He owned a laundry near the train station, and several other businesses. It was suspected that he had sponsored several Chinese immigrants under the stricter Head Tax rules. An easy-going man, the Negros considered him a brother. Hop Wo was an ambitious man, but like Chaz, gambling was his drug. It wasn't the first time they had played in Pearl's parlour.

If only Chaz didn't let things escalate so quickly.

If only Chaz hadn't asked Tina to hold his share of the stakes.

If only Tina hadn't let her dreams get the best of her.

If only Tina hadn't seized the opportunity to double cross Chaz.

If only Tina had simply left town.

If only Chaz didn't let his greed get the best of him.

If only Chaz didn't have such a quick temper.

If only Tina hadn't slipped the promissory notes to Alice before she fled.

If only Tina hadn't been slowed by her pregnancy.

If only Tina hadn't chosen to hide by the river after she stumbled and fell.

If only Chaz understood that his partners weren't half as decent as he was.

If only Chaz's partners hadn't employed a couple of thugs to clean up after him.

If only the thugs had found the promissory notes they sought.

If only the thugs hadn't set fire to the rooming house to cover their tracks.

If only the thugs hadn't drowned Tina and her unborn baby.

If only the cops had cared about the drowned hooker.

If only the cops didn't think she was just another drunk Indian.

If only Hop Wo hadn't felt double-crossed by Chaz.

If only Hop Wo had a son he could trust.

The whistle of the 12 o'clock train interrupted Alice's thoughts. She put the brush down and used the comb to make a part in her hair. She checked herself in the mirror and faked a smile. She frowned at the faint wrinkle lines around her eyes.

Alice lifted the tray up and unfolded the two halves of the promissory notes. When Tina had given her the torn pages, she believed the land would save them both. Tina thought the ranch land by Turner Valley would give her and her unborn baby a fresh start. She wanted to live off the land like her ancestors. Grow a garden. Sell some cattle each fall. But she couldn't do it alone. Tina needed Alice. Alice needed Tina. Deep down, Tina believed the land belonged to her without the promissory note. After all, it was the land of her people.

Alice ran her finger along the torn edges of the promissory notes. With Tina gone, Alice didn't care if she had land in Turner Valley or Chinatown. She just needed to find their matching halves, and prove she had title, and sell it off. She needed a good chunk of change to leave Pearl's, and to get her other debts paid. She needed something before the wrinkles around her eyes forced her to find a new source of income. Silver linings? She wondered at the irony of the torn pages and their silvery home. If only Chaz's partners were reasonable men. If only she didn't need Beatrice to help her find the matching sides. She hoped Bea would work with her. If all else failed, Alice guessed she could use her charm and a cup of magic tea. Again.

The River

Cottonwood fluff rides my currents, white, and brown, and black, and blue. A forest of skeletal fists raised, here just below the surface. My waters run red, then black with blood. This is what lies under my liquid breath. The razor's in my waters. I am a dazzling prison of your sins. You will feel their bony wrists at your throats as you sleep. I am noxious, anxious, enraged. I am engorged with your secrets. I am on the rise.

Beatrice

DESPITE WARNINGS THERE WOULD be repercussions if she opened the package, Beatrice felt it imperative to confirm its contents. She picked at the knot in the string with a long hairpin and managed to loosen a spot. She untied the knot and unravelled the string. She opened the bundle and found an assortment of unfamiliar dried nuts and berries. She'd been told there would be Chinese herbs, so it wasn't unexpected. But she knew there should be more. She walked across her room to pour the mixture into her washbasin, and she held her breath.

She inspected the paper wrapping. It appeared to be pages from a Chinese newspaper. If Bea could read it, she would have seen they were from the month before. A photo showed Dr. Sun Yat-sen shaking hands with local Chinese at a fund-raiser for the Chinese National League, but she wasn't familiar with their faces. She was curious about another photo. It showed land beside the Centre Street Bridge. The accompanying article about the escalating value of land in Chinatown might have helped her.

Her pulse quickened. She looked between the pages of newsprint and found nothing. The ink came off on her fingers as she tried to open them up. There was nothing more. Where were the two half pages of promissory notes? She didn't know whether to expect them folded and in the middle of the herbs, or between the pages of the wrapping. Not finding them was unacceptable. What if she had returned to Saskatchewan with this useless bundle of berries? The loss of promissory notes for land in both Chinatown and Turner Valley was definitely disconcerting.

Bea remembered the Chinese boy who would not make eye contact at the Negro party. The one from the laundry, what was his name? Yun Kee. He had taken the package from her hotel room, and Charlie Tucker had facilitated its return. Which one, or had both, double-crossed her? Could she trust Charlie? She was too exhausted to know anymore. The existence of the promissory notes would be a threat until they were all in her possession. Did Alice have them? Had she exchanged them for a deed? She had to find Alice.

Bea sat on the bed wondering what to do. She couldn't go to the police, and she couldn't expect Yun Kee would willingly give her the promissory notes. Not only was it her word against his, she knew she needed to have proof that she'd had the pages in the first place. All she had were the herbs, if that's even what they were. Chinese herbs from a laundry on 9th Avenue. Were they of any value or use to her? Did Alice need them? Did the Chinese man holed up on the cheese farm with her father need them? What was the boy's connection to the Chinese man? Was Charlie Tucker in on it? Who could she trust to help her get the two half pages back?

Bea's head was spinning with confusion. She'd been beaten, robbed, and raped, and had killed a man – but for what? She was angry and tired, though it was only midday. She needed to collect her thoughts. Midday? She hadn't eaten a thing since the party the evening before. Bea poured the herbs back onto the Chinese newsprint and retied them. She put them in her bag and determined to learn more about them. They were her only clue.

But first, she needed to eat. Wisely avoiding the two mystery men at the St. Louis Hotel, she headed to the Cecil Café.

"Sorry miss, you seem to have the worst timing ..."

"That's alright, Frankie, your cheese sandwich and a pot of tea will suit me fine. Perhaps you can help me in another way?"

"How's that?"

"Can you point me toward a Chinese herbal store?"

Frankie rolled his eyes. "Betty, wasn't it? You sure like the trouble spots, don't you? Whatever you need, I'm sure you can find it at Marshall's Pharmacy."

Beatrice persisted. "They won't be able to help me there. Please?"

Frankie considered this stubborn woman. Perhaps he had underestimated her. "Which Chinatown do you want to find?"

"There's more than one?" "Sort of. Chinatown used to be on 9th Ave by the train station, but there wasn't any room to expand. Another kind of popped up further south."

"And now?" Beatrice wasn't really interested in the history of Chinatown. She was peckish and frustrated and feeling like she'd been yanked around two provinces at the whim of others, and her own blind terror for her sister. She just wanted something to eat and directions.

"Property values soared, and the Chinese were basically expelled by real estate developers. But some Chinamen banded together and bought property for a third China- town." Frankie paused for effect, "You'd think they'd get the message!"

"Where is the new Chinatown?" Beatrice asked.

"For now, it's at the base of the Centre Street Bridge. Just south of the river. But not if we good Christian citizens can do anything about it." Frankie went to the cash register and brought back a petition. "Here, add your name to this and I'll get your yer food."

Beatrice wasn't sure if that was a command or a request. She scanned the letter addressed to the Mayor. The 'undersigned tax payers' urged council not to grant permits or licenses stating, "a nuisance to surrounding citizens" and "potential loss of income". She imagined the Chinese were taxpayers, too.

A complaint of Chinese wearing traditional dress specifically targeted women "masquerading in men's clothes', and asked, "Cannot something be done?" Beatrice felt an affinity for the foreigners. Why shouldn't women wear men's clothing? A lot of tasks were easier in trousers than in high heels and a dress. She wished she still had the suit jacket and scratchy wool pants that Alice had dressed her in.

Some tea spilled onto the table when Frankie set it down. "Don't go to Chinatown at night, and watch out for the opium addicts. Their eyes are wild and they're unpredictable. Even in the daytime."

"Opium addicts?"

"Yeah, they'll do anything for their habit. If they can't entice you to join, they'll steal your money to pay for a puff. The worst are the longtime addicts. You can't even tell they've succumbed to the drug. They're very sneaky." Frankie waved the cup under Bea's nose for effect. "Don't accept drinks from strangers."

"What if I'm parched, and someone offers me some water?"

"Then go to the river and use your hands. You're a target for some unpredictable and cunning opium addict." Bea wanted to protest his judgment but kept eating her sandwich. "You never heard of opium tea? It will have you doing things completely out of character. Days could pass without you knowing."

Bea swallowed; something clicked in her head. "Could opium pass for whiskey?"

"What do you think? It's odorless and colourless. It could pass for anything the addict tells you it is." Frankie poked the petition with his index finger, "Don't forget to sign this!"

The first thing Bea noticed about Chinatown was the unfamiliar smells. The rich aroma of roasted meats tickled her nose, but another smell made her nauseated. Under it all was the smell of horse piss, creosote and money. She noticed the buildings were made of brick rather than the sandstone used just a few blocks away in downtown. She supposed it was cheaper but safer than wood. She passed a restaurant, a laundry, and a barbershop. She peeked in a window at jars with Chinese script on them, and walls of wooden drawers. She was sure she'd hit the jackpot.

Bamboo chimes tinkled as she opened the door. A wave of new smells wafted around her. All she could recognize was some menthol. A Chinese man measuring out dried items ignored her. A young boy from the back room appeared and asked, "Yes, miss. Can I help you?"

Bea had planned her strategy on the walk from the café. "Yes, I've come into possession of what I believe are Chinese herbs, but I don't know how to use them." Bea pulled the package from her bag. She was addressing the boy, but hoping to catch the attention of the old man. He did not seem to be paying attention.

The boy unbundled her package. "Yes, these Chinese nuts and seeds. You make Ching Bo Leung soup?" Bea shook her head. "You soak in water to loosen dirt. Then cook overnight with pork bones. Only one cup per person."

"What are they for?"

"All-purpose good health. A tonic. Clean body, nourish your organs." The boy touched his lungs and made a circle around the kidney area.

Bea's frustration escalated. "Soup?" Served her right for trusting the Viscount and his Chinese acquaintance. What else could she have expected from Chinese herbs she'd gotten at a laundry? She reconsidered her strategy. "What if I needed something stronger? You know, to treat melancholy." She lowered her voice, "I can pay."

"You want Po Chai pills? Good for fever, diarrhea, over-drinking, over-eating." He opened a vial for her to smell. The smell made her step back. "How you say? The stomach …" The boy said slowly.

"Something even stronger," She deftly touched her purse, and lowered her voice again. "Like opium?"

The old man bundled the herbs and put the lid back on the jar. The boy asked something in Chinese. He pointed at Bea's purse and made a bow at the end of his request. In good faith, Bea opened her purse and slid a fiver across the counter. The old man got up, closed the blinds to the shop and indicated to Beatrice that she should not have loose lips.

The boy lit a lantern and told Bea to follow him. He opened a curtain in the back room and revealed a secret tunnel down-stairs. "Walk careful," he said. "Uneven ground." The wooden railing was smooth.

Beatrice's eyes were still adjusting to the lighting. At the bottom of the stairs, the boy parted another set of curtains and revealed an opium den. Chinese scroll paintings hung crookedly on the wall; makeshift mattresses lay on the floor. Patrons lay in repose sucking vapourized air through opium pipes that had been heated on oil lamps.

She really had hit the jackpot. In the back corner of the room lay Alice. It was hard to tell if Alice was dead or alive.

The River

*Teeth of ice, grinding one frozen beast against
another. Not good when it floods. Textures and
eddies, of my impossible chalk blue, sink to the
bottom. Dead branches. Dead women. Discarded whispers. I carry secrets in my depths.
They will walk again.*

Yun Kee

YUN KEE ROLLED OVER trying to find a better position on the cot.
Between his duties as a houseboy for prominent Jewish families, and serving food at the Negro house parties, how did
his mother expect him to put in full days at the laundry? Isn't
that what the other 'paper sons' were for? The real 'paper
sons'? Not he, Yun Kee, son of Lo Ying Tow and Hop Wo.
The 'paper sons' were new arrivals who owed his father for
bringing them over from China on false papers. Couldn't his
parents see he had higher aspirations?

Nobody knew the three of them were connected, not
even within the Chinese community. This fortunate misunderstanding sometimes worked to their advantage. At the
monthly mahjong games at Pearl's, for example, Yun Kee
had regularly helped his father assess how good an oppo-
nent's hand was. Mahjong was specifically designed to prevent
cheating, but the two had worked out a way to communicate
the number of points in a player's hands. When Yun Kee
refreshed the drinks and snacks between rounds, he would
choose a code item that would signal the points in a particular player's hand for the next round. It gave his father an

unfair advantage. Though it did not necessarily help him to win each round, Hop Wo was able to minimize his losses.

The chime on the shop door tinkled. Crap, he was just drifting off. Yun Kee pulled himself up and prepared to greet a customer. His friendly manner and nearly perfect English were key to the family's success. Some customers were amused by his slightly British accent, and all were glad they didn't need to venture into Chinatown to take their laundry. The slightly higher prices attracted prominent customers, and both father and son were able to use some of those relationships to their business advantage.

False alarm, it was just his mother, Lo Ying Tow, returning with fresh vegetables, meat and eggs from the market.

Lo Ying Tow

LO YING TOW'S TRIPS to the market were the highlight of her days. Not only a chance to get out of the shop, it was her opportunity to have social interaction and news from within Calgary's Chinese community. Since nobody knew that Hop Wo was really her husband, and Yun Kee her only son, many commiserated with Lo Ying Tow. Despite accepting gifts of food from potential suitors, she had managed to escape the efforts of the matchmakers.

Today's shopping trip had been particularly fruitful. The white woman who came for the package was asking about their use. Rumour had it that she even asked for opium. Lo Ying Tow knew the white woman was somehow connected to her husband's disappearance.

Absent for a month, Lo Ying Tow had suspicions something had gone amiss at one of Hop Wo's 'secret' business meetings. She was no fool. She knew they were not really business meetings. He was gambling again; it was his downfall.

Had it not been for his gambling problem, Hop Wo could have brought his wife and son over from China sooner than he did. One delay had occurred when the government raised Head Tax to $500. That had been a big disappointment. The bigger surprise was receiving a letter telling her he nearly had all the money needed for their passage, then learning in the next letter it would be several more years. She'd always suspected he'd lost the money gambling. What else was there for those Chinese bachelor men to do but work, drink, and gamble, alone in Canada? It was a hard life and some never managed to save enough to see their families again.

Now that she was here, Lo Ying Tow could keep a better eye on her husband's illicit activities. She was lucky Yun Kee looked out for their assets too, but his increasing confidence and bravado also put them at risk. She set the burlap bags on the counter and handed Yun Kee some eggs, "Steamed eggs tonight, your favourite. Put these in the icebox for now."

Yun Kee had been waiting to speak with her. In Chinese, he said to his mother, "Baba double-crossed me."

In English, Lo Ying Tow replied, "And you double-crossed the English woman."

Yun Kee knew she was angry. She rarely spoke English to him. He continued in Chinese, "How do you know?"

"You think your mother is stupid?

"The land in Chinatown will be my inheritance."

"You think a woman raising her son alone in rural China for 10 years doesn't learn a thing or two about survival?"

"It's not even worth that much."

"Someday it will be more valuable than you can imagine."

"Not if Baba loses the deed."

"Is that what happened? I thought you were there so that he wouldn't."

"I am there to keep him from going too far."

Lo Ying Tow wondered if her husband had jeopardized any of their other holdings. She wanted to ask, but she also sensed her son was afraid. Now was a good time for her to clip his wings a little. "You should not rely solely on the inheritance you will one day receive. You must also work hard."

Yun Kee knew better than to list his many jobs and prominent contacts to her. In his perfect English he said, "I am quite respected, you know. They call it success."

She was not as impressed by his British accent as others might be. "Success? You call it success that your father has been gone for a month, with no contact with us?" She blocked his path and said, "Don't get puffed up by the platitudes people give you. They are just watching out for themselves. Beware ambition, and never forget: They look at you and see a Celestial. If they have their way, those rich white men will send us all back to China and steal our businesses. We have no rights here. We are aliens. We are excluded. You are excluded, too."

"I am different, you will see. I haven't worked this hard to let it all be stolen from me, or you, or even Baba."

Hop Wo

HUA CHOW. THE CHINESE words for 'overseas Chinese' or immigrants, translate into 'bridge'. Indeed, Hop Wo had been a bridge between two cultures since his arrival from China in 1883. His timing had been fortuitous, there was no Head Tax at the time, and while some Occidentals resented the Chinese who were paid less than other workers to build the railway, others were more accepting.

Hop Wo landed in Victoria by way of San Francisco and made his way east. Men from his village in Guangdong province were already established in Calgary, and ready to help him find work and accommodation.

Hop Wo learned English quickly, and knew it was his ticket to getting ahead faster and further. Years later, he insisted his wife pay the British missionaries for extra tutoring for herself and their young son. The investment paid off, and both adjusted quickly to Canadian life once they finally arrived.

Perhaps Yun Kee had adjusted too well? Hop Wo sometimes wondered if he could trust his own son. Yun Kee seemed to forget his Chinese roots. Didn't realize complaints about the Chinese included their family. At the same time, Yun Kee was a resourceful ally. The family struggled under the pressure to pay back the money Hop Wo had borrowed to sponsor other 'paper sons' to emigrate to Canada. The idea was to bring over other men from the village to be a source of cheap staffing for the businesses Hop Wo had acquired. Once they arrived, they owed Hop Wo money, and at least until the debt was repaid, their loyalty was guaranteed. It was tricky to balance both sides of the books, and lately it seemed they owed more than what the businesses earned.

The mahjong games at Pearl's were a way for him to blow off steam and make new acquaintances. His friend, and sometimes business associate, Chaz Cohen was fascinated by Chinese culture. He loved Chinese food, and he implored Hop Wo to teach him how to play mahjong. The learning curve was steep, but Chaz had finally mastered the game and wanted others to love it as much as he did himself.

Who knew things would escalate so quickly the night Chaz brought Guy Weadick to play?

Chaz took a fountain pen and wrote a declaration on some parchment:

"*Whoever presents both sides of this promissory note to Chaz Cohen (or his descendants) receives the deed to ranch land in Turner Valley. This gentlemen's bet is to be honoured. No questions asked.*" He dated it, signed it, and slapped it on the table. The land wasn't even Chaz's to give, but his opponents didn't know that. In fact, Chaz only held the deed as collateral. Tina's friend Alice had borrowed against it to pay off the debts that fed her opium habit. Poor girl. She was in too deep. And Chaz was weak when it came to pretty girls. Hop Wo saw the way he looked at Tina, his exotic, birdlike lover.

"What's this?" the Viscount asked.

"Exactly what it says. Whatcha got to match this?"

The Viscount didn't hesitate. "I've got a cheese farm in Saskatchewan." He smiled to himself, knowing that only Hop Wo knew what a disaster that investment had turned out to be.

"Alright then, put that into the pot. Hop Wo?"

Yun Kee cleared his throat. "More congee, Mr. Hop Wo?" In public, Yun Kee and Hop Wo kept up the charade of being sponsor and 'paper son'. People knew that Hop Wo had brought Yun Kee to Canada, but everyone assumed the papers were false and the two were just pretending to be from the same family. The story was easy to maintain with their unrelated names, especially outside of Chinatown. "Or ginger, sir?"

Yun Kee's attempt to stop Hop Wo from joining the high stakes game failed. Hop Wo waved his arm to indicate there were matters far more important than a bowl of congee with or without extra ginger. "Okay, I've got some land in the new Chinatown. Write up another note and I will sign it." Yun Kee swallowed hard.

Guy Weadick slapped three bills down and declared, "Boys, I'm out. But this here's my gift to you. Another round of whiskey and more of this fine food. I will stay to witness this madness. Nobody told me this Chinese gambling game would get so intense!"

"Can we play with just three?" the Viscount asked. He still confused the complex rules of the game, especially when he was drunk.

Yun Kee started to answer, but Hop Wo cut him off. "Actually, three players is perfect. With one player less the rounds will go quicker. We deal the same but get our turns more often."

Chaz wrote up two more promissory notes. He added a witness line to his own and the other two. The Viscount and Hop Wo promised their deeds to the cheese farm in Saskatchewan and land in Calgary's new Chinatown. Guy Weadick signed as the witness for all three notes. They freshened their drinks and when the ink dried, Chaz tore all three notes carefully down the middle.

Each player received two half pages, one for the pot, and one for security, and chose one person to hold their stakes. Chaz chose Tina, who was sitting beside him. She was his lucky charm. Hop Wo asked Yun Kee, and the Viscount asked the visiting cowboy.

The mahjong game began anew.

Each round consisted of at least three games, with each player dealing one round. If the player won a round, he had dealt, then he would deal again. After the first round, the Viscount lost his promissory note to Chaz, and now Tina held both halves of his stake. The Viscount was so drunk he almost considered it a blessing. The men took another break. Tina left to powder her nose, and she looked very flushed when she returned.

On the next round, the Viscount was determined to win back his cheese farm but he was clearly the lesser player and the tiles were not in his favour. Tina complained of the heat, even after Yun Kee opened the window to create a cross breeze.

It was mid-afternoon when they started, and now the sun had set. Tina was already restless when Guy Weadick had stopped playing.

"Chaz, honey, I really can't sit much longer. How long are you boys going to keep playing?" Chaz noticed the sweat on Tina's brow. She was fanning herself despite the evening breeze.

"Ask Pearl if you can lie down a spell."

"Honey, the rooms are all full. Today was payday." She wiped her face for effect. "Why don't I go home and rest a bit. Perhaps I'll see you after the game ends."

Chaz took pity on Tina. Her pregnancy hadn't been easy and sitting for hours in the smoky parlour was probably not helping. He trusted her completely and didn't think twice to send her home. "You want me to hire you a carriage?"

"No honey. The fresh air and stretching my legs will do me well."

"But it's late. And dark out."

"Don't you worry. There's plenty of folks out celebrating payday. I don't have far." Tina kissed Chaz on the cheek and fled into the night.

The game continued and the Viscount's chances did not improve. Fortunately for him, luck was on Hop Wo's side. As was Yun Kee. Every time Chaz's hand looked pretty good, Yun Kee would pour his father fresh tea or congee and tell him it was hot. "Perhaps best to wait until cooler?" he warned.

Hop Wo felt bad about taking advantage of his friend, but he knew Chaz and his business associates were the ones forcing Chinatown to its third location. Hop Wo had been able to buy some land, but it hadn't been easy finding anyone willing to sell to a Chinaman. He needed more, and this was his chance. Selling the ranch land in Turner Valley would give him enough money to pay his own debts and buy another lot near the river.

Hop Wo won the next round. The promissory note for the cheese farm went back into the pot, and within the next hour, Hop Wo had won it all. Chaz had been so sure he could beat the Chinaman at his own game and had to laugh at his own foolishness. Still, he was a gentleman and he said he would honour the bet. The land had never really been his to begin with, and what would a prostitute with a fondness for opium do with a ranch anyway? Guy Weadick was relieved he'd bowed out early, his savings intact.

"That there is the craziest darn game I've ever seen. If I lived to be a hundred, I doubt I'd learn it," he exclaimed, slapping his giant hat back on his head.

The next day, when Hop Wo saw the burned out remains of the Chinese rooming house where Tina lived, he realized that while he known he could not trust Chaz's business partners, because clearly, they did not share his sense of integrity, he had trusted Chaz. Now he wasn't so sure. Hop Wo wondered if Chaz is a sore loser, with plans of his own for double-crossing the Chinaman. And what secrets, other than his love for Tina, did his partners hold over Chaz?

Rumour spread through the community quicker than the flames. Men had come looking for Tina, kicking down doors. When Tina could not be found, the hired thugs smashed her kerosene lamps, and set fire to her room.

Hop Wo found it difficult to believe his old friend could turn so ugly, but he'd learned long ago that pride and money held fierce power over people. It was time for him to disappear. Yun Kee knew those men. And Yun Kee knew his father held the missing halves of the promissory notes. If all the halves turned up, the deed holders could legally be bound to honour the bet. Hop Wo had weighed his options. The hacking cough that had plagued him for years, most particularly when he was tired and anxious had chosen this morning, of all mornings, to return.

He visited his old friend the Viscount at the Hotel Alexander at breakfast and returned both halves of the Viscount's promissory note, in exchange for the Viscount help. He collected the deed to his land in the new Chinatown, packed up a small bundle of clothes while Lo Ying Tow was out running errands. He left her a note in the deep pocket of the robe she'd brought from China and loved to wear in the morning before the laundry opened.

Wife – Trust me, but no-one else. I shall return when it is safe. I have erred, but I shall find a way.

And then Hop Wo joined the Viscount on an evening train to Saskatchewan, the long fingers of the setting sun tingling on the back of his neck.

Chapter Nine

by Dymphny Dronyk

Aaron – at home

THERE WAS TOO MUCH death. Turn on the news: Death. War. Mass shootings. Murdered and missing Indigenous women. Walk in his own front door: Bones. Secrets. Murder. Valeria – his friend and neighbour. And now she wasn't just a friend, but also his cousin! Murdered.

Aaron's head hurt. The past weeks had all been too much. His quiet life washed away in silt and confusion, the rage of the river seemed personal now, a portent. He'd left the Blackfoot Truck Stop after his meeting with Patricia, his mother's half-sister, feeling as though he'd had an out of body experience. All these years his mother had known she'd had another sister, and she had never mentioned a word of it to him. He was dazed. After a while, sitting in that diner booth, Patricia's words no longer registered in his mind. He had put his hand on hers, left it there covering her arthritic fingers, the worn golden rings. His energy had run out. He'd taken the two elderly women home and promised to call them in the morning.

Aaron sat in the clammy living room of his damp house, the chill creeping down the back of his neck. Now that the power was back, he could run a space heater, but the furnace was still full of muck, and the house felt cold and unwelcoming. The valiant little heater couldn't push out the gloom that had settled in his home. He longed for Valeria's rowdy warmth, the way she knew how to show up at the door at just the right time, always with some fresh East Village gossip, a new cause, or different tactic about how to protect some corner of their neighbourhood. But now he wondered about their friendship. She knew how lonely he was, his obsession with the history of East Village, which was in many ways, the history of his own family. Their own family! Why had she never told him? What had she been doing in his house? At first, he had imagined she had been checking on his safety – but what if she too had been looking for something? What if she was part of the badness?

For years Aaron had been haunted by the hints of stories that he read between the lines of history. The racism, the appropriation of land. East Village had been a corner of the city where the marginalized had always gathered. Settlement had pushed the First Nations people off the delta between the Bow and Elbow rivers. As Calgary grew from a Fort, to a town, to a city, his neighbourhood had absorbed the misfits. The strong Black community, including the porters on the railroad who couldn't find a room anywhere else on their overnight shifts, and the independent women such as Pearl Miller, who did not fit as wives or servants. Time and again the misfits had formed alliances and had found ways to survive. The Chinese and African Canadians, the new immigrants. In his lifetime, East Village had been considered more of a blight – a blemish on the city's skin, from which eyes were collectively averted. The Cecil Hotel was infamous as a refuge for drug addicts and the disenfranchised. Once again, the lost souls of the city were being banished elsewhere, to make room for swanky condos and a "lifestyle" that was colour coordinated and branded. The Golden Age Centre would be gone soon too. Yet another diaspora: the elderly people nobody really considered neighbours, but who understood the value of community better than anyone. Aaron would miss the friendly chit-chat, how it could take an hour to take the five-minute walk from his house to the café thanks to all the visiting.

His grandfather must have struggled too. Aaron's mother had told him how he'd never felt good enough, how the casual discrimination against Jews had chafed him. He was held up as a founding father of the city, a wealthy, successful businessman. The kind of man Aaron could never live up to, footsteps far too big to fill. But to be successful, sometimes you had to be ruthless. Aaron had seen that in others – even in his mother. It made him uncomfortable. He needed to understand how the deed he had found under the floorboards was connected to Valeria's death. Patricia was sure Valeria had become embroiled in a Cohen family game of greed, but something about that didn't quite make sense. Most of the Cohens were dead. And the deed belonged to a woman named Alice, signed in 1912.

Tommy Douglas glared at him from across the small room, flicking his tail, in that exasperated way he had, as if he meant "Idiot. Can't you see the answer? It's right in front of you."

"What now, TD?" Aaron muttered. "I guess the family secrets were even weirder than I suspected. What do I do now?"

Beatrice & Alice – in the opium den

"Alice! Alice, come on, wake up. You have to move." Beatrice propped Alice up on the greasy bedding. Alice wasn't dead, but she may as well have been for all the response she gave. The old man watched them fretfully, clearly nervous they would disturb the other dreamers and disrupt his business. His customers paid them no mind. They dozed or gazed into the haze of the room. It smelled of must and old sweat, and faintly, of burning maple sugar. Kerosene lamps flickered.

"Does she come here often?"

The old man looked away, his hands fidgeting with the edge of his jacket.

"Look, I don't care what you do here. I need to get my friend home. There are bad men looking for her. Will you help me? Please. You don't want them to come looking here, right?"

Desperation made Beatrice bold. Alice looked so vulnerable, and her fragility conjured up unwanted memories for Beatrice, memories about what happens when women don't look out for one another. Beatrice's anger and confusion slid over one another, and out of her mind. In their place, a desperate plan began to come together. She would have to take matters into her own hands, and deal with the root of their problems. She and the old man stared at each other. She held Alice in her arms and felt the girl's breath rattle deep in her lungs.

"Please?" Beatrice whispered. "Get Charlie, the blacksmith. Tell him to bring his wagon. He'll know what to do."

The man hesitated, clearly torn, then he nodded curtly and quietly left the dim room. Beatrice waited, anxious. She shifted Alice's weight so that she could get at the knife if she needed it. She felt exhaustion creep back into her being, into her bones, into her soul. She couldn't keep running. There was too much pain, too much death. It had to end. She had to end it. Enough. If she didn't end it now, there would never be an escape for her, or for Alice, for her sister Ida.

"Maman," she whispered. "S'il vous plaît aidez-moi. Je suis perdu. Dites-moi quoi faire."

The River - receding

*All the grandmothers in my belly are weeping
for the daughters I have carried away. Have you
learned nothing? Are you are only concerned
with profit margins and production values?
What about the glaciers, losing thousands of
years of stories? What about the bull trout?
What about the children? Clean water? The
wilderness?*

*I sing to you daily: I dance through you and
carry this ancient silt onward through my sisters,
all the way to the Hudson Bay. So few take heed
of my singing. Can you only notice me when I
am angry, when my rage washes away your com-
placency, your privilege? Bones wash clean, but
your sins stain my water. I will keep calling to
you until my last drop has flowed, until my dry
riverbed becomes a mausoleum, until you die of
thirst.*

Aaron & Chester at Chester's place

"Seriously, Chester, I don't know who to trust anymore. The more of the story I unravel, the less I understand. And you're part of it. What's your game? What do you want?"

Aaron stood in Chester's doorway, sodden and distraught. He had Tommy Douglas in his carrier, yowling. The cat had yowled the entire way to Kensington, and now his outrage echoed down the hallway of Chester's apartment building.

"Oh, landsakes, Aaron, get in here. This is a pet-free building. You'd think we were sacrificing him to the river gods the way he's carrying on."

"'Landsakes', Chester? Really? Who the hell says 'landsakes' anymore? What century are you in, Chester, or Phoebe Cardinal, or whoever you are?"

Chester grabbed the cat carrier and pulled them both inside. Aaron dropped his heavy backpack, several cloth grocery bags of cat supplies, and a damp sleeping bag on the tile floor of her entryway.

The warm apartment smelled of nutmeg and apricots. Candles burned crookedly in a cluster on the wooden chest that served as a coffee table. Chester let Tommy Douglas out of the carrier, her thick black hair tumbling over her shoulder. He began to explore the room, his tail still a spiky brush of indignation.

All at once Aaron felt like an idiot. "I'm sorry," he muttered to the puddle his boots were making on her clean floor. "I couldn't stay there tonight. I didn't know where else to go. I didn't mean to come in here yelling. I meant to ask if Tommy and I could sleep on your couch. What if they're trying to kill me too?"

Chester bustled about, finding towels, hanging up his wet jacket. "Just what we need, hey? More rain." she said. "Listen, it's okay. It's been a crazy few weeks. You can stay. Why don't you warm up in the shower? I've got some leftover borscht and rugelach for dessert. My brother left some of his stuff here. I'll dig out some dry clothes for you."

Later, they sat together on her sagging couch, under a worn Hudson's Bay blanket, Tommy Douglas contentedly kneading his massive paws into Chester's lap.

"Start at the beginning," she said, her strong hand in his. "You tell me what you know, and I promise to tell you everything I've learned too."

"TD doesn't usually like women," Aaron mused, stroking the big cat's head. "I'm surprised he's on your lap."

"Spill, Aaron," she commanded. "Enough of the crap."

"I'm not sure. It somehow ties back to the deed I found, land that doesn't belong to us. To my grandfather Chaz Cohen. Somehow to the secrets and lies that seem to be tangled up in every branch of my family tree. I phoned my mother tonight. She didn't give me a straight answer, about her secret sister, or about the cousin I never knew I had, but she didn't seem surprised that I was asking either. It was like she'd been waiting for me to call. She told me to keep Patricia out of the house. She sounded so angry and hard done by. I don't get it. She's always had everything. Grandfather looked after her. She was the favourite. Her older sisters, well, half-sisters I guess, died long before I was born. I didn't tell her about the deed, but I told her the cops think I killed Valeria. I asked her what she knew about Grandfather's business, about his involvement in forcing the Chinese out. I've always wanted to know if he was a crook, just another guy like Rodney, getting rich from screwing people."

"Okay, back up. Who's Rodney, again? And what exactly did Patricia tell you? How is that story different than what your mother told you?"

Aaron took a deep breath. "Sorry. It's all so confusing. Can't stop being an investigative journalist, can you? So today, after the funeral, Patricia told me a wild story. Some of it jives with what I thought was truth, what I'd told you. I knew my Mom was the illegitimate daughter, that she'd been raised in by her father's family, and that she'd only met her birth mother once. She'd told me that much, when I was in university. It explains a lot of her issues about abandonment, and not trusting people. But Patricia claims it wasn't quite that simple. When Mary Bannister, Patricia's mother, also my Mom's mother, gave birth to her daughter, my mother, the bastard daughter of my grandfather Cohen, in 1947, it was a huge scandal to be an unwed mother. Things were different. Mary was hidden away during her pregnancy, and the baby was taken from her when it was a few days old. The Cohen family took the baby in, said it was the child of a Jewish relative who had fled Europe in the war and ended up in New York, tried to make a life there, but eventually died of TB. It's true we have relatives there. Apparently, Aunt Ruth had been visiting New York around that time. It seemed legit. Our family looked heroic, which was better than a scandal. Patricia says Grandmother Sally knew the truth, and so did both my aunts, Ruth and Willa. The family wanted to keep its good name. Grandfather had started with nothing and built up his fortune. There was a lot to lose. Grandmother Sally's family felt she married beneath her standing, and they never really accepted the baby. Mom always said the Perelmans where terrible snobs. Ruth took pity on the baby and was closest to Mom. But both Ruth and Willa died of breast cancer, in their early 50s. More abandonment for Mom."

Chester had taken a stenographer's pad out of her messenger bag and was scribbling notes. "Wait, I think I need to draw a family tree. Truth is indeed stranger than fiction. So, your Mom grew up thinking she was an orphan, and so did the rest of high society. When did the story unravel?"

"At Grandfather's funeral, Patricia knew, but Mom didn't. Patricia's mother, Mary Bannister, had taken her. Mary wanted an excuse to see her lost child. Supposedly she'd never stopped loving Grandfather. The girls had an immediate affinity for each other. Mom thought she'd found her kindred spirit like in the Anne of Green Gables books. Not until Aunt Ruth died, a few years later, when Mom was 18, did she hear all the details. Grandmother Sally told her, perhaps out of bitterness, and warned her not to ruin the family name by telling anyone. She only told Patricia. Mom always said that Grandmother cared more about what the bridge ladies thought of her than about anything else. Mom inherited the family fortune. There was nobody left. Well, there's a bunch of Perelmans still, I imagine. We just never had much to do with them," he paused, suddenly far away.

"Patricia says they grew apart once Mom knew her real heritage. She was angry about the lies, and there was no one who knew the truth, after Grandmother died, except Patricia. Maybe she was jealous that Patricia and Mary had been close, despite Patricia's unruliness. Mom was young and unhappy. And rich, relatively speaking, although a lot of the family real estate turned out to belong to the Perelmans, not the Cohens. She travelled, tried to find herself. It was the 60s. Eventually she married my Dad, who is bat-shit crazy – two aging hippies finding each other – and they had me. A year later, Dad took off, and it was just the two of us, in our little yellow house full of antiques and Grandfather's books and papers."

Chester flipped through her notes and shook her head ruefully. "So, if I've kept track – we've got two lonely old ladies, half-sisters by your Grandfather, who both grew up in a web of lies. They were close as teenagers but now are suspicious of each other. And now one sister's only child is dead from blunt force trauma – and the other sister's only child has been accused of the murder."

Aaron rubbed his hands wearily over this stubble, as if to erase the ugly truth of what he was saying. "Yup. I guess that sums it up. Plus, a thrashed house. Some freak looking for something, maybe the deed. A land deed that doesn't belong to either sister, or either only child. Oh, and don't forget the skeleton that turned up under my porch. Can it get any crazier?"

Chester hugged Tommy Douglas close to her, "I think it can. I think your grandfather killed my Kookum's sister Tina, like she was garbage, just something that was in the way. I think they're still killing our women, just disposing of them, dumping them in rivers. I think those bones belong to Tina."

The big grey cat shot from her arms with a low growl, and landed on a windowsill, tail twitching.

"Your great-aunt was buried under my porch, murdered by my grandfather? What the hell? How is that possible? He tried to be an honourable man! I'm sure of it."

"Fine suits and a knack for making lots of money don't make anyone honourable, Aaron. You know that. Maybe you're right. Maybe you are in the way. They just might kill you too."

Beatrice & Alice at Charlie Tucker's shop

"I THOUGHT YOU WERE supposed to kill me, Bea," Alice murmured, finally starting to come to, where she lay on the cot in Charlie's back room. The curtains were drawn. Yun Kee stood watch by the front door. Charlie kept a wary eye on the back door, and on the two women.

"I decided that's too easy," Bea replied grimly. "Were you trying to do yourself in, with the opium? You need to start talking, Alice. I've had enough. Either we work together and save ourselves. Or we both end up dead by at the hands of pirates. I'm tired of running, so what's it going to be?"

Alice closed her eyes again. Her tight curls were coming undone. She looked shrunken, and none of the sass and vibrancy that Bea had encountered at the brothel was in evidence now. "I can't make it right, Bea. Tina's gone. Her baby is gone. The ranch is gone. If I wasn't such a coward, I would have drowned myself in that damn river."

"Save it for confession, Miss Alice," Charlie snarled. "We don't have much time. Whatever house of cards you two girls built is about to get blown down. And I don't want to go down with it. I just got out of jail, if you recall. Don't feel like going back."

"Alice, I'm not going to kill you. Then I'd be as wicked as the pirates, as bad as my father. You and me and my sister Ida – we can live, we can head to Vancouver, or to Paris. I'm going to throw the pirates off our scent. Now, tell me who your protector is, and why you'd rather take too much opium than have him keep you safe."

"And where's Tina?" Charlie interrupted. "Her sister has been asking for her, and so has Pearl. The rooming house burned down, and she's nowhere to be found."

"I'm not running anymore. I just want to go home," Alice said. She sat up carefully. "Tina's dead. She made a mistake. She got impatient and thought she could outsmart Chaz Cohen – or worse, his business partners, the Perelman's. Chaz had promised her the moon, but time was running out. She couldn't hide that she was with child. I went to check on Tina after the mah jong game, and saw her flee the rooming house, just before the men got there, and doused it in kerosene. They followed her to the river. I think they drowned her there. I didn't know what to do. Those men have nothing to do with me. Chaz is a fool. They were never going to let him keep Tina, no matter how smitten he is. It looks too bad for business for a man like Chaz Cohen to love a whore, and a half-breed at that. And me, well, the men I owe will never let me go. I'm too useful."

Charlie handed her a tin cup of coffee he had brewed. Alice wrapped her hands around it gratefully. "It's too late."

"Is it Weadick you owe?" Beatrice demanded, thinking of the money she'd pocketed.

"No, Guy is fine fella," Alice said. "He's got stars in his eyes about his exhibition, and he wouldn't hurt a fly."

"Your gentleman friend is ruining Chinatown, and the decent business we do," Yun Kee said to Alice. "Since the Opium Act has made the dreaming rooms illegal, we see more thugs."

"Opium pirates," Beatrice exclaimed. "Is that it? Is that who my father owes too?"

Alice looked at Yun Kee, and then at Charlie. "Everything's changing isn't it? It doesn't just stop with a little bit of fun. It seemed easy enough. Just ride the train back from Vancouver once in a while, carry their packages in my valise. Make sure I drop it off at the right place. Now they want more. They're putting the squeeze on me and on Pearl too. And I've got nowhere to run because I've gone and squandered my Daddy's ranch."

"My father came here a month ago, right after I came home from Europe," Beatrice explained. "He left with me with my sister Ida, saying he had business to attend in the city. A few days later he arrived back home, with a Chinese man; Father hid him in the milking barn. Father was worried. He kept returning to the train station, waiting for telegrams. I knew he'd made another of his deals, but not that it was with the devil. When they came to collect, they found all of us. He traded me for the one thing he cares about other than money – Ida. They sent me to get Alice, and with a message for the people at the laundry. Your people, Yun Kee."

"So it was your ranch that my father won in the mah jong game?" said Yun Kee to Alice.

She nodded. "Yes, my father died a few months back. Before I could go home and ask his forgiveness, before I could make it right. Even so, he willed me the ranch. There was no-one else. I had no interest in ranching, not until Tina told me she was with child. I liked her dreams for the ranch, and thought we could be together."

Then Yun Kee pointed at Beatrice. "It is my father who is hiding in your barn. Unless he is already dead."

"I think he is alive," Beatrice replied. "They believe he is part of the competition for their trade and are holding him hostage. Is he an opium pirate too?"

Yun Kee shook his head emphatically. "No, my father's weakness is gambling, not opium. Our family has never become embroiled in the opium wars. We have laundries, and we had a rooming house, until last night. We are businessmen not pirates."

Alice looked at Bea. "So, you're not running without your sister? Is that it?"

Beatrice felt her guts cramp at the thought of Ida. Terror flowed through her for a moment and strengthened her resolve. The mission became clear. "I should never have left Ida behind, this time, or when she was a child. They promised to do to her what they did to me if I don't bring them what they want. I can't bring them what they want. Their greed is the root of the problem. How do we stop them? Maybe I should just kill them all, like I did the pirate at the river."

Charlie crossed the small room to put his warm hands on her shoulders. "Now listen here girl. The only way to change something is by working together. You said that yourself. We need to make a plan. What have you come up with so far?"

"So, the men who killed Tina were sent not by this Chaz Cohen, but by his associates," Beatrice tried to keep it all in one clear line. "And the man who protects you, Alice, protects and enslaves you, is he not also an associate of Chaz. Perhaps the same man?"

"Yes," said Alice, nodding her head. "Yes! He is. You know how it is with businessmen. They all know each other. Drink long afternoons away at the Alberta Hotel. John owns a mine in Carbon. It isn't performing as well as it should. Now the mine is just a handy distraction from his opium running. John is a as bad for Chaz as he is for me, and for Chinatown. He wants it all."

"John Spencer is indeed wicked," Yun Kee confirmed. "The opium trade is blamed on the Chinese, but it has long been the British who have had a heavy hand in it. One must merely pay attention to the wars in the opium growing countries to understand this. Spencer will stop at nothing, unless he is stopped."

"What does he have on Pearl?" Charlie asked. "I can't imagine her doing anything to jeopardize her business. She's a good woman, and she's worked too hard."

"She borrowed money from him, but when she went to repay it the interest had gone up. And it keeps going up. He wants to keep it that way. Pearl's is in an excellent location. He is an evil man. He just likes to play with people," said Alice.

Beatrice frowned, and gritted her teeth. "We'll let the bastards double-cross each other, and then we'll kill them for good measure. We need Pearl to throw a party. We going to tell John that Hop Wo's masters are in town, ready to take over, but that they might be willing to make a deal. He'll believe the lie."

Charlie nodded slowly. "Perhaps that will work. Men can be swayed by both greed and lust. But it won't be guaranteed they'll come. And killing them ... well ... perhaps we don't need to go that far."

"You have to believe me, Charlie," she said, her voice choked with tears and rage. "Some men only understand the logic of a razor, or a bullet. But we need Chaz Cohen to help us get them to Pearl's."

"And we need Pearl to put her Bible aside long enough for the razor to do its work," Alice declared, her face ashen but resolved.

"Gladys said you kept my hair," Beatrice said looking at Alice. "We are going to send it to John as proof that I'm dead, that he needs a new assassin. You need to look like a lady, so you can make him believe it. And we need you back at Pearl's, to help."

"I am sure I can convince Pearl and Chaz Cohen to do what's right," Alice said.

Beatrice turned to Yun Kee. "I need to look like a man again. Can you find me some clothes at the laundry? Oh, and we're going to need some of those mattresses from the factory I've passed on my way to Chinatown. I've just thought of a way to dispose of the bodies."

The other three looked at her dubiously.

Charlie chuckled. "The mattresses?"

"Yes, mattresses," Beatrice nodded. "There's a lot of blood when a throat gets slit. And I imagine it wouldn't be the first time Pearl had to order some mattresses to keep her brothel respectable. Or dispose of soiled ones. Do any of you have a better plan? I don't have much left to lose, and neither do any of you."

185

"It's true that it wouldn't be the first time I've had to deliver mattresses and furniture to Pearl's," Charlie agreed, but he looked worried.

The silence was broken only by an ember snapping in the fire. The group peered at each closely, their eyes searching each other for a crack in the resolve, a less ugly solution. Finally, Yun Kee shrugged.

"Sometimes in life doing the right thing seems harder than it should. I do not believe the death of a few wicked men is as immoral as the evil they will continue to inflict on the innocent if they are allowed to live."

"The line between good and evil became confused for me a very long time ago. If good prevailed my mother would still be alive and my sister would not be held by these bad men who threaten her with violent rape." Beatrice whispered. Charlie put his arm around her and nodded reluctantly.

"What about my ranch?" asked Alice? "It's all I really want. Tina and I were saving to go there, so she could have the baby, and leave this life behind."

"If the promissory notes are destroyed, the deeds stay with their original owners," said Yun Kee, "and the bets mean nothing but drunken talk. Besides ripped notes in the hands of whores and Celestials have never held much sway."

"Chaz Cohen has my deed, and I have the promissory notes that Tina was holding. She stole them from the game, and left them with me," said Alice.

"I have the deed to my father's land," said Yun Kee. "He thought he'd taken it to the Viscount's cheese farm to exchange for safety, but I hid it away."

"My father has the deed to our farm," Beatrice said. "Perhaps he'll trade it for my sister's life, once they believe I'm dead."

The River - receding

*In high summer and in the depth of winter I
allow myself to rest. My waters slow.*

*In winter the cold replenishes the glaciers at
my heart, and the snows fill every cornice and
crevasse and valley of the mountains that are my
backbone. The snow makes me hopeful.*

*In summer pollen dances along my ripples as
I dream of rejuvenation. The bees flying above
my waters are slowed by the weight of the pollen
they carry, the tree roots stretch long toes into
my shore, and I remind myself that it is about
enduring, about finding a way to flow.*

Aaron & Chester & several dead ends

A COUPLE OF DAYS later, the sun shone hotter than normal for early spring. It seemed the whole city was out, neighbour helping neighbour, mucking out, rebuilding, making do. Rubber boots were sold out across the city. Evacuation centres had opened but remained almost empty, as people's hearts over-flowed even more widely than the rivers themselves. Amid the tears there was a peculiar comfort in the festival-like atmosphere of the streets. The downtown core was still a ghost town, pump companies pulling every bit of equipment they could find off oil patch jobs so that streets and parkades could be cleared of water. It was rumoured the mayor hadn't slept in days. The flood, epic in proportion, had been a terrible blow to the city and its residents. And yet there was also a hopeful element to it – the affirmation that when push came to shove, people joined hands and pushed right back.

Aaron's bank was still closed, and he was relieved to not have to slip into his corporate skin for a few more days.

"Maybe I've completely lost it," Aaron said to Chester one morning, stretching luxuriously in her soft bed. "But I think part of me will miss this camaraderie. It's inspiring to think that in a city of more than a million people, we still remember our good ole prairie barn-raising manners."

"It's something, that's for sure," Chester replied, searching her messenger bag for fresh camera batteries before she started yet another gruelling day of flood recovery stories for the Herald.

"I have to check at the police station again today. They said they'd try to have an answer for me about the skeleton. After that I'm going to track down Valeria's friend Reggie. They moved the DropIn Centre up the hill to Edmonton Trail. Maybe he knows something. Maybe he knows the guy in the jean jacket."

"The title search I did on the deed didn't uncover much. The land is listed under the Estate of Alice Herron, and a numbered company. Whoever that is owns more than just land. They own the mineral rights too. Could be worth a fortune if this shale development takes off in the foothills."

Aaron looked up. "What do you mean they own the mineral rights? I thought the Crown owned the minerals rights."

Chester shook her head. "That's true except for the landowners who are the descendants of Alberta's original homesteaders. They are still the registered owners of the petroleum or natural gas found below the few inches of top soil that most people own. Their annual cheques are a lot fatter than most people's!"

"It could be worth a lot more than it seems. Maybe it's my own mother. After she blew most of her father's fortune, she was pretty fixated on money. My cousin Dara was no help. She's a Barsky so it's not her side of the crooked family tree anyway."

"I'm more interested in how my great-auntie's skeleton got under your front porch," said Chester. "I'm sure Kookum's stories are true. She said Tina's man promised her safety, in return for one last favour. Kookum's memory was fading, but she never forgot her oldest sister. But for the white man a story isn't true without proof. It's like the Franklin Expedition. The Indigenous people new exactly where the ships had sunk. The knowledge was passed down through stories, generation to generation. But did any scientists believe it? Those ships could have been found more than a hundred years ago, if anyone had cared to listen."

"So, you want that deed to be proof that the land belongs to your family?"

"No, I don't care about the land. I want justice for Tina. I want her to have a name, and a burial site where we can pay our respects. We Indigenous women are invisible, we don't matter. And I want to know what else your grandfather was trying to hide."

"You're so cynical," said Aaron. "What if it's not that sinister? What if he was trying to protect someone, maybe even Tina?"

"I'm cynical?" You're the one who's sure someone is trying to kill you, but you have yet to figure out a motive."

Bea & Pearl & Charlie & Chaz & Alice – a heavy load

A WEARY LITTLE GROUP sat in Pearl's parlour. The mantel clocked ticked deeply, loud in the silence. Candlelight glittered off the edges of the crystal glasses, generously filled with whiskey.

Beatrice looked at her new boots. In the circus she'd learned it was all about the costume. People believed anything in the right setting, with the right props, maybe even things about themselves. The sturdy boots and the knife made her feel powerful. Maybe she'd never go back to corsets and the fussiness of being a lady. Her mother had been right – she should have been born a boy.

Charlie's head was in his hands, his broad back bent like those lithographs of Atlas, carrying the weight of the world. Beatrice reached out to stroke his back softly.

Chaz's neat bowler hat sat next to the empty whiskey decanter. He stared at it as if it would speak to him.

Alice sat in an armchair, wrapped in a throw. Tears flowed silently down her cheeks and she shivered. Her skin crawled, her bones ached. The drug whispered to her, and she knew she had to keep herself collected and fight through the suffering. She owed to Tina, and to her father.

Pearl held a worn Bible. She put her spectacles on and straightened in her chair resolutely. "If you will all indulge me. I feel that after the evil in which we have participated today we should perhaps ask for forgiveness together. It was necessary evil, but evil, nonetheless. I can see these acts do not sit well with any of us."

I thank you for your loyalty to me, and my girls, and my establishment. I try to keep my girls safe here. Sometimes I fail. Sometimes they fail themselves."

"It wasn't your fault, Pearl," said Alice. "How were you to know that John was such a wicked man? It was a horrid thing to do – but they had done much worse. At least they were dreaming, lulled by the opium tea, when Beatrice slit their throats. Lure them to the party, appeal to their greed, let them fall to their own vices. You're brilliant Beatrice. Smuggling them out in the mattresses was a stroke of genius."

Charlie looked up. "I suspected John was evil. That's why I didn't think twice about helping him get swindled when he bought that useless mine. The boys and I used the salt cannon out there, and he thought he'd hit the mother lode. We used the money for the Coloured People's Protective Association. I wondered if he'd ever trace the ruse back to me. But I never thought it would lead to all of this."

"It's my fault," Alice whispered. "It's all my fault. But now I want to make it right. What do we do now?"

Beatrice spoke up. "Now it's easy. John's body is being shipped to his mine in a crate. By the time they notice it smells bad and get Charlie's huge lock open, any evidence will be ruined. You and I are going out to your ranch, just as soon as Ida arrives in Calgary. Father can keep his damn cheese farm, but he can't have her. We'll figure out how to make a living somehow. I've learned a thing or two about trick ponies and cows. I'm going to be Ben, from now on, not Bea. It's easier that way."

"I'm going to bury Tina on the new plot I bought off Eighth Avenue," Chaz murmured. "And build a house there so nothing can ever disturb her again. The Perelman's may have kept her from me in life, but at least I'll be close to her every day. I'll marry Sally, as they've ordered, and keep the peace. I will keep the deed to your land safe, Alice, and take care of you as best I can. I promise you that, if you promise me never to speak of Tina. The ranch is in your name, and it will stay in your name. Your debt to me is paid, no matter what the Perelman's do next."

Yun Kee & Lo Ying Tow & Hop Wo – at the laundry

YUN KEE CAME IN the back door of the laundry, a basket of packages on one arm. His mother and father were sipping tea from the tiny cups they both loved in the thin light of an early morning.

"So again, you are helping the white woman," Lo Ying Tow snarled, crossing her arms angrily against the silk of her favourite robe.

Yun Kee bowed slightly in acknowledgement. "Yes, yes, I am. As Father would do. As anyone would do in a case like this. Miss Alice is fighting the dragon of opium. And these herbs will ease that journey."

"Yun Kee kept our family safe, in the moments when I was weak, and risked all we'd built up in this country," said Hop Wo. "He is doing no wrong. We must learn to trust each again. We are family. If we do not remember how precious this is, then all this suffering has been for nothing."

"Father is right." said Yun Kee. "We must also always remember our debt to Mister Cohen, for he is an ally we must foster."

Aaron & a man in jean jacket & a developer

"NOT YOU AGAIN," GRUMBLED Aaron. "I'm not signing anything. Can't you see I'm busy trying to put my house back in order?"

He had taken a load of ruined belongings from the basement out to the communal dumpster now parked in the alley, and found Rodney the developer, standing in a shiny pair of Hunter gumboots, staring at his house. Beside him was a thin, nervous man in a dirty jean jacket.

"Hey!" yelled Aaron, too surprised to be polite. "You're the guy! You're the jean jacket dude. Reggie told me about you. What did you want from Valeria?"

The man turned white and froze. Seconds later he bolted in the direction of City Hall's massive silvery wall. He didn't get far before he tripped on some debris left from the flood, skidded in the silt, and landed ass over teakettle, in one grungy heap, having knocked the wind out of himself.

Rodney and Aaron both rushed over, and dragged him upright by the arms, and yanked him in opposite directions.

"You killed her?" Rodney yelled, punching the man wildly. "Chase – you complete idiot. I didn't tell you to kill her. I told you to find out what she knew."

"It was an accident. I didn't mean to," Chase whined. "I didn't know how to tell you. She seemed to know a lot. She was so fierce about protecting his stupid crate of books. The crate killed her, not me. I brought you the goddamn crate of books. Nothing but a bunch of mouldy old journals and letters. What a pointless thing to die over."

Aaron wrestled to hold on to the squirming, dirty man and get his phone out of his pocket at the same time. "You bastard. Don't bloody move. I'm calling 911."

The River - flowing

And so I flow, full of secrets and castoffs. Full of the voices of the grandmothers. Will you dam me? Or will you cherish me; let me flow through you, full of seeds and dreams?

Chapter Ten

by Telmo dos Santos

The Cat

Aaron Cohen was not the type of person who would declaw his dear friend, Tommy Douglas. In fact, Aaron was suspicious of any cat owner who claimed to love their pet but would do such a cruel thing.

Some people did not understand Aaron's strong feelings for Tommy. During the flood, one Saturday morning, when TD and Aaron had been temporarily staying at his cousin Dara's place, she had abruptly ceased her vacuuming.

Looking over, he saw she was intently gazing at a shredded spot on the carpet ahead of her. Aaron's heart sank. He was in the midst of placing a segment of orange in his mouth. He managed to hastily gulp it down, just as his cousin turned her disgusted look from the carpet to him.

After almost choking on the orange, it was all Aaron could do to sheepishly blurt: "Tommy Douglas is really stressed out," while raising his hands pleadingly.

Now, home, a few months later, Tommy Douglas had quickly readapted to his familiar environment. Tommy remained very much the same cat. His large fluffy paws concealed his intact claws. He had a soft grey coat.

Tommy's behaviour, however, was unusual in some respects. There were idiosyncrasies. Even before the flood Tommy always avoided the porch.

After the flood, Tommy Douglas started acting strangely in a different way. Once every few days, while Aaron slept, the temperature in the house would suddenly drop a few degrees. No doubt this was because the furnace had been affected by the flood.

On these occasions too, as if by some odd coincidence, the slow drip from the bathroom faucet would quicken. This was likely because the plumbing had also been affected by the flood.

It would also happen that if a light had been left on in the house, it would flicker unevenly during these moments. It was odd that the thermostat, plumbing and electric grid could all be affected at the same time; however, it was an old creaky house, one damaged by a powerful flood.

What was stranger was the way Tommy Douglas would react. The grey hairs on his back would slowly begin to rise and he would arch his back. His ears would point backwards. His eyes narrowed. He would bare his fangs and hiss. Then he would become increasingly agitated and pace back and forth before suddenly darting off.

On these odd nights, nights after Valeria's body had been found face down in the water at the bottom of the basement stairs, Tommy Douglas would quickly and silently run to Aaron's room, a grey streak, and jump onto the queen bed where his master slept.

Once settled in a compact ball, Tommy would stretch his paws out in front. From the toes of his paws, with eyes narrowed, Tommy Douglas' sharp claws would continuously and rhythmically extend and contract. He would stay that way, silent, crouched, facing the doorway, until dawn.

The Rat

DETECTIVE STANSKY STARED AT the video monitor a few more seconds. It showed a small bare room, only large enough to fit a small table and two chairs. The camera angle was from above, facing one of the two chairs. A man sat on that chair opposite the overhead camera. He was wearing a dirty jean jacket with a dark T-shirt underneath. The man sat perfectly still, stooped over the table.

Eventually Stansky quietly spoke: "The victim's mother, Patricia Claxton, is sure it's murder. The alleged motive is a dispute over a land deal that dates back to her grandfather's shady dealings in 1912."

Constable Kim Radar remained silent for a few seconds. She knew her partner was expecting more than a careless analysis and deliberated before speaking.

Radar was wearing the standard issue dark blue Calgary Police Service uniform. She looked good, despite her diminutive size, sharp and crisp. Although it was past two in the morning there wasn't a black shiny hair out of place in her tightly pulled bun. Her service cap was immaculate and neatly placed on the nearby table.

Her partner, Detective Stansky wasn't in uniform. His slacks and blue shirt didn't look too shabby, but they weren't exactly of the latest fashion either. It was hard to guess his age. He had a kind of timeless, if worn, look to him. His eyes, a little watery, were a reassuring pale blue. Standing next to Constable Radar, he could have been a decade or two older. His calm demeanor subtly conveyed experience and authority.

After a few moments Radar spoke: "ID checks out: Daroza, Chase. Thirty-two-year-old male, single, unemployed. Rents a small basement apartment out in the northeast, close to

Marlborough Mall. No criminal record hits on PIMS or CIS...
He hasn't said anything since his arrest except that he wants
to talk to a lawyer. We gave him his phone call. The lawyer
he called was Sam Bernstein. Not exactly a lawyer who takes
Legal Aid files, if you know what I mean. So, what we have
is a suspect who is unemployed yet has money to hire an
expensive lawyer."

Radar waited for Stansky to speak, but he remained silent.
They both stared at the video monitor and the top of Daroza's
head onscreen. Kim eventually started thinking out loud, "It
doesn't really make sense. At best we have a second-degree
murder case, because we don't have any evidence of the planning or deliberation, we need for first degree, but even that's
a stretch because we need a specific intent to kill for second
degree murder. Do we have specific intent to kill? According
to the witnesses he blurted out that he didn't mean to kill
anyone. He basically said it was an accident."

"So, while that puts him on the scene," she continued, "and
he's the last person to see her alive, if he assaults her and she
dies accidentally then maybe we have a reasonable likeli-
hood of conviction on a manslaughter charge. Maybe. But
the problem is we have no evidence of any assault preceding
the blunt force trauma that caused her death. There is some
statement about fighting over a crate of books, but nothing
is reported stolen. Dead bodies can't talk, and it's doubtful
the medical examiner is going to be able to turn up anything
further given the state her body was in when it was found
in the water. So at best we have a manslaughter, at worst we
have a pure accident. Seems kinda shaky to charge him, I
think. Could charge him with second degree and hope to
get manslaughter."

Stansky nodded. "You're right, we got fuck all. All we
have is a half-assed confession that makes it sound like it

might have been an actual accident. ID is not an issue; he was there when she died. The question is, did he kill her? We have no evidence of that. The deceased may have simply fallen, or, our boy with the spiky hair may have been trying to prevent her from committing a robbery. At least that's what Sam Goldstein is going to tell the jury. He's going to tear this case apart. The other thing is this, gel boy over here has no criminal record and, take him out of that ratty jean jacket and he looks presentable. His real estate developer buddy, what's his name, Rodney, he's probably footing his legal bill and will serve as a character witness. They'll blame the victim."

Stansky continued: "I checked her out. Her criminal record is three pages long. Mostly small stuff, theft under here, drug possession there, no violence. One solicitation charge, withdrawn. One obstruction of justice, a couple of breaches of probation and a couple of failures to appear. Nothing in the last seven or eight years. Looks like she might have cleaned up. But what was she doing trespassing in that house anyway? Turns out she's related to the owner but he hadn't given her permission to go in the house or to take any crate of books. I can see already how all of this is going to play out at trial. They're going to say Daroza followed her in, suspected she was breaking in, right? It's a flood, looting happens. He's got a reason to be at the scene, he's working for that real estate guy who wants to know how the house has weathered the flood. So our girl Valeria sees him and maybe panics and has a bad fall. Or maybe he's trying to prevent her from stealing stuff. That's not an assault, he's being a good Samaritan. The bottom line is we don't have a motive for any murder or even a manslaughter."

Kim looked up to meet her partner's gaze. "What do we do now?"

"I'm going to tell our boy with the gel and the expensive lawyer that I know everything about his boss and the shady real estate dealings and tell him he might as well confess to everything."

Kim looked confused, "But we checked that out, there's no evidence ..."

Stansky cut her off. "Well, maybe Daroza knows something we don't. Maybe he'll sell out his buddy to save his own skin."

"One thing I know," he said, "is nobody likes a rat."

The Pig

"CHASE DAROZA?" STANSKY ASKED as he walked into the small room.

"Yeah, that's me," Daroza said, looking Stansky squarely in the eye. "Who the hell are you?"

The suspect was either too smart or had been too well briefed by his lawyer to want to give any incriminating statement. Stansky knew right away that bluffing was not going to work. These days the police relied on fear. A very small and uncomfortable interview room took the place of the "bad cop". Fear of the unknown. It was enough to make the most inexperienced accused want to talk. Want to try to help themselves.

Stansky didn't bother to sit down. He met the suspect's gaze evenly.

"Look, I'm not here to waste your time or mine. You don't want to give a statement, that's fine. But we have two witnesses who say you put yourself at the scene and that you said you didn't mean to kill her. So you got problems, kid."

"How about screw you."

"How about you rot in jail until your trial? We have grounds to lay a second-degree murder charge and if a judge or jury goes down the middle you may end up with manslaughter. How does five to ten years in prison sound to you? You have a good lawyer so maybe you'll get sentenced to six and with remission serve three. Not bad for killing someone, pretty good deal, right? Three years is still plenty of time in jail though. Lots of stuff can happen in three years, right?"

Daroza gazed up at the camera behind Stansky, slightly uncomfortable, "My lawyer told me not to say anything and that's what I'm going to do. I just want my bail hearing. Okay?"

"Bail hearing? You think you're getting bail? I don't know what your lawyer told you, but this is a murder investigation. Protection and safety of the public is the paramount consideration. You really think a judge is going to put his ass on the line and release you on the street after you allegedly drowned some poor woman?"

"Look, I didn't drown anybody, that's not what happened."

"Why don't you tell me what happened then, because you know a human being, a woman, was found dead, face down in the water. We know it wasn't the guy who owned the house, and you admitted you were there. You admitted to taking stuff. How do you think it's going to play out in front of a judge or jury when they learn you had your chance to give your side of the story but you deliberately chose not to say anything? How do you think that's going to make you look?"

Daroza was still for a few moments then looked up again, meeting Stansky's gaze "I didn't kill her, it was an accident. Do whatever you want, say whatever you want. We're done."

Stansky closed the door to the observation room. Kim was waiting for him, having watched the entirety of the interview by CCTV. "He didn't break."

Stansky poured himself a coffee. "He didn't break, but he knows something. He wasn't in the East Village during the flood acting like the good Samaritan, I'm pretty sure about that. He's been prepped for questioning, knew this was coming. That's a bit strange if it was all a complete accident".

"Should we consent to his release, and then see if we can get a wiretap?"

Stansky took a slow sip of his lukewarm coffee.

"No. We have to oppose the release; no one ever consents to release on a murder charge. If you consent to release you might tip off Goldstein that we're going for a wire. Too easy, he'll think. Make sure you oppose release as usual. Take the full 24 hours to allow the Crown to prep the bail hearing. If they need more time they can ask for another 48 hours, it's in the code."

"Might as well give our man a taste of jail. Kim, I want you to try to get that wiretap warrant personally. Make sure the paperwork is filled out correctly. No guesses, no exaggerations, no fabrications. If we get it, we get it. If we get the warrant and there are holes in the application, any evidence we collect might get tossed out at trial. Then the whole thing is a point-less exercise. Dot it right. Whether we get the wire or not, I want surveillance on this guy when he gets out, if he gets out."

"You think he did it?"

"I'm not sure, but he's hiding something."

Stansky sat alone at his round kitchen table. The house was silent. A simple conical lamp hung overhead, casting a pale circular luminescence on the table, and dark shadows all

202

around it. Stansky's face was partway in the shadows and partway in the light. On the table was an open bottle of Smirnoff vodka, a shot glass, and Stansky's handgun, on its side, pointing away.

Daroza hadn't said anything, either in the interview or to the undercover in the cell afterwards, as he waited for the bail hearing. There were no leads on surveillance either, despite Constable Radar constantly tailing the suspect.

Stansky had attended the bail hearing in court two days later. His heart sank when he saw who the Crown had assigned to the file. He could only guess why the powers that be had assigned a murder file to such a junior prosecutor. Probably had to do with the victim. The case had obviously been classified low priority. Stansky felt sickened by it.

He tried talking to the prosecutor before the bail hearing.

"Sally, hi, I'm Detective Stansky, I'm the lead investigator on this file."

"Good to meet you Consta-"

"Detective. Look, I don't want to step on your toes. I know you guys know what you're doing here, I just know Sam Goldstein is the defence on this and he's going to try to argue it's a weak Crown case.

"Sam is defence counsel?"

Stansky saw Sally Armstrong was annoyed that he knew more about the file than she did. She didn't look too interested in hearing what he had to say. She had the air of a school-teacher who already knows the right answer and is impatiently indulging a mixed-up child.

"Look the strength of the Crown case is relevant to all three grounds for detention." Stansky continued, doggedly. "Sam Goldstein is going to argue it's a weak Crown case, he's probably also going to argue the deceased Valeria was a prostitute and a criminal and was up to no good."

Armstrong snapped back: "Well, I don't see a lot of evidence for second degree murder. How do you know this Daroza guy intended to kill her? This thing about the crate of books, the owner of the house doesn't say anything about it in his statement. I saw her record, she's a bit of a rounder, how do we know she didn't just accidentally get hurt when she was caught in the middle of a break and enter?"

"Ya, she has a criminal record, but it's dated. The other thing is if you read the Cohen statement, they were friends, he trusted her and doesn't think she would steal from him. Hell, he didn't even think he had anything worth stealing! Goldstein is going to play the game of blaming the victim, you have to make the judge realize this picture he's going to paint of the deceased is not the real story."

Armstrong was been visibly annoyed now, with arms crossed in front of her chest.

"What do you want me to do exactly? This guy has no criminal record and I can't see any motive for murder. We have three character references that were faxed to our office, they all check out. The evidence for murder or even manslaughter is weak. Frankly, I'd be surprised if this guy gets convicted of anything."

"Look, this isn't just another prostitute." Stansky felt he wasn't getting through. "You can try to remind the judge about how marginalized women are treated by the system, about the missing and murdered aboriginal women. There is an epidemic, over a thousand have been killed. Make the judge understand it's not just one isolated woman but that this is part of something larger. Something needs to be done, focus on the tertiary ground, that detention is necessary to maintain the public confidence in the administration of justice. With all these women dying, getting killed, if their accused killers, are constantly released, it creates the wrong impression that women's lives don't matter. It creates a risk."

Armstrong now gave off the vibe that she was actually bored by the turn of the conversation. Stansky realized she wasn't going to do anything he was suggesting during the hearing. He gave her an even look. "Good luck in the there."

When Sam Bernstein and the judge finally had come in, the bail hearing had looked like a formality. Stansky had stayed in the courtroom during the bail hearing, and had stayed sitting after the judge, defence lawyer and accused had all left the courtroom. Sally Armstrong had walked off like she didn't even care.

Now, at the kitchen table, Stansky grabbed the half full bottle with his right hand. He filled the glass, took the shot, filled it again and took another. When he righted the bottle the liquid inside undulated beneath the one third mark.

The warrant for the wiretap had been denied. There had been no clear confession from the accused. Bail had been a forgone conclusion and granted without much of a fight from the Crown Prosecutor. The trail of possible leads on this case was fast disappearing.

Stansky had even gone to the forensic examiner's office to look at Valeria's body firsthand. His last resort. When the attending clerk had slid the tray out of the metal refrigeration unit, he had been surprised that Valeria's remains were in a body bag.

"The body is already in an advanced stage of decomposition," the clerk had explained apologetically. "Because, you know, it was found in floodwater."

As Stansky slowly opened the zipper, he heard the squishing sounds the liquefying body made as it moved with the opening body bag. The face was unrecognizable, more skeleton than flesh.

The smell of the remains hit him hard but Stansky didn't flinch. The skull was turned slightly to one side. He could see a large dark hole in the back of skull where they had removed her brain. He knew this was standard autopsy procedure when a corpse is discovered under suspicious circumstances. Stansky had intently stared inside the dark recess for a few moments, trying to get answers. Valeria, he had thought, what happened? He felt a heavy sadness wash over his heart.

Now Stansky couldn't taste the vodka. The house beyond the kitchen table was completely silent. He couldn't feel the alcohol. He could only hear his own even breath.

He kept thinking of the darkness inside the hole in Valeria's skull. The darkest darkness that said nothing. It drew him in. Perhaps he had stared for too long. The light from the lamp over the table dimmed, and the darkness around the table seemed to close around him.

Stansky reached his hand forward again, but this time he did not touch the bottle.

In pitch black and eerie silence, the unmistakable click of the Glock safety switch reverberated.

The Eagle

AARON WOKE WITH A start. Something felt wrong. The faint smell of putrid floodwater. The house was cold. There was a sound. Gradually he realized he could hear water running in the nearby bathroom. Had he left the water on? Aaron forced himself to get up. When he got to his feet he had to steady himself for a few seconds.

Aaron felt along the walls of the dark house. It was only a few feet from the bedroom to the bathroom, but his head felt foggy. When Aaron got to the bathroom he heard the steady flow of water coming from the sink faucet. He felt for the light switch and flicked it. Nothing. He flicked it again. Still nothing. What the hell, the power is out and my water is running, Aaron thought.

The water was running steadily in the sink and had almost overfilled it. Aaron tried to turn the tap off.

The tap was already in the off position and only budged a few millimeters. I'll have to get that fixed, Aaron thought. He fumbled with the tap until the flow slowed to a drizzle. As he stared at the malfunctioning faucet, suddenly he realized he had not seen Tommy Douglas.

Where was the cat?

Aaron groped his way to the kitchen and picked up the cat food box, shaking it. Usually that was enough to make Tommy show his face. Aaron waited for a second, looking around the dim living room. He strained his ears. He couldn't hear Tommy at all. It was unusual for TD to be out of sight for very long. The house wasn't very big.

Aaron was going from room to room now, with a flashlight he had retrieved from the kitchen, trying to find Tommy.

Tommy wasn't in any of the rooms. Aaron even tried looking behind and under the living room couch. He then stopped and thought that maybe he should go back to the bedrooms to see if somehow Tommy had become trapped in one of the closets. But Tommy would be meowing like crazy if he was locked in a closet.

Unless. ...

Aaron shuddered and quickly rushed to check the bedroom closets. He checked the main bedroom first. He held his breath as he opened the accordion style doors and shone the flashlight inside every lower corner. He felt relieved not to see Tommy there, just the usual shoes and boxes. He rushed to the second bedroom closet.

Tommy wasn't there either.

Aaron went back to the living room, stopping by the bedroom first to put on a sweatshirt over his pajamas. The house felt unusually cold. The gas furnace hadn't been right since the flood even though he had had it checked.

Aaron eyed the door that led to the basement. Tommy couldn't be down there. He'd installed a latch and padlock on that door that he always kept locked and closed. In the beam of the flashlight he could see the latch and lock were on the door.

The truth was he hated going down to the basement since the flood. Since he had found Valeria's body there, at the bottom of the stairs. And the deed, the one he had found beneath the floorboards, he kept it in the basement too. He didn't know what to do with it. Aaron knew he would have to go down to the basement eventually, not just to check on Tommy. The breaker switch was also down there, as was the furnace.

"Tommy?" Aaron called one more time, hoping the sudden emergence of his beloved friend would give him an excuse not to descend into the damp bowels of the house. Tommy did not appear. Aaron stood up and walked to the bedroom door to retrieve his keys. He found the keys on the dresser, where he always left them. He walked back to the kitchen and faced the basement door as he sorted through his various keys. When he grabbed the padlock to insert the key, he realized the padlock was unlocked.

The u-shaped shackle of the padlock was not depressed and swung freely on one arm, away from the locking mechanism. Aaron slowly removed the lock from the latch and brought it closer to his face, shining the flashlight ray on it. There were a few small beads of moisture on the padlock.

That's just the sweat from my hands, Aaron told himself. He felt deeply uneasy. The house was freezing cold, and he knew his hands were not sweating.

Aaron had a flashback of Valeria's floating body, facedown at the bottom of the basement stairs. Floating. Dead in the water. He couldn't help wondering if the person who had murdered his friend, his cousin, had come back to hurt him. Aaron knew the suspect had been released on bail, a certain Constable Radar had given him a call to warn him. Told him to call her if anything suspicious happened. Anything suspicious like this I guess, Aaron thought. He considered using his cellphone but rejected the idea. I'm being silly, he thought. Aaron finally managed to push his fear aside, he reached for the door handle.

As Aaron prepared to turn the handle he heard a heavy knocking from the other side.

Aaron froze. He could hear his heart thumping heavily in his chest. Suddenly he was indeed starting to sweat, the cold sweat of spine-chilling fear.

Aaron still had his hand on the handle when he heard the heavy knocking again. This time he realized that it was not coming from behind the basement door, but rather the knocking appeared to be coming from his front door. I'm losing it, he thought.

Aaron closed the latch and placed the padlock on it, making sure to click it shut, even pulling on it to make sure it was locked. Aaron heard the knocking again. "Coming!" he yelled. He felt relieved to have company and rushed over to the small foyer.

When Aaron opened the main door to his home, he found himself looking at an unfamiliar face.

"Hey there friend. I think your bell is busted." There was a First Nations man standing on his new porch, which was little more than the top of some stairs. It had been replaced since the flood had torn it away. The man was dressed in black and wore his hair in a single braid. His eyes were clear and friendly.

"The bell is not busted; my power is out. Can I help you?"

The man seemed to be in a cheerful spirit. "Your power is out you say. So you don't think your bell is busted. I see, I see. Well, it's possible your bell is busted AND your power is out, but that would be an odd coincidence. Too odd a coincidence." He stood very straight. He was smiling now.

Aaron had no idea who he was speaking to and was just about to ask him if he could help him for the second time, when the man became very serious.

"I don't think so," he said.

"What?"

"You asked if you could help me. I don't think you can help me. I came here to help you."

Norman Eaglespeaker, from Whitehorse, sat on the chair across from the love seat. Aaron had lit a candle on the coffee table to give off some extra light, though there was now pale sunlight coming through the window. Norman had a tall glass of water and he took a small sip from it now and again, placing it carefully back in front of him.

"Nice place you got here. Cozy."

"Thanks, it was my grandfather's. I grew up here with my mom. Doesn't seem to be in very good shape now though. We were hit pretty hard by the flood. The power is off and the taps don't work. I can't even find my cat."

Norman looked straight ahead for a few seconds.

"You say you can't find your cat?" he asked.

"Why have you seen him?" Aaron asked excitedly. "I think maybe he's still here somewhere".

Norman continued to look straight ahead for a few seconds. He looked deep in thought, as if he was listening to something.

"No, I'm sorry I have not seen your cat." He sat upright in the chair, refusing to lean back. His arms rested formally on the armrests.

The house was still. With the power off, not even the intermittent hum of the refrigerator interrupted the silence. Only the dribble of water from the faucet in the bathroom, which was not too far away, could faintly be heard.

After a few more awkward minutes Norman Eaglespeaker broke the silence.

"You know, the animals ... The animals are not like us. The animals are sacred. We are sacred too, but the animals are different from us. The animals are made perfect by the Creator, so they can't make mistakes. They are pure, innocent. But we can make mistakes. We make lots of mistakes. We are not so pure, not so innocent. Some accident are not accidents."

"Some ... accidents ... are not ... accidents?"

Norman smiled. "The animals are sacred."

"So what does that mean about my cat?"

Norman did not speak but looked serious again. Then he swiftly got up from the chair.

"I must be leaving now. Thank you for the water. Thank you for inviting me in. Thank you for speaking with me."

"Wait, you came from far away. You said you could help me. How can you help me?"

Norman slowly turned back and looked at Aaron, facing him squarely once again.

"It is true, I came to deliver a message, if you are ready to receive it. I did not know what the message was, but now I know what the message is."

Aaron was having an increasingly strange morning, but at this stage he thought things had reached their maximum possible strangeness.

"What do you mean message, who is the message from?" He was exasperated.

"It is from a friend. My Elder and the Elder of your friend have spoken to each other. These things did not happen in our world, they happened in what we call the spirit world. My Elder spoke to me, and now I am speaking to you. We cannot understand these things, yet they are true."

Aaron looked at Norman, mouth open, head slightly tilted, not sure what to think or say.

"Valeria".

The word hit him squarely, like a push to the chest. Suddenly it sounded to Aaron like a high-pitched ringing was rising in his ears. His vision clouded. He could only faintly see the man in front of him.

Norman Eaglespeaker's voice came through strong and clear; deep.

"Your spirit animal has departed. You must leave this place."

Aaron Cohen passed out.

The Madam

PEARL MILLER ROCKED SLOWLY back and forth on her wooden rocking chair. She had some knitting on her lap, but the needles and yarn were down beside her folded hands. It was late in the night, and although the night was her domain, sometimes even she needed a rest.

The kerosene lamp beside her flickered nervously behind a thin glass shield. The room was drafty, as most rooms in the brothel were. Now, in the cold of night, beside the flickering lamp, she had time to reflect.

Pearl had gone along with the plan even though dead bodies were, generally speaking, bad for business. It wasn't the first time a mattress or two had discretely been carried out. In a brothel it was to be expected that every once in a while, a mattress would need to be replaced.

She didn't feel too bad about John Spencer. He had been trying to extort her for a long time. He wasn't the first to try to bully her and Pearl Miller had enough wisdom to know he wouldn't be the last. That's what had set Pearl Miller alert. She knew men, she understood them. She knew their greed, their selfishness, their cowardliness, their pettiness, their sexual desires. Their perversions. Now John had paid for his abuses in cold blood. Pearl wasn't happy about what had happened on her premises, but she was a practical woman, and she knew John was a bad man who would not be missed.

The plan had not gone smoothly. The idea had been to lure John and his associates, and when they were dazed from opium to finish their wicked lives. The men had come, as planned, but they were suspicious, cautious. They had carried in their guns. They had found Alice and Beatrice behind a curtain, knives shaking in their hands. The girls' bravado had suddenly evaporated in the face of a six shooter. Charlie and Chaz had stared glumly, caught. Only Yun Kee had kept his composure.

"This is a misunderstanding perhaps?"

The plan was poorly and too hastily thought out. Now the room was like a powder keg waiting to ignite. Guns were drawn everywhere, there was shouting and yelling. Pearl, nearest to the door, and trusting her intuition, had fled. She had paused in the hallway, expecting gunshots. When none rang out, she had cautiously peered into the room through a crack in the doorway.

In the middle of the room Charlie held a dripping knife in his hand. Four bodies of grown men were slumped around the room in awkward positions only the dead can occupy.

Pistols dangled on the ends of their dead fingers uselessly or lay on the floor beside them. There was crimson shiny blood everywhere. It was all over Charlie's white cotton smock and suspenders, on his face and arms. Charlie had his head down and was breathing heavily. Blood and sweat dripped from his curly brow. His thick muscled arms bulged with adrenalin. Alice and Beatrice cowered in the corner as did Chaz. Yun Kee still sat calmly, palms on his knees, back straight. A long thin crimson splatter of blood was sprayed across his face.

"Yes, a misunderstanding perhaps," he said without moving his head.

John Spencer held both hands to his throat as blood seeped out in time with his fading heartbeat. Finally, his eyes rolled back, and he released his hands.

Now Pearl rocked in her wooden chair alone, as the flame flickered. The girls had left together. Beatrice and Alice had gone to the ranch. They had promised to do anything in repayment for Pearl's help and secrecy. She had taken up their offer. A bargain was struck that she could send some of her girls there, when they were too sick or tired or old for the kind of work that was done on her premises, or perhaps if they were heavy with child. Pearl liked the idea of being able to provide an escape, an escape she herself she had never been afforded.

There was a light thumping at the window. She looked over and was surprised to see the faint outline of a cat face staring back from being the glass. The green eyes were captivating. Pearl Miller could hardly believe a cat was there, oddly perched on the window ledge.

She opened the window.

"Why hello there big fellow."

Pearl gently reached for the cat. The cat meowed quietly and shivered. Pearle was surprised when she touched the cat to feel it was soaking wet beneath her elegant hands.

It was not raining.

The Blacksmith

CHARLIE REMOVED HIS SUSPENDERS and let his loose pants fall to the floor around his powerful legs. He removed the bloodstained cotton smock. He stood for a few minutes enjoying the air against his naked dark body. There was a fire burning in the hearth, but he was a dozen feet removed from it. He could feel the coolness of the air.

Charlie clenched his hands into fists and flexed his powerful forearms. They were thick and marked with muscles that he had earned at the heavy price of countless hours of work. Heat, hammer, cool. Heat, hammer, cool. Repeat until the iron was ready. This was the art and science of blacksmithing. Just as he had fashioned countless pieces of metalwork, so too had the metalwork fashioned him.

Flecking his arms were scars where numerous sparks had burned and etched their permanent mark. The heavy leather gauntlets he sometimes wore did not keep every burning flash out. After all these years he barely noticed when there was a new burn to add to the collage. The smell of his own burning flesh was familiar, almost comforting. But his arms were still powerful, as the events from earlier in the day at Pearl Miller's had so clearly revealed.

It's strange what hitting metal with a hammer repeatedly can do to a man, Charlie thought. On the one hand, it takes a lot of physical energy, and is exhausting. Charlie knew there was also another aspect of blacksmithing too though, a hidden aspect. If you could get past the physical exhaustion

215

and keep going, after a while the body would become almost like a machine, almost automatic, and the physical exhaustion would become unnoticeable.

Then a different kind of energy would start to enter, rather than leave his body. It was not a physical energy, but something mental or spiritual. It felt like a coil being tightened. A kind of angry energy. That energy would accumulate slowly with each hammer stroke. Minutes, hours, days, weeks, months, years would go by. The energy would accumulate and be stored in his body. Eventually that energy would have to escape.

That was how Charlie understood what had happened. He had not acted consciously. He had seen the first gun come out, he had heard some shouting. Then he had acted automatically. Everything had happened instantly. Suddenly Charlie found himself in the center of the room in the brothel, with the knife dripping blood clenched in his hand, bodies and blood everywhere. He had not thought to stab anyone, yet he knew he had killed them all.

He didn't feel it was his fault. He was like a coiled spring. A coiled spring waiting to be released.

Charlie was sore all over. He walked back towards the tin tub of water he had warmed. He closed a thin curtain behind him. He squatted down awkwardly in the small tin tub. Finally, he sat with his knees, chest and arms exposed above water. Still, the hot water felt good against his tight muscles and he allowed himself to relax in the heated water.

Charlie's thoughts turned to Beatrice. She had offered for him to join them at the ranch, but he had refused. He had instinctively understood Alice would not welcome the idea of a man like him around. Besides, it was not something he wanted. Even a woman as exotic as Beatrice only held a certain aesthetic appeal for him. He had wished them both well, told them he would visit, and they knew where to find him also, should they need him.

Pearl Miller had also offered to repay him for his help, not just for the killings but for the cleaning up and body disposal afterwards. Her currency was the kind of services she was in the business of providing. "Any girl you want," she said. "Hell, take two!" But he had simply shaken his head. Pearl had looked at him quizzically, but she had not pressed the matter.

Charlie saw the movement of a slim silhouette reflected on the curtain.

"The girls are on the train?" Charlie asked.

"Yes."

"And the deed?"

"I gave it to Mr. Cohen."

"Not your father?"

"Father has many businesses. Besides, the deed is not lucky. Gambling is not lucky. I will find other ways to help father. A misunderstanding, perhaps."

"Chaz Cohen is a fool."

"Mr. Cohen is not a bad businessman. He has a good heart. He has made some mistakes."

There was a prolonged silence. The fire crackled in the hearth. The shadow became larger on the curtain.

Charlie saw the fingers of a slender hand reach around the side of the cloth, preparing to draw it sideways.

Charlie stood up in the small tin tub, letting water drip downwards from every part of his strong black body.

"I've been waiting for you."

The River

THE RIVER NEVER SLEEPS. Or perhaps the river is always sleeping, dreaming, carrying our thoughts and spirits downriver, downriver towards the ocean, towards their demise, like a prolonged, undulating, and fatal somnolence.

If you ask the experts what caused the flood, they would have you believe the rivers were sleeping, and then awakened suddenly, like a sleeping dragon. Or perhaps, more aptly, like a sleeping serpent.

There was a large amount of rainfall, up to 200 millimeters in some places. Add in the ground that was already saturated preceding the deluge. Combine that with areas that were still frozen not far below the surface, and a local geography that encourages water to run downhill quickly, and there's a recipe for devastation.

There was a dead body hidden beneath a porch. The dead body of a pregnant Aboriginal woman. It had been there too long. It was crying out for justice. It was crying out for recognition. The baby was also crying out. They were crying out together in a song.

The deluges were the result of some unexpected weather. Along with the torrents of rain, there were unpredicted wind patterns and the convergence of two huge weather systems.

Aaron awakes to find Chester in his home. She came over in the evening when she could not reach him on his cell. Aaron thinks he has dreamt up Norman Eaglespeaker. He is still confused and ignores the partially filled glass of water and candle on the coffee table.

Chester and Aaron go post missing cat pictures together. At the same time, unseen by anyone, Tommy Douglas stealthily approaches the river edge. It is fast-moving, swollen with grey floodwater. Tommy arches so his front is lower than his back. Then he does something no one would expect any cat to do. Tommy Douglas silently jumps, completely splayed, into the freezing Elbow River.

He immediately disappears.

The massive weather system responsible for the storms was trapped over southern Alberta by a high-pressure system to the north and winds blowing toward the west, the opposite direction of prevailing winds throughout Canada.

The steady water flow from Aaron's broken faucet quickens, spilling onto the bathroom floor. Eventually water flows past the threshold of the living room, where the cord from the electric space heater is stretched. Another flood, of a sort. The heater cord reaches into the electrical socket, which previously appeared to be without current.

The river hears the song.

Valeria's bones, inside the body bag, begin to jerk and slosh within the liquefied remains of what was her body. This happens inside the refrigeration unit at the Calgary forensic laboratory. No one notices. Constable Kim, naked in bed, sends a text message to Detective Stansky. She receives no reply.

The snow packs were kind of average. The snowmelt had been a little late in the mountains, but nothing spectacular. Then came the deluge. It rained on the tops of the mountains, and that caused a rapid snowmelt. In some places another 110 millimeters of snowmelt contributed to the rainfall water.

Aaron and Chester return to the yellow house to see it being devoured by flames. The bright yellow and orange colours contrast sharply with the opaque night sky. The fire emanates heat, light, and a crackling roar. It is mesmerizing.

Aaron briefly considers running into his house, to save everything, or perhaps to destroy himself, but he remembers

TD is no longer there. "Your spirit animal has departed," he faintly hears.

Chester gasps, "The deed! My Kookum!" She runs into the burning house before Aaron can stop her.

Aaron wants to follow her, but something holds him back. He powerlessly watches Chester enter the fire.

Aaron falls to his knees.

A cat hisses.

The river never sleeps.

Across the East Village sky a lonely shot rings out.

Chapter Eleven

Epilogue – Historical Notes by Harry Sanders

In 2015, Noir on Eighth was conceived and composed in tandem with the re-conception and re-composition of the district itself. The writers' imagined version of historical East Village was the perfect setting for a crime drama; new East Village provides a retrospective viewpoint.

East Village

Though it was so named no earlier than 1969, Calgary's Downtown East Village is as old as the city itself. As part of Section 15, Township 24, Range 1 west of the 5th Meridian, it became property of the Canadian Pacific Railway (CPR), which subdivided it as the Townsite of Calgary in 1884. For most of its history, the district was regarded as "skid row," a term applied by none other than the city's medical officer of health in 1941. It was the meeting point of immigrant families, marginalized communities, down-and-outers, and criminal elements. Its few-dozen blocks included family homes, butcher shops, corner stores, hide and fur vendors, hotels, and mechanics' garages. Light industry offered local employment.

But the district also contained bootleggers and brothels, and it was wedged between familiar, though forbidding, boundaries: the Bow River to the north; the CPR tracks, maintenance yards, and roundhouse to the south; the business district to the west; and, to the east, Fort Calgary (the mounted police barracks until 1914) and the Grand Trunk Pacific Railway yards (the GTP, a precursor to Canadian National Railways, or CNR thereafter). After decades of neglect, the district became the focus of city regeneration and gentrification early in the 21st century.

Prologue *by Deborah Willis and Kris Demeanor*

Aaron Cohen

In the very first sentence of the text, we meet Aaron Cohen, whom we learn to be a resident of his grandfather's old house in East Village. Chaz Cohen, Aaron's grandfather, would hardly have been alone in the district in 1912, the period when much of *Noir on Eighth* is set. Jews were well represented among the area's diverse population, and local businesses included H. Hoffman's Fish Market & Grocery and two butcher shops owned by the Friedman brothers (one kosher, one not). In 1912, the Calgary Hebrew School was located on or next to the present site of the Calgary Drop-In Centre, and the House of Jacob Synagogue stood on the future site of Bow Valley College. There was even an Aaron Cohen, who in 1912 lived at 428—7th Avenue East, right about where the CTrain tracks now turn north from 7th Avenue toward the northeast LRT

222

line. The real Aaron owned a cigar shop a few blocks west on the present site of Arts Commons, where *Noir* contributors participated in Word Fest in October 2015. It might have been on the very site of the Electric Theatre (corner of 8th Avenue and 2nd Street East) that Beatrice de Seychelle—Bea—reads about in the *Calgary Daily Herald* in Chapter One.

Simmons Building

In that same first sentence, Aaron is distracted and nearly crashes his bicycle into the Simmons Mattress Factory. This building was constructed in 1912 as the Alaska Western Bedding Company factory, which Aritha van Herk references in Chapter Five. (In keeping with the noir theme, in real life, the factory's manager, Edwin Bromley, went missing in the spring of 1928, and his body was found two weeks later on the roof of the building.)

Aaron refers to the sound of construction. The present, in *Noir on Eighth*, is when the East Village is being gentrified and is a construction zone.

Ice jams and flooding on the Bow River

The source of Aaron's distraction is the Bow River, which is jammed with ice and has overflown its banks. This occurrence has repeated itself through time, and each episode has written itself as part of the history of East Village and of Calgary itself. Aaron mentions the historic floods of 1897, 1915, and 1932.

Langevin Bridge (renamed Reconciliation Bridge)

The text refers to the Langevin Bridge, a steel structure built in 1910 to replace the original wooden Langevin Bridge that had been built in 1888. Around the time *Noir* was conceived, the name of this bridge became controversial. It had been named for Sir Hector-Louis Langevin, the public works minister in Sir John A. Macdonald's government in the 1880s and the first federal cabinet minister to visit Calgary. At the request of Calgary citizens, Langevin's department built this bridge, and it was named for him in gratitude. The new bridge retained the old name when it was completed a generation later. But a century on, the release of the Truth and Reconciliation report in the spring of 2015 quoted Langevin's long-ago speech in the House of Commons in which he expressed the government's residential schools program for First Nations children in positive terms. Speaking for the government, Langevin— who had previously been Indian Affairs Minister—outlined the need to separate children from their parents in order to impose non-Native culture on Native children. Through broadcast, print, and social media, many Calgarians voiced a desire to rename the Langevin Bridge.

This issue arose at the same time that many Canadians were calling out for a national inquiry into missing and murdered indigenous women. These ongoing disappearances and murders (hundreds in number over the years), and the perceived absence of a serious effort to solve them, is a recurring motif in *Noir* (as it was in reality during the time it was written). As *Noir* was being composed, this matter became a federal election issue, with the Conservative government resisting the call for a national inquiry and the opposition New Democrats and Liberals promising one. Justin Trudeau's Liberals defeated Stephen Harper's Conservatives in the October 19, 2015 election that occurred during the fortnight between the release of Chapter Nine and Chapter Ten of *Noir on Eighth*.

Aaron's House and Grandfather

Aaron lives in a bungalow built in 1914 by his grandfather, who was a tanner. The house is as fictional as the Cohens, but it could easily have been East Village's sole remaining house at 521—8th Avenue SE, which still stands immediately west of Loft 112, the real-life writers' centre where contributors met through 2015 to develop and celebrate *Noir*. In 1912, it was the home of stock inspector Peter D. Sanders. Aaron has refused a developer's offer to buy his property, and his is the last remaining house in the district. His story recalls that of Wilmot Baldwin, who resisted urban renewal efforts in 1970 and, for as long as he could, refused to leave his house at 320—5th Avenue SE, which was targeted for demolition to make way for the new Young Women's Christian Association that was built just west of East Village.

In 1914, the year of *Noir on Eighth,* Chaz Cohen builds his yellow bungalow, the real-life Cecil Morris Cohen was vice-president of the Calgary Tannery Co. Ltd., which was located on Elbow Avenue in East Calgary. Cecil Cohen lived at Pirmez Creek, west of Calgary, where he was one of the owners of the Belgian Horse Ranch. Also in 1914, the Alberta Rope & Tanning Company was located at 415—6th Avenue East in the East Village.

Aaron's Historic Walks

Aaron is an active member of the Historical Society of Alberta, and he researches and conducts historical tours through the streets of Calgary. The society really exists, and it was established by the Historical Society of Alberta Act in 1907, just two years after the creation of the province. Aaron is researching East Village; besides the Simmons Building and his own house, he plans to include the following in his tour: the Cecil Hotel (built in 1911, closed in 2009 and scheduled for demolition at the time *Noir* was written); the King Edward Hotel (built in 1906, expanded in 1907, closed in 2004, dismantled in 2013, and reconstructed as a façade—using the original bricks, *in situ*—as part of the National Music Centre complex at the time *Noir* was being written); and the St. Louis Hotel (opened in 1914, closed in 2006, and undergoing restoration at the time *Noir* was written).

Tommy Douglas

Aaron lives with his cat, whom he has named for the late Saskatchewan politician Tommy Douglas (1904-1986). Long before Aaron's birth in 1982, Douglas spoke in Calgary—in 1952, during his term as premier of Saskatchewan, and in 1961, when he addressed the Men's and Women's Canadian Clubs at the Palliser Hotel as the newly-minted leader of the federal New Democratic Party. Aaron is certainly familiar with Douglas' reputation as the founder of Medicare (and the grandfather of actor Kiefer Sutherland).

Central Library

When he returns to his house the day after the flood, Aaron wonders if Valeria has gone to the Central library. This is the Wm. R. Castell Central Library at 616 Macleod Trail SE, which opened in 1963 a short distance west of East Village and was expanded a decade later.

The Bones Under Aaron's Porch

The flood has washed away Aaron's porch; with it gone, he uncovers shards of bone that play a large role in *Noir*. This is based on a real occurrence. In 1910, William J. Gourley built Gourley's Garage at 617—7th Avenue East. This business had become Steele's Garage by the 1930s. It had become Lee's Garage by the early 1970s when contractor Ernie Bengert was hired to build a front porch. Bengert excavated in front of the garage—until he uncovered the feet of a human skeleton that lay buried. He called the police, who examined the site and then told him just to cover it up. Bengert built the porch over the skeleton, and there it remained until the garage was demolished some years later. In 2004, with East Village redevelopment in the news, Bengert told his story to the *Herald*, which published an article about it on March 29, 2004. Research determined that there had been no official burial on the site.

Chapter One *by Deborah Willis and Kris Demeanor*

Public Market

Beatrice hustles down 1st Street past the public market. Not long after this part of the story is set, three markets opened in this general area: the Calgary Public Market in 1914, the New Calgary Market in 1916, and the City Hall Market in 1920. Half of the merchants at the New Calgary Market were Chinese (even Hop Wo had a confectionery there in 1925-27), and the text mentions that Bea would likely have found the mixture she needed in a Chinese shop.

The Calgary Public Market opened kitty-corner from the

Cecil Hotel in 1914, and the portion of this building that survived a 1954 fire still remains extant as Booker's Crab Shack. (A re-creation of the building is represented at Calgary's Heritage Park Historical Village as Gasoline Alley.) The City Hall Market opened on 2nd Street East (now Macleod Trail SE) in 1920 and remained in operation until 1952; Olympic Plaza was developed on its site in 1987. The New Calgary Market opened in in 1916 in two adjacent buildings further west along 7th Avenue: the Delemere Block (125-127) and the former Calgary Stock Exchange (129). Both remain extant in 2015.

Cecil Café

Beatrice enters the Cecil Café, which stands next to the hotel, and there she accepts a meal from Frankie. In Beatrice's time, the restaurant was in the hotel; the Cecil Café that many Calgarians remember was built years later.

Calgary Daily Herald

At the Cecil Café, Bea glances at a copy of the *Calgary Daily Herald*. That was the title of the *Calgary Herald* in Bea's time. At that time, all of the major newspapers in the Southam chain styled themselves in that manner, including the *Toronto Daily Star*, which informed the original name of Clark Kent's employer in the Superman comics—the *Daily Star*. (Original artist Joe Shuster was originally from Toronto.) The fictional newspaper was later renamed the *Daily Planet*.

Bea sees the story "Socialist Organizer Speaks" and the advertisement for Walk-Over Shoes; both appeared in the January 24, 1910 edition of the *Herald*. The Socialist organizer, William Gribble of Toronto, had spoken the previous night at the Princess Theatre (310a—8th Avenue East), which stood on the future site of the Calgary Municipal Building. (Again, in keeping with the noir theme, William Gribble was also the name of a Philadelphia murderer in the 1990s.) Glass Bros., where Bea wishes to go to buy Walk-Over Shoes, was in the Clarence Block, a sandstone building that remains extant in 2015 at 120—8th Avenue SW.

Bea also reads an article about the suspicious-sounding accident that injured John Ricks in his home at 618—4th Street East. That article dated from October 18, 1909; Ricks died of his injuries and is buried in Union Cemetery.

Costello Block (502—8th Avenue East)

Frankie refers Bea to a hardware store in the Costello Block, which stood about five blocks south of the Cecil. William Alphonse Costello built this business block in 1908, and in 1912 it housed the Dominion Weights and Measures Office (occupied by Chief Inspector John W. Costello, presumably William's father) and the Provincial Coroner's office (occupied by coroner Dr. Thomas J. Costello, William's brother). Dr. Michael C. Costello, one of William's brothers, later served as Calgary's First World War-era mayor. Michael was also a physician and coroner, and he attended Calgary's last execution in 1914, only a year before he became mayor. (The procedure was botched.) The Costello Block of 1912 also housed a drugstore (McCutcheon and McGill), and a liquor dealer, Patrick J. McManus. Upstairs, about half-a-dozen tenants lived in furnished rooms. During Prohibition (1916-24), McManus became a partner in the nearby King Edward Hotel, and a series of liquor violations landed him in court and nearly cost the hotel its business license. McManus left Calgary to farm in the Morrin district, and he eventually retired to Edmonton but is buried in Calgary. The Costello Block was demolished sometime after 1961.

Charlie Tucker

When Bea leaves the Costello Block, a thief grabs her billfold with "Dickensian speed," and Bea trips in an attempt to catch him. Charlie Tucker, a blacksmith, subdues the thief and recovers Bea's billfold, and he invites her into his nearby blacksmith shop to wash up after her fall. Probably none of the characters (nor the chapter's authors) are aware that the action takes place just blocks from the 8ᵗʰ Avenue East watch repair shop of Charles Dickens, a distant relative and namesake of the British author who created Oliver Twist.

Charlie is Black, his workplace (and presumably his home) are located near the homes of the majority of Black people in Calgary at the time. Many Black men worked as porters for the railway companies, and they lived with their families in East Village. Unfortunate racist attitudes meant that Black people were barred from certain restaurants and hotels (including the King Edward until the late 1940s), and in a 1940 riot, white men attacked a Black musician and vandalized establishments owned by Blacks.

There were several blacksmiths shops like Charlie Tucker's in the vicinity of the Costello Block, including one on 8ᵗʰ Avenue East, just east of the Queen's Hotel (on the future site of the Calgary Municipal Complex). It was built for William J. Gourley, whose nearby garage was also the scene of the mysterious human burial that inspired the story of the skeleton under Aaron's porch.

Laundry (corner of 9th Avenue and 3rd Street East)

Bea picks up a package at a laundry business on the corner
of 9th Avenue and 3rd Street East. There were many such laundries in the East Village in Bea's time, but there wasn't one
on that corner. In reality, Bea would have found Ho Lem's
rooming house and a Christian mission (on the northwest
corner, where the Calgary Municipal Building now stands)
or Sykes & Bramley, blacksmiths (on the northeast corner,
where construction of the new Calgary Public Library was
still pending at the time *Noir* was conceived and written).
However, two blocks east (just past Pearl Miller's house), near
the northwest corner of 9th Avenue and 5th Street East, Bea
would have seen Chong Lee's laundry.

St. Louis Hotel (430—8th Avenue East)

Next, Bea walks the equivalent of about a block to the St.
Louis Hotel, where she enters the tavern to find someone who
can tell her how to get to Pearl Miller's house. The St. Louis
opened on April 7, 1914, and it remained in business until
2006, when the city acquired it in preparation for East Village
redevelopment. The text notes the adjacent barbershop, which
long-time Calgarians remember as the European Barber Shop.
The building (434-8th Avenue East) was constructed in 1910,
and it originally housed the Saville Dry Goods store. It was
stuccoed in 1943, and it housed the European Barber Shop
by 1962.

Pearl Miller's house (526—9th Avenue East)

Bea now walks another block or so to the small house where
Pearl Miller (ca. 1882-1957) operates a brothel. The real Pearl

Miller was evidently an American woman who had settled in Rossland, B.C. and married a man named Rose before leaving him and moving to Calgary, where she started working as a prostitute. She arrived before 1914, when there is a record of her arrest. Historically, Pearl initially worked on 6th Avenue East, and the small East Village bungalow that later became Calgary's most famous brothel was still the home of CPR car inspector George Ash (1886-1976). The house was built around 1902. Pearl established her 9th Avenue brothel by 1926, and she later relocated it to the city's tony Mount Royal district (reportedly with assistance from the son of a prominent lawyer, as referenced in Chapter Seven). But Pearl continued to own or live in the 9th Avenue house at least until the 1940s. She spent three months in prison in the early 1940s, and apparently there she found religion. Thereafter, Pearl tried to talk prostitutes into reforming themselves. She died in 1957, and her 9th Avenue house was demolished sometime after 1971.

Chapter Two *by Natalie Meisner*

Near the beginning of the chapter, Bea examines "a city still not as old as she was". Her age is never revealed, but in 1912, 18 years had passed since Calgary's incorporation as a city, 28 years since its incorporation as a town, and 37 years since the North-West Mounted Police had established Fort Calgary.

We learn that Bea's father is a French nobleman. It would not have been unusual for a titled European to settle on the prairies, even in Calgary. One example includes Alexander von Mielecki, a Polish-German nobleman who planned to develop an eponymous Calgary subdivision. Another, somewhat related example is Colonel Armand Trochu (1857-1930), who led a group of fellow cavalry officers in establishing the ranching settlement that became Trochu, Alberta. Trochu's uncle was the Paris governor who defended the city during the Franco-Prussian War.

The hotel where Bea has registered is unidentified, and we later learn that it is near the Hudson's Bay Company store. In 1912, the Bay store was located at Centre Street and 8th Avenue West; the present HBC store, which opened a block to the west in 1913, was still under construction. Bea could have been staying in any one of a dozen hotels. The Alberta Hotel, which remains extant kitty-corner from the present Bay store as the Alberta Hotel Building, was still in operation; it closed in 1916 when Prohibition began. (It was in George Lane's room in the Alberta Hotel that Guy Weadick, whom Bea meets on the train in Chapter Five, pitched his Frontier Week idea to three wealthy ranchers—Lane, Patrick Burns, and A.E. Cross—in 1912. The three wealthy ranchers promised financial backing for what became the Calgary Stampede, and they guaranteed the support of a fourth man, A.J. McLean, who was also the provincial treasurer, thereby rounding out the group that has been immortalized as the Big Four.)

Bea might have been staying at the Queen's or Imperial hotels that stood a couple of blocks east of the Bay store of 1912. But it would be a satisfying coincidence if Bea had checked in at the Empress, which stood just a few blocks away at 219—6th Avenue West. Years later, the Empress' elevator operator, Armand La Brosse, lived in Pearl Miller's old 9th Avenue house after she moved out. The Empress began in 1911 as a temperance hotel on 6th Avenue West; eventually, it became the favourite drinking hole of Calgary Herald reporters who worked in the nearby Herald Building. Had the Herald not moved to a sprawling new plant in 1980, nor the Empress demolished later that decade, it might have become the hangout of *Noir*'s fictional Herald reporter, Phoebe Chester.

Mrs. McGonagall's rooming house, where Bea aspires to live, is fictional, as is McGonagall herself. (So too was her contemporary, Peter J. McGonigle, along with the imaginary *Midnapore Gazette* that he supposedly edited. McGonigle and the *Gazette* were foils created by their real-life counterparts, Bob Edwards and his satirical newspaper, the *Calgary Eye Opener*.) But there were many rooming houses in 1912 Calgary, including one on the same block as Pearl Miller's house (Edgar L. Albertson's establishment at 514—9th Avenue East), one a block west (John Smith's Victoria Rooming House, 430—9th Avenue East), and two side-by-side rooming houses a block east (Nellie Knowler's at 626—9th Avenue East, and the Homestead Rooming House at 632). The Van Dyke rooming house operated nearby at 501—4th Street East.

Flesher Marble & Tile Company

To avoid a suspected follower, Bea presses herself against the Flesher Marble & Tile company. In 1912, it was located in the Bruner Block in the Beltline district, at the northeast corner of 13th Avenue and 1st Street West (now the location of a Starbucks). The Bruner Block was converted into the Noble Hotel in 1919. Half a century later, the New Noble Hotel opened around the corner on 12th Avenue, and the old Noble was demolished. Eventually, the New Noble was revamped and renamed as the Hotel Arts.

Chapter Three *by Ian Williams*

James Joyce Pub

In a passage set in the present day, the text refers to the James Joyce Pub. The building that houses this Irish-style pub was completed in 1912 as the Molson's Bank Building. Historically, Molson's Brewery and Molson's Banks were founded by a father and son. John Molson, the brewery founder, was also a banker; his son, also named John Molson, founded the bank but was also a brewer. The James Joyce Pub serves only Irish beer, with the consequence that one cannot buy a Molson's beer in the Molson Bank Building.

Oil Industry

In 1912, we learn that oil lies underneath Alice's property, and this is what motivates the people who have sent Bea to kill Alice and steal her title deed. The Turner Valley oil boom lies two years in the future, but Alberta's oil industry is already over a decade old at this point.

Chapter Four *by Jani Krulc*

In 1912, Bea dons a man's clothes, asks Alice to cut her long hair, and sets out in a man's guise to find work. Calgary had just such a case eight years after Bea tries this. In September 1920, Helen A. Howard ran away from her home in Missoula, Montana, and refashioned herself in Calgary as Harold Pete Leighton. She worked briefly as a messenger for the Northern Electric Co. Ltd. (which is later renamed Northern Telecom, and, ultimately, Nortel). But after only two days, her masquerade was uncovered, and police presumably sent her back to Montana.

In the present, Valeria declines a spot on the bus evacuating East Village residents, coyly citing the need "to make sure them zoo animals don't get out". This is an evident reference to the Calgary floods of 2013, when a hippopotamus escaped from the nearby, flood-damaged Calgary Zoo.

Chapter Five *by Aritha van Herk*

Bea walks past the Alaska Western Bedding Company, a new mattress factory that, back in the prologue and over a century later, Aaron nearly crashes into with his bicycle.

Later, en route to buy boots at Glass Bros., the text notes that Bea crosses Centre Street. Historically, this was the dividing line in Calgary between the respectable part of town (west of Centre Street) and the rest of the city centre to the east, where people who did not have cause to go would not.

The new railway to Prince George that Bea imagines herself taking is the Grand Trunk Pacific Railway, which historically reached Calgary in 1914 and established its railyard and station on the former Fort Calgary site adjacent to East Village. Less than a decade later, the GTP was amalgamated into the government-owned CNR.

In a flashback to Bea's train journey to Calgary, she meets Guy Weadick, the American showman behind the original Calgary Stampede in 1912. He gives her the handkerchief that she already had in an earlier chapter, when we learned that it is monogrammed with the initials 'GW'. Weadick refers to his wife Flores, who is Flores LaDue, a trick rider and Guy's partner in his career, which reaches its zenith with the Calgary Stampede. Weadick describes the irresistible smell of Calgary, which comprises creosote, horse piss, and money. As *Noir* was being written, creosote—the aromatic wood preserving agent that had been used to treat railway ties and sidewalk boards—returned to the news in Calgary. In August 2015, the owners of the Calgary Flames and Calgary Stampeders proposed redeveloping the city's unattractive West Village (so named in counterbalance to the East Village) as CalgaryNEXT, a sports and entertainment complex. The project would require a multimillion-dollar cleanup of the former Domtar creosote plant site, where the cancer-causing substance remained in abundance underground.

Chapter Six *by Cheryl Foggo and Clem Martini*

As a background to Chapter Six, Cheryl Foggo provided the following historical notes:

Almost all of Calgary's Black citizens lived in the East Village at that time for a variety of reasons, including proximity to the train station where some were employed, safety in numbers, discrimination in housing in other neighbourhoods and cheaper rents. The size of the community is hard to pin to an exact figure, but in October of 1910, 150 Black people attended a ball thrown by the Coloured People's Protective Association (CPPA) in Calgary, held at Eagle Hall in the Beltline. There were so many Black people in East Village that sometimes the newspapers referred to it as "darktown". The CPPA was formed in response to discrimination. The organization did a lot of things, as mentioned in our chapter, as well as arranging social functions like the "Colored Ball" as it was headlined in the *Calgary Daily Herald*. Harry and Bertha Palmer, the hosts of the party in our chapter, moved around a lot, always in the East Village, providing rooming-house lodgings and a

hang-out spot for Black porters. In 1912 they were living at
611—1st Avenue East. The Palmer's places were often raided by
police who most often tried to get them on charges of selling
liquor or running a house of ill repute. Sometimes they were
acquitted, and at least once that I know of they were sentenced
to six months' hard labour. The CPPA helped them out of a few
jams. Life was a real conundrum. Most of the hotels would not
accept Blacks, but the porters had to have somewhere to stay
overnight. However, the white neighbours and police hated
these Black boarding houses. The powers that be and the police
also really hated the CPPA. They considered it a "Secret Society"
that smacked of communism and they seemed to resent Black
folks helping other Black folks out, even though they were bla-
tantly excluded from employment opportunities and housing.
All the Black people named in our piece (except Charlie, who
was Kris and Debbie's brilliant invention! Charlie absolutely
could have existed) were real people living in Calgary circa
1912, and some were board members of the CPPA. Spencer
and Jesse Lewis were John Ware's wife Mildred's siblings and
really did play frequently at parties. I've seen Spence's violin
and case! Bobby Ware is John and Mildred Ware's oldest son,
who was living with his grandparents and a multitude of siblings and cousins at that time, as his parents had both died in
1905. The Lewis's did not live in East Village in 1912. Daniel
Lewis (their father) was an incredibly skilled carpenter, who
had built a huge house on the site where Westbrook Mall is
now. William Herbert Darby was the first cook at the Vulcan
hotel as mentioned in the story, but for at least part of the
year of 1912 he and his family were living with the Lewis's in
the big house. His wife Mary was another daughter of theirs.

Although relations were not always positive between the
Black and Chinese communities, most often they were. Here's
a quote from an article I wrote years ago:

Black men who arrived in Calgary from the east as porters on the railroads, often denied service in the hotels and restaurants, soon enough began to figure out where they *could* go. They were welcomed by the Chinese proprietors of a few café s in particular in the 20s and 30s - the Crystal Café and the Canadian Café, and the white owner of another - the Palace Café. The early Calgary pioneers loved to reminisce about Hop Wo, who owned one of the cafés, and who fed many a hungry porter with recipes he adapted to their tastes. "We called him our brother," said Dick Bellamy.

Another historical name that appears in this chapter is Clinton Ford. This is Clinton J. Ford (1882-1964), a Calgary lawyer who became city solicitor in 1913 and ultimately became Chief Justice of Alberta. He was the grandfather of well-known journalist Catherine Ford.

Teatro (200—8ᵗʰ Avenue SE)

In the present, Aaron and Phoebe Chester have drinks at Teatro. This upscale restaurant opened in 1994 in the former Dominion Bank Building, a Beaux-Arts style building that opened just blocks west of the East Village in 1912. Bea probably walked right past it on her way to buy boots at Glass Bros. (The text also mentions the Hub Employment Agency and adjacent Grand Central Hotel, both of which stood on 9ᵗʰ Avenue East on the present site of the Marriott Hotel/ Glenbow Museum/convention centre complex.)

Claxton family

This chapter establishes Valeria's family name as Claxton, a name that resonates in Calgary's history. In 1885, F. Claxton (his first name is unknown) established a skating rink—Claxton's

Rink—on the southeast corner of McTavish Street (later Centre Street) and 6ᵗʰ Avenue. William Roper Hull (1856-1925), who made his fortune in the ranching and meat businesses, built the Calgary Opera House (also known as Hull's Opera House) on the site of Claxton's Rink in 1893.

Chapter Seven *by Lisa Murphy-Lamb*

Peace Bridge

The chapter opens with Aaron crossing the Peace Bridge, which traverses the Bow River west of downtown, across the business district from East Village. This pedestrian and bicycle bridge opened in 2012 to considerable controversy, including criticism of its location and the presumed extravagance of its design by Spanish architect Santiago Calatrava. But the bridge had many enthusiastic supporters, and by the time *Noir* was written, it had become a popular symbol of the city.

Orange Lofts (535—8ᵗʰ Avenue SE)

Completed in 2003, this condominium complex was part of the redevelopment of East Village that was still in progress when *Noir on Eighth* was written. It houses both Loft 112 (the writers' centre on which the *Noir* project centred) and Hear My Soul, the café where Aaron meets with Phoebe Chester in Chapter Seven. The complex occupies the former site of three homes on 8ᵗʰ Avenue East: 523 (occupied by Mrs. Jean Bagnell in 1912), 531 (Charles E. Isleib), and 537 (Gertrude Landry, the widow of Daniel Landry).

St. Patrick's Island

On her way from the party to her hotel room, Bea walks along St. Patrick's Island. Just two years before this part of the story was set, St. Patrick's—along with St. Andrew's and St. George's islands—had been outside the city limits and property of the Dominion government in Ottawa. Construction of the St. George's Island Bridge in 1908 had met Ottawa's condition for transfer of the islands, which were transferred to the city in 1910 for parks development. The auto club that the text references was developed in 1921 and remained in existence at least until the 1960s.

Hotel Alexandra (226—9th Avenue East)

Bea is now staying at her second hotel, and this time it's the Hotel Alexandra, which opened in 1911 as a high-class establishment where Conservative politician (and future prime minister) R.B. Bennett kept a table until the Palliser Hotel opened in 1914. Owner Albert Dick and his wife Vera travelled first-class on the *Titanic* and were among the doomed ship's survivors. The Alexandra's grandeur had long since faded when it was demolished in 1980 to make way for the Calgary Centre for Performing Arts. Just months before *Noir* was conceived, the performing arts centre was renamed Arts Commons.

"Negro Dive Raided"

In her hotel room, Bea reads the *Calgary Daily Herald*'s account of the previous night's police raid that she escaped. The story appeared in the May 11, 1912 edition, placing the historical event on Friday night, May 10. *Noir* moves the event from its real-life location at 620—6ᵗʰ Avenue East (Gladys Dorrington's establishment) to the home of Harry and Bertha Palmer at 611—1ˢᵗ Avenue East and establishes the Palmers—who, as noted above, were historical personalities (as was their East Village home on 1ˢᵗ Avenue East).

Bannermans and Perelmans

The chapter establishes that Chaz Cohen had married Sally Perelman, whose family lived in Calgary, and that he later had an illegitimate daughter—Aaron's mother, Felicity—with a younger woman named Mary Bannister. These are fictional characters, but both family names resonate in Calgary's history, albeit with an alternative spelling in one case. The historical Mary Bannister (1902-1951) was the daughter of Billy Bannister (1866-1934), who until 1902 managed the Bow Valley Ranch (on the present Fish Creek Provincial Park) for its owner, William Roper Hull.

This is the same William Roper Hull who, in 1893, built his eponymous opera house on the former site of Claxton's Rink. Billy Bannister later worked as a cattle buyer for P. Burns and Company. That company's founder, Patrick Burns, was one of the Big Four ranchers who backed Guy Weadick's original Calgary Stampede in 1912. (Each of the Big Four promised to pay up to $25,000 if the Stampede racked up debts—which it did not.) Abraham and Benjamin Pearlman, Jewish brothers from Winnipeg, moved to Calgary in 1924 and purchased Polar Aerated Water Works, a factory adjacent to Chinatown where they produced 7-Up and Orange Crush under franchise.

Golden Age Club (610—8th Avenue SE)

Valeria's funeral takes place in the Golden Age Club, a senior citizens' organization that was founded in 1951 and moved into this East Village address in 1984. Around the time *Noir* was conceived, the club was threatened with closure due to financial difficulties, which Dymphny Dronyk mentions in Chapter Nine. In 1912, the future club quarters were more or less occupied by the homes of George Lore (604—8th Avenue East), Ernest Frazee (612), Edward Farren (614), Lulu Harrison (616), and Daniel W. Rathvon (618).

Blackfoot Truck Stop

Aaron dines with Patricia Claxton at the Blackfoot Truck Stop, a real-life diner beloved by truckers and Calgarians at large. Edna Taylor (ca. 1933-2011) opened this roadside establishment in 1956 in the Inglewood district, one of Calgary's oldest neighbourhoods and a nearby neighbour to East Village.

Chapter Eight *by Dale Lee Kwong*

Tina Whiskeyjack, Plains Cree

Tina Whiskeyjack is introduced as a Plains Cree woman who finds employment at Pearl Miller's brothel, becomes pregnant by Chaz Cohen, and is murdered by thugs. In 1912, only 36 years had passed since the signing of Treaty 6, the instrument of surrender for Tina's people's land. Calgary lies within the territory of Treaty 7, which was signed in 1877 and involved the Tsuu t'ina, Siksika, Kainai, Pikani, and Stoney Nations.

The Chinese rooming house where Chaz establishes Tina

is destroyed by arson. By including an archival photograph in the chapter, Dale Lee Kwong associates this fire with the one that took place in Chinatown in October 1912.

Hop Wo, Yo Ling Tow, and Kun Yee

Hop Wo is an historical figure from Calgary's history, immortalized through Herald photographer William J. Oliver's image of his laundry business being moved in the 1920s. From about 1910-25, he operated a laundry business at 302—7th Avenue West; the building was later moved to an unknown location. He might also be the Hop Wo who, in the mid-1920s, operated a confectionery store in the New Calgary Market (which still stands at 125-129—7th Avenue SW between the laundry and East Village). Cheryl Foggo notes that Hop Wo fed many of the black porters at a café he owned.

Hop Wo's story in Noir is fiction; similarly, his wife, Yo Ling Tow, and their son, Kun Yee, are fictional characters. Yo Ling Tow would have been one of the few Chinese women in Calgary. Because of the head tax imposed on Chinese immigrants—established in 1885 and raised to an exorbitant $500 in 1903—very few men were able to bring their wives or children from China. Louie Kheong, one of Chinatown's founders, brought his wife to Calgary in 1905, and their first child was also the first Chinese-Canadian born in the city.

Dale Lee Kwong named her character Yo Ling Tow for her own paternal grandmother who raised 15 children (nine of them her own) before spending her final years in a bungalow on 17th Avenue just west of 14th Street SW. Her name is inscribed (as "Low Ying To") on a park bench in Chinatown's Sien Lok Park.

Chinatown

Calgary's present Chinatown was two years old in 1912, and the text outlines its development and that of its two predecessors. The first, in the 1880s, was at the corner of McTavish Street and Atlantic Avenue (changed to Centre Street and 9th Avenue in 1904, when Calgary changed from street names to street numbers), within sight of the CPR station. The second was in the Beltline district south of downtown, right around 10th Avenue and 1st Street West. When the Canadian Northern Railway (a forerunner to the CNR) obtained a right-of-way along 1st Street, the real estate market forced out Chinatown. (In *Noir*, it is Chaz Cohen and his business associates who push out the second Chinatown.)

Louie Kheong led a group of Chinese businessmen who established a new Chinatown on Centre Street, one where Calgary's Chinese community owned its own property and could escape the uncertainty of tenancy. A group of citizens petitioned the city to deny the building permit, but the effort was unsuccessful, and Calgary's third (and permanent) Chinatown became a reality. The later petition to remove Chinatown, dated May 26, 1914 and referenced in the text, was similarly unsuccessful. It took decades for the attitudes of non-Chinese residents of Calgary to regard the district as a cultural asset rather than a source of fear (based on newspaper headlines about police raids on opium and gambling dens) and the object of racist scorn.

Kheong and his partners built the Canton Block, which still stands at 202-210 Centre Street SE as Chinatown's sole remaining original building. In 1911, Dr. Sun Yat-Sen, a revolutionary against China's imperial government, spoke at a fundraiser in the Canton Block; the event is referenced in the text. Within a year of his Calgary speech, Sun was president of the Chinese republic.

Chapter Nine *by Dymphny Dronyk*

Hudson Bay

The voice of the river says that it flows "all the way to the Hudson Bay." This natural phenomenon had an important consequence in Canadian history. In 1670, the Crown issued the Hudson's Bay Company's charter, granting it exclusive trade privileges in all the lands whose waters drained into Hudson Bay. Since the Bow River ultimately drains into Hudson Bay, southern Alberta was included in Rupert's Land, as the Hudson's Bay Company's territory was called.

In 1869, the company surrendered its charter to the Crown, and the British government arranged for the transfer of the territory to Canada. Circumstances of the transfer triggered the Red River Rebellion in 1869. The NWMP was dispatched west in 1874, and a series of treaties in the 1870s extinguished indigenous rights to the land and established land reserves where the nomadic peoples were now made to settle. With the introduction of the Dominion Lands Act (which established the homestead farm system), the construction of the CPR, and measures that allowed for large-scale ranching leases, conditions were complete for the superimposition of a non-Native population and an agriculture-and resource-based economy in western Canada.

The homestead system was intended to facilitate agricultural development. It allowed applicants to gain title to a quarter-section of land (and, subsequently an additional quarter section called a "pre-emption") for a nominal $10 fee and the performance of certain tasks—" proving up," it was called—including the cultivation of a certain number of acres, construction of a dwelling and other buildings, and fulfilling a residency requirement. And, crucial for *Noir*, it

gave mineral rights as well as surface rights—until the regula-
tions were changed and mineral rights were reserved for the
Crown. Only the early homesteaders gained mineral rights,
and these include Alice's family in *Noir on Eighth*. To this day,
mineral rights are retained by a few families in Alberta who
have managed to maintain original land title.

The Jewish Community

This chapter establishes that Chaz Cohen had "felt chafed" at
the casual discrimination that Jews encountered in his time,
and such discrimination certainly did occur. Calgary's permanent Jewish community began in 1889, and it has always
remained a tiny minority, peaking in the 1920s and again
in the 1940s at two per cent of the city's population. After
the Second World War, the community took in Holocaust
survivors, war orphans among them. This is the context in
which Felicity Cohen's arrival is explained in 1947. Felicity is
Chaz' illegitimate daughter and Aaron's mother; Chaz' family
adopts her and proffers the explanation that she is the child
of a relative "who had fled Europe in the war" and later died.

Drinking at the Alberta Hotel

In a discussion with Bea, Charlie Tucker, and Yun Kee, Alice
talks about the men who spend long afternoons drinking at
the Alberta Hotel. Historically, a clique of important men
in Calgary used to gather at the Alberta Hotel to drink, and
this is verified by the diary of Calgary's 1890s mayor, Wesley
Fletcher Orr, which is preserved at the Glenbow Archives.

Aftermath of the flood

The text describes the aftermath of the flood, with both tears and a festival-like atmosphere of neighbourly assistance. All of this is equally descriptive of Calgary in the wake of the 2013 floods.

Chapter Ten *by Telmo dos Santos*

In the present, Tommy Douglas the cat disappears from Aaron's house; he re-appears in 1912 in Pearl Miller's house. Aaron's yellow bungalow is not necessarily intended to represent the real-life house at 521—8th Avenue SE (next door to Loft 112), even though both are the sole remaining historic homes in their respective East Villages. Nonetheless, the location of 521, which was built around 1904 and where Peter D. Sanders lived in 1912, presents an interesting coincidence. It stands directly across the lane from the site of Pearl Miller's brothel. If the Sanders house was indeed the Cohen house, then Tommy Douglas' travel through time would cover only a short distance through space—the width of a back alley.

In this 1911 fire insurance map, Pearl Miller's house is represented near the upper left at 526—9th Avenue East. Peter D. Sanders' house stands directly opposite the lane, at 521—8th Avenue East to the right. The map also shows the future site of the Orange Lofts (535—8th Avenue SE), which includes Loft 112 and Hear My Soul Café; two Chinese laundries stands east of Pearl Miller's house and south of the future Orange Lofts at 911—5th Street East and 538—9th Avenue East (bottom left).

BIOGRAPHIES

SAJE DAMEN is a freelance graphic designer, illustrator, and animator who champions all things independent and local in Calgary, AB. She graduated from Alberta College of Art and Design in 2018 with a BDes in Graphic Design.

KRIS DEMEANOR is a songwriter, poet, theatre and film artist. He's released seven recordings of original songs, most recently 'Entirely New Beasts' in spring 2016, featuring co-writes and beats programming by Rae Spoon. Kris was the inaugural Poet Laureate of Calgary (2012-14) and co-edited as his legacy project the book 'The Calgary Project – City Map in Verse and Visual', a compilation of poetry and visual art by Calgary writers and artists. In 2015 he was nominated for a Canadian Screen Award as best supporting actor for his role in the film The Valley Below. Recent work includes Making Treaty 7, a multi-disciplinary show featuring First Nations and non-aboriginal artists illuminating Alberta's history; writing songs for CBC's The Irrelevant Show; collaborating with Ian Tyson on two songs for his latest record; and Shelter from the Storm - a songwriting project with clients of Calgary's Drop-In Centre. Kris was awarded the Lieutenant Governor General's Established Artist Award at the Mayor's

Lunch in 2017, and has released his first print publication, the instructional booklet '*How to be an Asshole of Calgary*'.

DYMPHNY DRONYK is a mediator by vocation, and communications/engagement consultant by default. She works as a Qualified Mediator for Alberta Justice, as well as privately, and is also an editor, translator, and a story doula. She is passionate about the magic of story and has woven words for money and for love for more than 35 years. Her first volume of poetry, *Contrary Infatuations*, was short-listed for the Pat Lowther Award and the Stephan G. Stephansson Award for Poetry. She is co-publisher and co-editor at House of Blue Skies Publishing, whose bestselling anthologies include 2014's *The Calgary Project – A City Map in Verse and Visual*. Dymphny has served on the boards of the Writers Guild of Alberta, the League of Canadian Poets, and the Creative Nonfiction Collective.

CHERYL FOGGO has been published and produced extensively as a journalist, screenwriter, poet, playwright, writer of fiction and non-fiction, and as a young adult novelist. She has a particular interest in sharing the history of Black pioneers on the prairies and has written extensively on that subject in books, magazines, and anthologies.

She received the Sondra Kelly Screenplay Award from the Writers Guild of Canada and was named Professional of The Year by the Black Gold Awards Society of Alberta in 2013. Her latest children's book is *Dear Baobab* and her most recent play, *John Ware Reimagined*, garnered sold out houses in Calgary. She is delighted to have had the play shortlisted for the WGA Drama Award. Cheryl is working on a documentary film with the National Film Board called *John Ware Reclaimed*, as well as collaborating with two Edmonton writers on a new book about historical Black life in Western Canada.

ARITHA VAN Herk is a cultural commentator as well as an award-winning Canadian novelist whose work has been acclaimed throughout North America and Europe. She has given readings, lectures, and workshops on culture and community, literature and life, in the United Kingdom, the United States, Singapore, Australia, Spain, Germany, Belgium, Holland, Austria, the Baltics, and Scandinavia. Her popular, creative and critical work has been widely published and her work has been translated into ten languages.

AvH was born in central Alberta, read every book in the library at Camrose, and studied at the University of Alberta. She first rose to international literary prominence with the publication of *Judith*, which received the Seal First Novel Award and which was published in North America, the United Kingdom, and Europe.

Her other novels include *The Tent Peg*; *No Fixed Address: An Amorous Journey*; *Places Far From Ellesmere*; *Restlessness*. *In Visible Ink*; and *A Frozen Tongue* collect her essays and ficto-criticism.

Mavericks: An Incorrigible History of Alberta offers an unorthodox narrative of that province's past. *Mavericks* so inspired the Glenbow Museum of Calgary, that they created a permanent Alberta gallery and named the gallery after the book. AvH returned to her Alberta stories to create *Audacious and Adamant: A Maverick History of Alberta*, the companion book to the exhibition.

AvH is a member of the Royal Society of Canada, and a Professor who teaches Canadian Literature and Creative

251

Writing in the Department of English at the University of Calgary, but first of all, she is a writer who loves stories.

JANI KRULC's first collection of short fiction, *The Jesus Year*, was published in 2013. She holds an MA in English and Creative Writing from Concordia University and a BA (Hons) in English from the University of Calgary. Jani is a founder of Scribe YYC, a boutique writing consultancy based in Calgary, Alberta. She has taught creative writing to youth and adults, mentored new writers, and edited multiple manuscripts.

CLEM MARTINI is an award-winning playwright, novelist, and screenwriter with more than thirty plays and twelve books of fiction and nonfiction to his credit, including the W.O. Mitchell Book Prize–winning Bitter Medicine: A Graphic Memoir of Mental Illness, the anthology, Martini with a Twist, and The Unravelling, and The Comedian. His texts on playwriting, The Blunt Playwright, The Greek Playwright, and The Ancient Comedians are employed widely at universities and colleges across the continent.

He is currently the Chair of the Division of Drama in the School of Creative and Performing Arts at the University of Calgary.

NATALIE MEISNER (www.nataliemeisner.com) is a writer from Lockeport, Nova Scotia. Her plays have been produced across the country, won numerous awards, been collected in book from and appear in numerous Canadian Anthologies. Her book, *Double Pregnant: Two Lesbians Make a Family* is her lighthearted and informative true account of two lesbians who want to have children. (2014 Fernwood Publishing.) She published a children's book, *My Mommy, My Mama, My Brother, and Me*, in 2019.

Her plays have won the Canadian National Playwriting Competition, been shortlisted for the Herman Voaden, and been produced by CBC Radio. Stage productions include *Speed Dating For Sperm Donors* (Lunchbox Theatre), *Burning In*, a play about a Canadian Journalist inspired by Susan Sontag's *Regarding the Pain of Others* (Gateway Theatre), and *Pink Sugar: A Dark Tale of Love, Betrayal and Missing Body Parts* (BSMT Theatre, Solo Collective). Her plays have been published in *Outspoken: A Canadian Collection of Lesbian Scenes and Monologues* and *Lesbian Plays: Coming of Age in Canada*. Her early plays have been collected in book form: *Growing Up Salty* (Roseway/Fernwood).

Natalie Meisner is a wife and mother of two great boys and divides her time between Lockeport, NS and Calgary, AB. She holds a Doctorate in English (University of Calgary), a Master of Fine Arts in Creative Writing (University of British Columbia) and Bachelor's degree in English from Dalhousie University. She has taught at the University of Regina, University of Calgary and currently is a Professor in the Department of English at Mount Royal University where she teaches creative writing, drama and literature.

LISA MURPHY-LAMB has a Bachelor of Education from the University of Calgary and a Master of Education (Inclusive Education) from McGill University. She taught with the Calgary Board of Education, Bow Valley College, Mount Royal University as well she consulted privately. In Houston, Lisa became involved in Writers in the Schools (WITS), an organization that sends professional writers into Houston classrooms.

For five years, Lisa was the Director of WordsWorth Creative Writing Residency for Youth, a summer program for teen writers sponsored by the Writers' Guild of Alberta. She mentors teen writers; is a founding member of the People's Poetry Festival; an active member of the Writers in the School Alliance (WITSA); and a creative writing student at the University of Calgary. Currently she is director of Loft 112, an inclusive creative space for artists and writers in the East Village.

She is the author of *Jesus on the Dashboard* (Stonehouse Publishing), has published several articles in both Canada and the United States, an erotic short story, a nonfiction book which was banned from her youngest son's classroom in Texas, and a piece for CBC Television. Experiencing and surviving Hurricane Ike in Houston, Texas was the subject for two photography exhibitions and her contribution to a photography and essay book.

HARRY SANDERS is a historian, freelance writer, historical consultant and speaker. He was born in 1966 in Drumheller, Alberta where his father owned and operated the Whitehorse Hotel. Spending his early youth in and around this old hotel gave Harry a lifelong appreciation for heritage buildings, and this influenced his decision to study history and to follow a career as a local historian.

Harry was educated at the Calgary Hebrew School and Bishop Carroll High School (class of 1984). In 1988 he earned a Bachelor of Arts (First Class Honours) in History at the University of Calgary. During his university years, Harry spent his summers working as an interpreter at Heritage Park Historical Village.

Harry has worked at the Calgary Public Library, the City of Calgary Archives, the Jewish Historical Society of Southern Alberta, and the Glenbow Library & Archives. Since 1995 Harry has been a self-employed historical consultant, contract researcher, and freelance writer. He is the author of *Watermarks: One Hundred Years of Calgary Waterworks* (2000), *Calgary's Historic Union Cemetery: A Walking Guide* (2002). *The Story Behind Alberta Name: How Cities, Towns, Villages and Hamlets Got Their Names* (2003), *Historic Walks of Calgary* (2005), and *Calgary Transit: A Centennial History* (2009). From 1996-99, Harry continued the late Jack Peach's '*Looking Back*' column in the Calgary Sun. From 2006-09, Harry appeared weekly on CBC Radio One as 'Harry the Historian'.

Harry is married to Kirsten Olson, and they have two children, Jonas and Anna.

TELMO DOS SANTOS is a criminal defence lawyer, a human rights advocate, a martial artist, a poet and writer. As a poet Telmo previously received a scholarship to attend the Banff Centre international spoken word program. Telmo regularly performs at open mic and poetry slam events throughout the city. In his legal work Telmo has successfully defended racial minorities charged with serious criminal offences including attempted murder and second-degree murder. Telmo's human rights advocacy focuses on the area of indigenous issues. Telmo has previously published feature articles on subjects including the over-incarceration of Indigenous people and missing and murdered indigenous women. Telmo is the founder and current chair of the Calgary Criminal Defence Lawyers Association's Indigenous Criminal Justice Committee, which advocates on Indigenous criminal justice issues. Telmo also founded and heads Calgary Creative

Dimension, a collaborative group space for artists to work on their individual creative pursuits. Telmo currently holds the rank of fifth-kyu (blue belt) in Chito-Ryu karate, under Sensei Gary Sabean.

IAN WILLIAMS is the author of *Reproduction* (Random House, 2019).

His poetry collection, *Personals*, was shortlisted for the Griffin Poetry Prize and the Robert Kroetsch Poetry Book Award. His short story collection, *Not Anyone's Anything*, won the Danuta Gleed Literary Award for the best first collection of short fiction in Canada. His first book, *You Know Who You Are*, was a finalist for the ReLit Poetry Prize. CBC named him as one of ten Canadian writers to watch. In 2018, he became a trustee for the Griffin Poetry Prize.

Williams holds a Ph.D. in English at the University of Toronto and is currently an assistant professor of poetry in the Creative Writing program at the University of British Columbia. He was the 2014-2015 Canadian Writer-in-Residence for the University of Calgary's Distinguished Writers Program. He has held fellowships or residencies from the Banff Center, Vermont Studio Center, Cave Canem, Kimmel Harding Nelson Center for the Arts, and Palazzo Rinaldi in Italy. He was also a scholar at the National Humanities Center Summer Institute for Literary Study.

DEBORAH WILLIS was born and raised in Calgary, Alberta. Her first book, *Vanishing and Other Stories*, was named one of the the Globe and Mail's Best Books of 2009, and was shortlisted for the Governor General's Award. She was a bookseller at Munro's Books in Victoria, BC, a writer-in-residence at Joy

Kogawa House in Vancouver, BC, the 2012-2013 Calgary Distinguished Writers Program writer-in-residence at the University of Calgary, and the Writer in Residence at MacEwan University in Edmonton. She currently works for Freehand Books in Calgary and is a proud volunteer at The Women's Centre of Calgary.

Her second collection of short stories was published in February 2017 by Hamish Hamilton, the literary imprint of Penguin Random House Canada, and W.W. Norton and Company in the U.S, and will be translated into Italian by Del Vecchio Editore. *The Dark and Other Love Stories* was long-listed for the 2017 Giller Prize, won the Georges Bugnet Award for best work of fiction published in Alberta, and was named one of the best books of the year by *The Globe and Mail*, the CBC, and *Chatelaine Magazine*. Her fiction and non-fiction has appeared in *The Walrus*, *The Virginia Quarterly*, *The Iowa Review*, *Lucky Peach*, *The Wall Street Journal*, and *Zoetrope*. Deborah is currently working on a novel.